High-Rise Chronicles:

Every Lease a Different Life, Every Life a Different Story

High-Rise Chronicles:

Every Lease a Different Life, Every Life a Different Story

Written by **Kia Monique Crooms**
Cover by **Mary Anne VanderLaan**

iUniverse, Inc.
New York   Bloomington

High-Rise Chronicles

Every Lease a Different Life, Every Life a Different Story

iUniverse books may be ordered through booksellers or by contacting:

iUniverse
1663 Liberty Drive
Bloomington, IN 47403
www.iuniverse.com
1-800-Authors (1-800-288-4677)

ISBN: 978-1-4401-4077-8 (pbk)
ISBN: 978-1-4401-4079-2 (hbk)
ISBN: 978-1-4401-4078-5 (ebk)

Printed in the United States of America

iUniverse rev. date: 5/22/2009

Foreword By Mary Anne VanderLaan

Little do we know of what goes on behind the scenes.

If you have ever gone to look for an apartment, you know what you are shown by the leasing professionals. It is a picture-perfect home. A high-rise community with a doorman—who remembers your name and that your daughter is still in college; security guards—who promise to protect and serve; shiny elevators; lovely carpeting; spacious rooms; and everything you could wish for!

The stories within these chapters smash that illusion. It is a compilation of what you will never be shown, and probably will never hear.

Human nature is quite confounding. Few get the opportunity to see into tens of thousands of people's lives through their homes like Property Managers. When you are surrounded, 52 weeks a year, by people living their respective lives, it can become quite a weave. Lives ranging from people who receive federal funds in order to pay their rent to people who pay their rent a year in advance, because they don't want to try to keep up with the triviality of "paying the rent". Then there are those who cannot pay their rent at all. And they may all live right next door to one another.

You realize some think "normal living" is being surrounded by roaches and infested with bed bugs with the occasional mouse meandering through. Then there are those whose entire apartments look spectacular—like pages torn from a Pottery Barn catalog.

Among tenants, there are people being evicted, bounced checks, disruptive parties, crime, and cons. Excuses, experiences, life, love, compassion. In some cases, your heart gets caught up. In others your adrenaline boils through your body, directing you to scream or slap.

Sometimes it bursts into chaos. It all goes on in these pages. The author shares a collection of stories that will take you to those places. This is human interest at its best.

Dedicated to the angels on my left and the angels on my right—grand-mother, Mary Lou; uncle, DeWayne Anthony; father-in-law, Amos Jr.; step-father, William Harold—Rest In Peace.

Allow me to start by giving all honors to God who heads my life and meets me at my needs. Thanks to my husband, Derrick, for your love, friendship, support and encouragement. I'd like to also thank my mother, Pam, for giving me life and for always supporting everything that I set out to do. Thanks to my father, Gregory, for praying for me daily. Thanks to my sister, Patrice—I know you think I am your hero...but actually you're mine! To my brothers, Gregory Jr. and Micah—love you both to pieces. To my first cousin, Mina, lots of love to you.

A very special thanks to my pastors, Rev. Gregory A. Simmons (Detroit) and Dr. Jamal Harrison-Bryant (Baltimore). You are more relevant than you know. Your teachings have taken my spirituality and personal walk with God to new heights. More thanks to two women who have dedicated their lives to education and early child development: my God-mother, Marion Lemon Cunningham— for the life lessons, support and encouragement; and God-sister, Janet Marie Cunningham— for your love, advice and assistance with the title.

A very special thanks to a very special friend, Mary Anne VanderLaan, the creativity, the maturity, the blessing that you brought to this project as a gifted artist yourself...I cannot articulate into words what it means to me. Thank you.

More special thanks to my grandmother, aunts, uncles, cousins, in-laws, friends, colleagues, and supervisors (former and present). I would be remiss if I didn't also thank those Detroit Public School teachers who inspired me to achieve excellence: Mrs. Flecksteiner (O.W. Holmes), Mrs. Rose Jackson (Munger Middle) and Ms. McCormick (Cass Technical High).

And to my beautiful and intelligent nieces: Danielle Monique, Jordan Alexis, Chloe Chanel...be encouraged, continue your education and know that I will always love you!

Chapter 1

There's an old saying: "If you never lie, you never have to remember anything."

"Welcome to The Highlands, how may I assist you?" A leasing professional answered the phone. "You will love our two-bedroom floor plans. You'll especially love the price, as we are running an awesome special on two bedrooms only." Maureen was selling to a charming caller on the phone. "It sounds like you are primarily looking for a one-bedroom suite, but you also mentioned that you work out of your home. Our one-bedroom units are not equipped with a den or the office space you desire. Keep in mind; if you search for a one-bedroom with a den elsewhere, you're gonna pay an arm and a leg. Reserve a two bedroom over the phone with me using your credit card, and I'll throw in a $500 gift card to the Great Indoors. That will at least furnish your kitchen and bathrooms," Maureen closed the deal over the phone.

She was a great salesperson with an astounding 60 percent closing ratio. Maureen updated her Blackberry with client-specific information, sending them birthday and anniversary cards via e-mail and E-cards. Some of her co-workers believed that people preferred to be left alone, but until someone proved otherwise, Maureen was the best salesperson at The Highlands. With bright eyes and a smile that would light up the star that tops the tree, Maureen carried herself as a respectable businesswoman at all times. Unlike most, she began her shift an hour before the office opened and stayed behind two hours after it closed. She worked her leads like a true entrepreneur and with such finesse.

Her clients totally respected and looked to her long after they had moved and settled in.

As many managers would guess, because Maureen was such a good salesperson, her administrative skills left a little to be desired. She could not keep her client files organized, even when her job was once threatened.

Stan, another leading salesperson on the leasing team, was pretty much the same way. He resembled the likes of a sharp car salesman with a crisp suit and coordinating tie. His shoes shined as if he was in military training, and his Versace brand eye wear made a resounding fashion statement. With an average closing ratio of 57.5 percent, he struggled with a lot more than paperwork. Stan came from a long line of alcoholism in his family. It was no secret that he relished an occasional nip—and often. One holiday season a couple of years back, the property manager received a complaint that Stan had made sexual references in the presence of a female resident. The following day, Stan was written up and warned to stay off the bottle or risk losing his job.

He was ordered to attend AA classes and sensitivity training to redeem himself. After sixteen days of being sober and miserable, it was observed that Stan could not function without the alcohol in his system. The boozing associate was now the opposite of a model salesperson: late for work, forgetting appointments, and consistently closing on half his original ratio.

One Monday morning, the property manager, Cole, put a bottle of Bombay Sapphire under Stan's desk with a note; *I can only pray that I'm doing the right thing ... You cannot afford for your career to end based on the numbers that you are producing. And I can't afford to lose my job based on your numbers ... so enjoy and Merry Christmas!* Stan just sort of nodded his head in acknowledgment after reading the note, but the two never spoke of the bottle again. They went on to lead the entire real estate portfolio by accomplishing great things at the site.

After the holiday break was over, Maureen had a ton of clients lined up to move into the Chicago high-rise community. The lobby was professionally decorated by the daughter of a 1920s famous couturier who worked as a curator of gowns and dresses for Marshall Field's in Chicago more than eighty years ago. The panache ambiance was absolutely amazing, with white, hand made silk poinsettias in large terracotta planters and variations of purple, lilac, and lavender décor on the twelve-foot holiday trees in every corner of the grand lobby.

Mr. Borland of Connecticut was among the many to check in that week. Mr. Borland was the hard sell who gave Maureen his credit card number over the phone to reserve a $2,400 per month two-bedroom unit—sight unseen. Because of his line of work, he assured Maureen that he would not have time for a grand tour of the building or its amenities upon his arrival. He would only have time to show identification, sign the original fifteen-page lease agreement, and retrieve his keys.

"Can I get you any coffee or Artesian bottled water?" Maureen offered after shaking Mr. Borland's hand and sitting him at a stainless-steel table in the café. His olive skin and wavy hair made him easy on the eyes.

"No, really, I must be going. I'd like to just get the paperwork out of the way and collect my keys," The businessman stressed while shaking the light snow off of his Burberry trench coat and matching scarf.

"Right away, Mr. Borland," Maureen said, as she hurried to her desk to retrieve his file.

She returned quickly with the original paperwork for him to sign. "The first five pages require your initials and date, while the final ten require a full signature and date at each highlighted 'X,'" Maureen explained, as Mr. Borland started immediately by quickly initially without even taking a seat at the stainless-steel table. "While you continue with that, could I please take your driver's license or passport to photo copy for our records?" Maureen asked.

Mr. Borland took out a brown leather wallet and flipped through the many plastic cards looking for a driver's license, and then he proclaimed that he must have accidentally left it in the backseat of the airport taxi that transported him to the building. "I know that I faxed a copy to you several weeks ago, can I bring in my passport when I get a little more unpacked?" The tall, dark, and handsome gentleman asked.

"Sure. I have a copy here with your paperwork. Please be sure to bring down an original, as it is our policy to verify original identification when taking an application over the phone," Maureen answered.

"I for one can understand and respect your policy. Several years ago, I was a victim of identity theft," Mr. Borland admitted. "Hey,

I've got to run … movers will be here shortly. Maureen, it is a pleasure to finally meet you, and I look forward to a lengthy landlord–tenant relationship. See you in a couple of days. Ciao." He exited her sight to take the elevator to the lobby area. *What a nice man*, she thought to herself. Then, she proceeded to assist the next client.

Months go by, and springtime in Chicago is at its best. The cold winter hawk is an inconvenience of the past, and the streets are filled with shoppers, sightseers, and locals. From beachgoers playing sand volleyball and watching the sailboats go by on Lake Michigan to rainbow-inspired tulips lining the Magnificent Mile, there's no place like Chicago during spring. The Highlands was experiencing some good press after hosting a successful pre-spring fashion show that turned out to be a star-studded event. Proceeds from the fundraiser were donated to a cancer institute, in an effort to support their continuation in curing cancer and producing more survivors. It was a dilatory day for business. The phones rang infrequently, the appointment book was light, and it was the perfect day to catch up on filing and other loose ends.

The phone rang, and a male voice on the opposite end asked to speak to a manager or supervisor. "Certainly, though I would be more than happy to assist you with any questions you may have," Stan said.

"No offense, but this may be a matter above your pay grade," the snotty caller insisted.

"Cole, there's an extremely rude guy for you on line one," Stan buzzed Cole's office line.

"Put 'em through," he retorted. "Thank you for calling The Highlands, this is the property manager, Cole. How may I assist you?"

The caller went on to inquire about the exact whereabouts of the building and why his credit card was being used to secure such an expensive apartment in Chicago. Cole looked up the name and credit card number offered by Mr. Victor Borland of Connecticut.

"Sir, I am showing that you have a rental account with us, but it sounds like you have no knowledge of initiating such an account," Cole said, puzzled. "Sir, unfortunately, there is nothing I am allowed to assist you with over the phone. This is a matter that will need to be handled in person," Cole explained to Mr. Borland.

Mr. Borland stated that he was actually at the airport with his wife, and both were on their way to the building. Cole ended the call and began to research which consultant was awarded the sale.

"Maureen, can I see you in my office for a moment? And please bring Mr. Borland's rental file in with you," Cole said, after he buzzed her extension.

Maureen sat in a chair at Cole's desk with the file in hand. "Is something wrong?" she queried.

Cole went on to explain the strange call he had just received and inquired about the entire process of how Mr. Borland had come to rent an apartment at The Highlands. Maureen summarized her experience with the handsome gentleman and admitted that she failed to follow up with him on his original identification.

"My gut tells me that the real Vic Borland is on his way here," Cole warned.

Maureen felt horrible. Her imagination got the best of her as she imagined getting thrown in jail for conspiracy to commit fraud along with Mr. Borland—or whoever he is.

A distinguished Canadian gentleman entered the management office with a beautiful blonde on his arms.

"How can we help you?" Cole asked, extending his hand for a firm handshake.

"Victor Borland and this is my wife, Laura," Mr. Borland extended his hand as his eyes perused the room in observation. The two followed Cole into his office with Maureen close behind.

"As I'm sure you understand, I will need to see your identification before we delve into this thing," Cole started to say.

"I would hope that was a consistent policy, especially prior to initiating a $30,000 lease with someone," Mr. Borland expressed angrily.

Cole made a colored copy of the Connecticut driver's licenses for Mr. and Mrs. Borland. He began to explain how an impostor entered into the agreement with the property and how credit card sales over the phone were totally legal and acceptable.

Mr. Borland explained how he went to purchase a small piece of real estate in Dallas, when he was turned down for the loan due to an outstanding credit debt in excess of $125,000. "That obviously drew a red flag and caused me to pull my credit report for answers," Mr. Borland explained.

Cole encouraged Maureen to describe, once again, her sales experience with the "other" Borland. Cole showed Victor Borland the photograph that was obviously cut and pasted over his picture on his Connecticut license. Victor recognized the gentleman as a representative at the Yacht Club he frequented in Westport. Victor remembered losing his driver's license at the club, but, apparently, it was either stolen or lost and found by the suspect.

"Well, let's see this apartment of mine," Mr. Borland said with sarcasm.

"Sir, I don't think that's a good idea," Cole stated.

"Why not? Technically, it's my apartment, right … so let's see it," Mr. Borland said, as he grabbed his wife's hand and started toward the elevator.

Cole whispered, "Please pull the key to Mr. Borland's unit and have security meet me on the fortieth floor with it."

"Wow, fortieth floor, huh? The guy's got taste—that's for sure," Mr. Borland, who obviously overheard Cole's request, said.

Everyone, including a security person, was standing in front of the unit and knocking at this point. Maureen knew that the impersonator would not be home, because he traveled so frequently.

"He's actually in Boston this week; there shouldn't be anyone home," Maureen assured them.

"Yeah, he's probably racking up frequent flyer miles on my credit cards," Mr. Borland said, with more apparent sarcasm.

After turning the locks, the group was unprepared for what they saw next: an absolutely stunning and fabulous apartment home. Never had anyone residing in or visiting this downtown Windy City building seen such style and décor within four walls.

The California-style closets were aligned with high-end men's dress shoes and suits. Oxford styles, wing tips, and British and Italian name brand shoes in different shades and hides of burgundy, cognac, and black were neatly lined in the master suite closet. Flat panel televisions and the topmost electronics were mounted in every room. Standard GE appliances were replaced with the Sub-Zero brand appliances, while Louis Vuitton luggage and garment bags were stored in the coat closet alongside a brand-new set of golf clubs.

"Like you said, honey ... he's got good taste," Mrs. Borland mimicked her husband, after feeling the fabric of the bedspreads.

"I don't know how far you've gotten from a legal standpoint, but I think it's time we get the police involved," Cole suggested.

"I think you're right. Can we give them a call from your office?" Mr. Borland humbly asked.

"I just have one question," Mrs. Borland began. "Was it not a red flag for your office when this man asked to pay for an entire year of rent all up front?"

Cole pointed at Maureen to give her the opportunity to respond. "Actually, many of our clients opt to do just the same, primarily due to their traveling schedule or purchase points, depending on the card being used. It is more common than you think," Maureen explained.

"Gee, I guess it has been a long time since I've rented an apartment," Mrs. Borland smiled and exited in front of her husband as he held onto the small of her back.

The group reentered Cole's office to place a complaint with the local police department. After many phone calls to creditors and detectives, Mr. Borland was close to putting the fraudulent purchases and trips to Chicago to rest. The strategy was to set up a sort of sting with the Chicago police to enmesh the deceiver while he luxuriated in his fortieth floor apartment and arrest him. There was no certainty to his true identity. Every other name or alias associated with the address for purchases and shipments was additional victims of the impostor. What was known was that the impostor had fraudulently achieved credit and identity theft in excess of a quarter of a million dollars. Maureen would be instrumental in the sting, since she was the only person who had built a rapport and trust factor with him. It turned out that the fake Victor Borland traveled extensively and had to be called via cell phone to prompt his return to Chicago.

With a wire tap in place, Maureen initiated a telephone call to the con artist. "Mr. Borland, long time no see. How are things in Boston?" she asked.

He was surprised to hear from Maureen but was very cordial over the telephone. "You know, I never did get you to come in with your identification as per our policy. My manager has been all over me and even went as far as to deny paying out the commission I earned for your apartment." Maureen played along with detectives coaxing her in Cole's office.

"Maureen, I am extremely sorry. It totally slipped my mind. Tell you what … I can briefly stop through Chicago this Thursday before heading to Minneapolis for a meeting," the smooth talker promised.

"That would be super. Thank you, thank you!" Maureen said excitedly.

"See you then, kiddo." He ended the call abruptly.

"All we can do at this point is wait," said a detective.

The next phase of the plan included officers setting up in the vacant apartment across the hall from the suspected apartment on the fortieth floor. Other officers would pose in the office as employees in suits and plain clothes, while a sixth officer would replace the security guard at the front desk in the grand lobby.

Thursday morning came, and everyone was in place. The phony Borland entered the office with an Illinois driver's license in the name of Victor Borland. He had obviously committed to being a local and applied for a license in Chicago. Maureen had small talk with him, while she photocopied the ID. She thanked him profusely as he helped himself to a mint chocolate cookie on a platter outside of the office.

"You know, I'm never in town long enough to enjoy my apartment or any of the other cool amenities you all offer here," he admitted.

"I guess your line of work is very demanding," Maureen said with her hand slightly trembling as she returned the license to the phony Borland.

"I was hoping to catch a little TV in my apartment this morning, but I really better run," he said.

"Actually, I was hoping you could check on your apartment while you were here," Maureen swiftly responded. "The lady above you overflowed her tub last week. Our maintenance guys think they intercepted it prior to it leaking in your apartment, but it sure would help if you checked for damages and reported back to us." Maureen felt redeemed after some quick thinking on her part.

Detectives radioed upstairs for the officers to apprehend him as soon as he turned the key to his apartment. The officers were anxiously watching through the door viewer from across the hall. "You're probably right; I better verify that there aren't any damages before getting back on the plane. My apologies for any inconvenience my delays caused you. Ciao." He exited the office in a hurry.

"Be ready; he moves like lightning," a detective radioed again.

Officers rushed out of their door when phony Borland disengaged the deadbolt lock on his door. "Freeze! You're under arrest! Put your hands up where I can see them!" officers instructed while tackling the suspect to the ground and handcuffing his hands behind his back. Finally, he was captured. Remaining detectives had taken the service elevator up to where the action took place and began reading him his rights. The fake Borland was escorted out of the building in handcuffs and sat in a Chicago squad car waiting out front.

The maintenance supervisor showed up to the apartment to change the locks and secure the apartment. Upon opening the door, they found the police officers collecting the goods in dark duffel bags. One officer looked up after hearing the door creek and said, "We're collecting the stolen property for our evidence room, so you're gonna have to come back within the next hour for the locks." He rushed the maintenance supervisor back to the corridor and locked the door behind him.

Yeah right. I'd like to see just how much of the goods actually end up in that evidence room of yours, the maintenance supervisor thought to himself.

Chapter 2

For she said to herself, "If only I may touch His garment,
I shall be made well." —Matthew 9:21

Sherry was responding to a call from a sixth floor resident claiming that
Volda Slack in 613 was beating one of her foster children again. This
was the second call this week, and Sherry was not up for a confrontation
this time. As she responded to the initial call on Sunday evening, Sherry
recalled Ms. Slack invading her three feet of personal space by getting
in her face screaming, "You wanna raise 'em! Be my fucking guest,
because as long as they're in my house, eating my food, using electricity
that I pay for … they are going to get the black smacked off of them
when they disobey me!" Ms. Slack continued to yell.

"Ma'am, I'm not trying to tell you how to raise your children. I
don't believe in spanking, but that is my own philosophy. But you're
gonna have to keep it down or I will be forced to call the police,"
Sherry said. Volda slammed the door in Sherry's face.

Sherry was the head of security at City View at Meridian, standing
5'9" and weighing in at 285 pounds. One could always catch her
snacking or observe residents bringing her desserts. She was a devoted
vegetarian, but definitely made up for her absence of meat with
sweets. "This woman is going to make me lose my job," Sherry told a
colleague.

Outside of being an irascible mother, Volda was also a principal at
an inner city high school. Prior to moving to City View at Meridian

two and a half years ago, her permanent residence was that of a motel. She rented a room by the week and a different vehicle every month. Rumor had it that she lost everything to gambling years ago. Her credit score was horrific; she couldn't finance a vehicle at a 50 percent interest rate. Never married, no biological children, but several foster children passed through her home. Neighbors suspected she was in it merely for the money. She couldn't genuinely care for the children—the way she yelled at them. Standing 5'10" herself with mid-brown skin wearing a mushroom hairstyle, much like Condoleezza Rice, Volda was just a miserable woman and made everyone miserable around her.

Volda's assistant principal was a well-educated, well-spoken Caucasian woman from Chicago. She complimented Volda well, because she possessed all of the proper skills required to run a tough school in the inner city. Nancy had the respect of the school board members and most importantly the children, while Principal Volda Slack had only the support of the primary school investor, Bishop William Gunns. The dichotomy of ideals between the bishop and the school board mixed like oil and water—they didn't. The bishop was a wealthy slum lord of many project communities in the inner city. He also owned many franchised fast-food restaurants. He made national news years ago when he closed the doors to one of his fast-food restaurants, unbeknownst to the crew members. Apparently, Bishop William, also known as "Dollar Bill," had become quite delinquent in business taxes. A lien was placed on his restaurant, forcing him not to open for business as usual one pay Friday afternoon.

Staff members rallied around the restaurant, throwing foreign objects through the windows and vandalizing the padlock placed on the doors in hopes of finding their payroll checks on a countertop in the store. Police arrived to silence the mob, and the local news anchors pulled in to cover the story of many single parents and minimum wage earners looking forward to their earned and due pay. Bishop Gunns' publicist held a press conference the Tuesday following the store closing to personally and publicly issue prepaid debit cards to all staff members in hopes of keeping the media out of Bishop Gunns' church. "This is a place of worship for God's sake," Bishop Gunns was quoted as saying, while pushing past a camera crew waiting for his chauffeur-driven Cadillac Deville to arrive one Sunday morning.

It was suspected that Volda Slack was either the bishop's love child or mistress, primarily due to the way that complaining letters against her went unanswered and the way that people were transferred to grimy assignments or terminated if they raised issues against her. Volda claimed to have received her doctorate from a university in Texas, which accounted for her southern accent, but it didn't add up when measuring her professionalism or leadership skills.

Once during a teachers' strike, Volda was asked by the chairman of the board to prepare a letter to go out to all of the parents in the community asking for their support and patience during such strike. Volda, as she did most things, delegated the letter writing to Nancy and asked her to have it on her desk to proofread by noon the following day. After several red markings, Volda kicked the letter back to Nancy to be rewritten. Once again, Nancy left a draft on Volda's desk—only for it to sit atop the desk for seven days before Volda proofed it. And, once again, Volda marked up the letter and returned it to Nancy for a third attempt. Meanwhile, Nancy had sought the professional advice from English teachers in the school and her husband, who was writing a dissertation for his doctorate. All found no changes to be necessary.

On the morning the board was looking to release the letter, an e-mail came across Volda's desk asking the whereabouts of such notice. Volda grew frantic and blamed Nancy, "How dare you make me miss such an important deadline." Nancy snapped back that it was Volda's inadequacies that caused her to miss yet another deadline. The school board's attorney drafted a moderately toned notification and rushed distribution to the parents of the students that attended the high school.

Of Volda's foster children, there were three boys—all fewer than ten years of age—and two teenage girls. The girls were Volda's biggest opposition as they challenged every rule she set and constantly reminded her that she was not their biological mother. "Don't you ever put me in the same sentence as that crack whore!" Volda would lash back. "She may have brought you into the world, but I will take you out!"

One evening, Volda sent the two girls—Bridget and Pheona—to the grocery store to pick up some whole milk, cheese, and bread for the boys' lunch the next day. "If Rita is there, go through her lane, and see if she will let you get a package of cigarettes for me," Volda instructed the fifteen- and seventeen-year-old girls.

They skipped to the grocery store in hopes of seeing Neil and Solomon—two of their romantic interests that often hung out in front of the fuel station near the store. "How's my hair?" asked the eldest of the pair, Pheona.

"It's fine. What about me, how do I look?" Bridget inquired.

Pheona stopped to tease her sister's hair and add a little pink lip gloss to her thin lips. She coached as she applied the makeup, "This is the plan … we're going to get the groceries, get one of the guys to buy the pack of cigarettes … take it all back to the apartment, and wait for mom to fall asleep before we come back out. Okay?" Pheona checked for her sister's understanding.

"What if he asks me to stay out with him?" Bridget asked. Bridget always looked up to her sister for answers.

The girls' plan worked like a charm. They arrived back at the sixth floor with whole milk, cheese, bread, and an off brand of cigarettes. Volda made a grilled cheese sandwich for herself and the boys, lit a cigarette from her new pack, and headed toward the master bedroom offering final instructions, "You heifers clean up that kitchen before bed, and leave a message on the maintenance phone that my master bath toilet is stopped up again."

Bridget mumbled under her breath, "If you stopped eating all that damn cheese, the toilet wouldn't stop up." Volda yelled for her to repeat her last comment, but Pheona came to her sister's rescue by making up a lame and more respectful phrase.

With the entire kitchen clean—stove and microwave spotless, linoleum floor air drying, and all dishes put away—the girls grabbed Volda's cell phone and made their way to the rear door of the apartment building. A roving security guard cut them off as they rounded the building. "Where are you girls running off to?" the guard asked.

"Uh … hi, Ms. Payne, we were just doing something for our mother," the girls fumbled.

"I know for a fact your mother wouldn't send you out this time of morning," the woman said. "I'm going to tell you like my mother used to tell me; there is nothing open after one in the morning except legs and liquor stores. You girls watch yourselves; those boys are hardly worth it," Security Officer Payne warned as she walked away.

The girls ran off to meet Neil and Solomon at the swimming pool. The four had made a plan to go skinny dipping together. Bridget was a little unnerved by the plan, as she hated for her little brother to accidentally walk in on her while in the shower, let alone exposing herself to a strange boy. She was a virgin and planned to stay that way at least until she was eighteen. The boys were standing by the pool gate in dark clothing, just as planned.

Pheona and Solomon got started almost immediately. Seconds after hopping the fence, Solomon had removed his hooded sweatshirt and sneakers, while Pheona had pulled her dress over her head and was shivering in her underwear and ballerina slippers.

"You scared or something?" Neil asked Bridget as she stood fully clothed on the opposite side of the pool gate from the others.

"No!" she snapped back.

Bridget finally joined the others poolside and watched as her sister and Solomon made out in five feet of water, with his arms wrapped around her to shield her bosom from the others.

"Are you going to do this or not?" Neil asked. "Because I can be at another chick's house...." But Bridget assured him that she was getting in. Though chagrin took over her emotions, she took her sweet time removing her tennis shoes and jeans. Pulling her T-shirt down over her buttocks after she removed her panties, Bridget sat down on the concrete stairs leading into the pool. Her resolute suitor smiled as he swam over to the steps, tugging on her dark T-shirt.

"We don't have to do anything if you don't want to. I just want to hold you," Neil reassured her, as his penis stood erect in the swimming pool. Bridget giggled and allowed him to pull her up off of the stair. The two begin kissing, touching, and rubbing. Neil tried to pressure Bridget to allow him to insert himself in her, "I'll go slowly. It won't hurt. I promise," he pledged.

Bridget continued to refuse, trying to reassure Neil that someday he will be her first, "But not tonight," she said.

Her amber eyes displayed timidity along with yellow pigments glistening under the pole lighting. Neil continued to hold her tight around her waist; he whispered how she must not care about him and how he wished he had gone over to "what's her face's house," because he's used to dealing with mature girls. Bridget finally succumbed to Neil's pressuring and allowed him to enter her while she clung to the poolside handrails. What was probably over in less than two minutes seemed to have lasted a lifetime to Bridget. Tears ran down her face as she felt him forcefully enter her walls over and over and over. "Damn, you tight," was all that she could hear him say. As Neil pulled himself out to ejaculate, he noticed the red water filling the space between Bridget's navy shirt and his bare chest.

"Damn, are you bleeding?" Neil asked, as he backed away from her. Bridget's left cheek was lying on the concrete deck of the pool while she held her stomach.

Her sister rushed to her side, "What happened? Did you start your menstrual, girl?" Bridget just cried silently and never said a word. She couldn't help but think about the woman in the Bible who suffered from a twelve-year hemorrhage. *Is this what it felt like to her as she bled and bled and bled?* The only difference was Jesus wasn't walking around the swimming pool with the hem of his garment exposed for healing.

The boys quickly got dressed and hopped the fence to the other side. "Aren't you going to help me?" Pheona called out to Solomon, but he just kept running. Pheona got her sister dressed and assisted her as she tried to walk back to the building. Security Officer Payne had been making her rounds back near the pool when she saw the girls again. "What happened to her?" Payne called out.

"I don't know. I think she is just cramping from her period."

"I hope your mother is home, because she is going to need to talk to this girl," Payne said. Payne tried probing questions to get Bridget to talk, but she just sobbed uncontrollably.

Payne knocked on the apartment door with her night stick, while Bridget sat on the floor in the hallway, covered in blood. "What in the hell happened?" Volda asked when looking down at Bridget. Something snapped in Volda, after helping Bridget up to her feet and into the apartment, she immediately began physically attacking Pheona. "What did you do? What did you do to this girl?" she yelled as Officer Payne dialed 911 on the cordless phone sitting atop the TV stand in the living room.

Soon thereafter, police and sex crime detectives arrived to question the family and transport Bridget to Children's Hospital for a rape kit. Volda remained hysterical until officers were able to restrain her and calm her down. They separated Volda from riding in the ambulance with her wounded foster daughter. The two remained separated for three hours while police and detectives questioned Bridget. The rape kit was performed by a female doctor, who examined every crevice of her body—ears, nose, mouth, throat, rectum, and vagina. No speculum was used. Just a gloved hand and a robotic instrument entered the young girl's crevices checking for semen.

At age fifteen, Bridget was being tested for syphilis, gonorrhea, Chlamydia, and HIV. The nurse advised Volda that she should bring her daughter back every three months to be retested for HIV—at least for another year. After fourteen hours between police custody for questioning and doctors and nurses poking and prodding, Bridget was finally reunited with Volda and returned home. Pheona was staying with a friend from school, as she was cursed by Volda never to step foot back into her home again. Bridget didn't make it farther than the sofa upon her return home. Volda tucked her in with a white chenille blanket to sleep for the remainder of the day. The doctors recommended sleep aides, and Bridget slept for hours. She finally woke up to get a glass of water around midnight and decided to sit up in a chair on the balcony to watch the stars.

Bridget found comfort in the stars as a child. She stared out of the window in the foster home where she shared a room with a dozen other unattached children. Bridget began to think about life after this ordeal. Her mind clouded with negative scenarios and hypothetical questions. Would Volda send her back to a foster home? Was Volda being silent and supportive long enough until the visits from the police wore off? What foster parent would want a troubled teen that was recently raped and possibly contracted HIV? It was definitely not what she had bargained for as her first sexual encounter.

Police had Solomon in custody for questioning. Neil, who actually penetrated Bridget, was still at large. Based on Solomon's statement, Neil was twenty-six years of age, though Bridget told police in her narrative that he was nineteen. Obviously, that was his misrepresentation to her. In the beginning, Solomon was being intentionally ambiguous during the police interrogation. He seemed to have been influenced by some obvious street code against snitching. He even went as far as plopping his feet on the table, "In my hood, snitches get stitches … and I ain't no snitch." After detectives poetically described how he would be charged for rape as an accomplice, a first-degree felony, Solomon stopped thinking like a jailbird and began singing like a song bird.

The phone rang early the next morning. It was Detective Lourdes Cruz advising that Brian Neil Obeng was arrested and in police custody. Volda was so relieved. She rushed to Bridget's room to share the good news, when she was stopped in her tracks by frantic knocking and pounding at her apartment entry door.

"Just a minute!" Volda screamed at the door just before snatching it open.

"Ms. Slack, I'm afraid I have some terrible news for you," an officer said.

"Terrible? I just received great news from Detective Cruz that you have the scum bag in custody," Volda replied out of confusion. In the meantime, the other two officers walked by Volda to enter the apartment toward the balcony railing.

"What's going on?" Volda queried, still in a confused state. Volda recognized the white chenille blanket tied and thrown over the balcony rail. Outside of the second floor terrace hung Bridget's slump body approximately eight feet from the ground level. She finally touched the hem of his garment.

Chapter 3

It wasn't misty eyed, it was eyes wide open.—Unknown

The property's focus had changed from raising rents, dumping the buildings, and weeding out the riffraff to discounting rents to occupy the building. The owners were cash strapped; thus, they were trying to refinance the mortgage to achieve lower interest rates. However, the financial institution put a freeze on all assets, including cash, until the owners made good on their end of the agreement—realizing and maintaining the 90 percent occupancy they proposed.

Have you ever met someone who was so evil and had such negative characteristics and work ethics that they were always suspicious of everyone else? Meet Wendell Nubbs. Wendell was the property manager at Sawyer Heights, a thirty-two-story building built in the 1930s. In its days of glory, The Eldorado, the building's original name, was home to some of the most infamous movie stars, politicians, and prominent businessmen in Chicago. After government subsidy programs materialized and some of the city's lower class people overran the building, it closed its doors to the world in the early 1980s. Along came a group of investors, restoration advisors, and a citywide petition, and Sawyer Heights became home to some of the Windy City's wealthiest clientele. Apartments and lofts featured complimentary cable television, oversized garden tubs, laminate cherry wood cabinetry, blue slate linoleum flooring, washer and dryer connections, Frieze carpeting, and chair and crown molding throughout.

Sawyer Heights boasted luxury amenities such as a uniformed doorman, business center with Wi-Fi hot spots, an underground parking garage, secured entry system, clubroom for social events, rooftop swimming pool, fitness studio, and a conference room for board meetings.

Wendell, with his medium curly hair and broad, flat nose, was closet gay and had a significant plight with drug abuse. He took over managing the community within the past three and a half years. Though he earned the respect of his staff by showing his willingness to roll up his sleeves and work alongside them in a pinch, Wendell didn't trust anyone. He had the highest staff turnover rate in the owners' portfolio, and many often wondered why one had never contributed such turnover to Wendell's poor management style. Other than those few dire situations, on the scale between zero and the company's minimum is where Wendell's work ethic usually laid.

Once, Wendell planted an empty snack bag in the lawn on the property and set up a hidden camera to record how many times one of his staff members would walk by the debris without picking it up. He captured a maintenance technician walking by the bag four times within three hours and never bending down to pick it up. That maintenance technician was written up and had a negative mark against his once-perfect employment record. On another occasion, Wendell fired an exterminating company from the property for not spraying an apartment's cabinet for roaches. Prior to the company's scheduled visit, Wendell entered the resident's apartment home to tape shut the kitchen cupboards with invisible tape to prove that the exterminating company was not being forthright in doing all that they could to rid this family of roaches. "They're coming out of the alarm clock in my bedroom," Mrs. Woods complained.

Many suspected that Wendell's unscrupulous behavior was due to his mother's untimely death in an automobile accident when he was a teenager. Though he didn't speak much of his mother's dying, Wendell often told the story of an encounter with his aunt after the funeral. Wendell came from a very modest and humble upbringing. His aunt, on the other hand, married a very wealthy New York Stock Exchange banker and lived in a seven-bedroom, five-bathroom mansion in Rancho Cucamonga, California. As Wendell sat on the porch step after his mother's funeral, his aunt pulled him upstairs in her sister's bedroom. She discreetly closed the door quietly behind them, pulled a plastic bag out of the closet, and patted the mattress for Wendell to sit beside her. Wendell's heart began to race. He'd heard rumors concerning his aunt's fortune and often dreamed that she would leave him and his siblings a trust fund, since she was unable to bear children of her own. His palms began to sweat, and his mouth watered uncontrollably.

"Now, you keep this between the two of us," Aunt Elizabeth prefaced before pulling out a bill and folding it in Wendell's hand. When he opened his hand, which felt as though it was crumbling, he observed a single bill, a crinkled ten-dollar bill. "Put that away, and go on back downstairs so no one suspects us," Aunt Elizabeth continued as she waited for Wendell to exit prior to hiding the plastic bag again.

"You would have assumed it was a million dollars versus ten," he joked while telling the story to his personnel.

Sawyer Heights had evolved—once again—into this undesirable edifice for loathsome tenants. With the new goal reverting to improving the community's occupancy by offering an abundance of concessions and rent discounts to attract a larger quantity of people, the quality of people suffered. Delinquency problems resurfaced. By the fifteenth of the month, $160,000 was still outstanding. This was absolutely unheard of. Obvious drug dealers and other illegal activity mongers occupied many apartment homes, with large amounts of traffic visiting select apartment homes. One dealer on the first floor kept a Rottweiler chained up on his balcony while he sat in a porch swing dealing. On the fourteenth floor, Linda tied a black scarf to her balcony, which indicated that the whore house was open for business. She would cross the street from the apartment building to flag down cars by lifting her top revealing her sagging breasts while verbalizing her apartment number.

However, Wendell didn't buy his drugs from his building. In some ways, he had more ethics than to mix business with pleasure. Wendell was a southern boy and hung out with a group of friends also imported from Atlanta, Georgia, better known as "Hotlanta." The three amigos would drive home as often as possible—holidays, birthdays, and some weekends. They frequented a bar in Atlanta that did not serve beer or liquor. They served bottled water and bowls of Ecstasy pills and GHB.

Wendell's drug of choice was "Tina" and "K." "Tina" was short for crystal meth, and "K" was simply ketamine—a cat tranquilizer that doubled as a powerful hallucinogen.

Wendell's buddies often teased about a time when they were driving back from a gay marriage ceremony in San Francisco. Wendell was so high off GHB, Tina, and "X" that he was shaking like a leaf in the backseat of the car he was riding in. The two friends in the front seat had done a lot of drugs too and were often distracted on the road by Wendell's backseat shaking. The driver pulled off to the side of the road and called a college buddy of his, Dr. Ray Keller. "What kind of drugs did he take?" Dr. Keller asked while laughing. "Oh, he's just dehydrated," he said, after learning which drugs were on the menu. "Don't panic; pull into a 7-Eleven and buy a pack of Gatorade and calcium pills to cure his dehydration. He'll be fine within a couple of hours," the doctor advised.

Once during a backyard party, Wendell got so high that he put his grandmother's white wicker rocking chair on top of his friend's vintage Jaguar and rocked off onto the concrete. "I'm done. I'm done!" Wendell screamed, throwing his hands up in surrender after falling to the ground. He wasn't severely hurt, but ten stitches were required.

Back at the property, an eviction was taking place. Bailiffs from the City County's Office were on-site with a third-party moving company transferring the delinquent resident's personal belongings from his apartment to the city street. While movers were riding in the elevator returning to the twenty-fourth floor for another load, three maintenance men were conspiring to steal the pricey items being brought down—a fifty-two-inch flat-panel TV, iPods, brand-new rental furniture, attractive wall art, a Rolex watch in a mahogany jewelry box, 450-count Egyptian cotton linen sets, and lots of other electronic equipment.

Meanwhile, the tenant—a twenty-something mamma's boy—rushed in the management office with a cashier's check for $4,584.34 while his mother was carrying another cashier's check for $8,700. "This should cover his next six months of rent," she said, holding the check between her thumb and index finger. Her nails were beautifully manicured, her makeup was flawless, and her Burberry poncho was fierce. At least, that is what Wendell was thinking. Wendell smiled and accepted both payments while calling the bailiff's cell phone to terminate the eviction process. "Thank you, Mr. Nubbs. Here is my cell phone if my son gives you any more trouble," the stylish mother offered. "Please don't get the wrong idea that Ian will be bailed out of every situation. He's a good kid that makes bad decisions. Besides, I'd rather pay for him to stay here than pay a different price with him in my guest room," she said, making light of an embarrassing situation.

Ian rushed down to the loading dock with his mother looking through the pile of furniture debris, "Where is my watch?" he screamed after turning over the mahogany jewelry box. "Where in the hell is my flat screen? Where is my stuff?" he yelled at pedestrians passing by.

Ian's mother marched back up to Wendell's office, "My son's belongings were being stolen either before or after they hit the street, and I would like some answers." Wendell tried to calm the woman, assuring her that state law requires a landlord to wait twenty-four hours prior to selling, taking, or doing otherwise to a tenant's belongings. However, she was still furious and demanded the phone number to the corporate office or owner's office to pass on to her attorneys.

Meanwhile, Ian's neighbor in apartment #2408 entered the office and said, "Wendell, I think there is something you should know," she said prior to noticing Ian standing near the file cabinet.

"Oh, hi Ian. Actually, I need to tell you too … one of the maintenance guys just tried to sell me a fifty-two-inch plasma TV, and I believe it's yours." Ian raced out of the office to the elevator to try and find the maintenance person or his television.

"Thank you, Donna," Wendell said, trying to coax Donna out of the office.

"See, you are attempting to obfuscate a crime, Mr. Nubbs. You are making no effort to get off your behind and try to catch some of your seedy maintenance men from stealing any more of my son's things," she said. Ian's mother was growing more and more hostile, and the entire ordeal started to spin out of control.

Weeks later, an attorney representing Ian and his family sent a letter of representation indicating the family was filing a suit for $55,000 to reimburse Ian for his stolen personal items and suffering. Because of the property's cash-strapped position, the owners decided to submit an insurance claim with their liability carrier. After a $10,000 deductible was paid and the three maintenance men that conspired to steal Ian's items were terminated, the parties agreed upon a $20,000 settlement.

Chapter 4

Dance as if no one's watching, sing as if no one's listening, and live every day as if it were your last. —Irish Proverb

"Thank you for calling Castleton Towers. My name is Randall, and I can assist you."

"We noticed you all were having the party room painted. Will it be available at seven o'clock for this evening's tenants' association meeting?" a voice inquired on the other end of the call.

"Absolutely, the penthouse suite will be available for the tenants' meeting," Randall answered while rolling his eyes after recognizing Mr. Wells' voice. Randall was careful not to adjust the professional tone of his voice. "Lindsay? Absolutely, she will be attending the meeting, and light refreshments will be served," Randall said, while swiftly waiving his pen in the air in an attempt to capture Lindsay's attention to observe his call.

"Please pass a message on to her … she may want to alert her babysitter; this is going to be a long meeting," Mr. Wells almost promised.

"I will do just that. Is there anything else, sir? All right, have a good night." Randall sprang out of his chair barely securing the telephone receiver on its cradle.

"That was Mr. Wells, and, from the sound of his voice, honey, you are going to need back up at that tenant meeting tonight," Randall shifted from his ultra professional tone to his usual homosexual melodramatic self.

"The primary topic will be the elevators, I know. I am prepared for verbal attacks. Hell, I have survived many of them in this building. I'll be fine," Lindsay assured him.

Lindsay was a tall, voluptuous African-American woman in her early thirties. Her sienna complexion, huge brown eyes, and high cheek bones gave her an attractive yet exotic look. She was very well endowed, with breasts that stood like torpedoes at a size of 44DD. Her hair was naturally kinky. She wore it in a high puff with a decorative hair accessory to coordinate, with her wardrobe.

Lindsay had a commanding presence, yet she was a soft-spoken woman. She would give her last of anything to anyone who needed it.

Upper management had recruited her from an urban housing project that was eventually bought out by the city and converted to condos. She had managed the development for close to seven years and had made miraculous strides in implementing neighborhood crime watch programs and extracurricular activities for troubled youth.

With a predominantly African-American resident base in this high-rise acquisition, owners conceded that Lindsay was a great replacement for the rumored racist shoes she filled.

The Alexandre Martinot wall clock displayed only ten minutes to spare. Lindsay smiled at residents arriving early as she signed the credit card receipt from caterers. Usually, management provided menial refreshments such as bottled water, fresh coffee, and butter cream cake slices due to substandard budget restraints. This time, Lindsay sought approval to spring for wing platters, potato wedges, and Caesar salads.

"Please come in, make yourselves comfortable, and thank you for coming," Lindsay pledged as more and more dwellers started to fill the room. Some began to pick up plates immediately and whispered amongst one another that they did not want to be at the end of the line when the food ran out, as it tended to do at every function hosted by management.

"Please, please. Food will be available after the meeting. Let's allow time for others to get in," Lindsay announced with her hands up. One male resident had already piled his Styrofoam plate with what looked like twenty-five wings and had tongs in hand to hoard the potato wedges. "Sir. No. No. This is not meant to replace your dinner. We are providing complimentary hors'doeuvres only. I'll take that plate, thank you," Lindsay scolded. Others observed in disgust not understanding why it was necessary to wait for the room to fill, realizing that most people attended these meetings just for the free food.

The penthouse suite was a generous-sized room on the twenty-fifth floor of the high-rise community. The space showed definite signs of age and deterioration with wooden floor boards protruding from their flat, secure position. The walls were discolored from water damage, and the leaky windows rattled in the high altitudes of the wind. The downtown skyline was breathtaking, though most windows were obscured because of the precipitation allowed to seep in between panes. Appliances, nevertheless clean, looked as though they had seen the best of days.

Owners had budgeted to offer the room a makeover; however, investors had put a damper on many building improvement plans as income plummeted.

"Ahh, what smells so good?" Mr. Wells asked prior to entering the suite. "Trying to bribe us with chicken, are they?" he quipped.

"Please take your seats," Lindsay said, trying to ignore his sarcasm.

Mr. Wells handed a middle-aged woman a yellow-lined note pad as he announced her to take the meeting minutes. "Good evening, ladies and gentlemen. I have a church program to attend immediately following this meeting, so I assure you we will be brief. I'd like to thank Ms. Lindsay Waters for taking time out of her busy schedule to answer a few questions for us tonight. As you all are aware, we have been after management for several weeks now to do something with these elevators. Many of you have been trapped inside of them or experienced long waits to ride them upon returning home from a hard day at work," he announced before getting interrupted with peanut gallery comments from attendees. "Ms. Lindsay, we would like to think that ownership is aware of the thirty-year-old elevators and concur with the need to upgrade them. Is that a true statement?" Mr. Wells asked extending his right arm and bowing as if to invite Lindsay to take the podium space beside him.

"That is correct. I have passed down information to the owners regarding the challenges with entrapments and such. I have also met with representatives from Reptile Elevator Company that have ordered parts to repair the guides and doors of the freight cars. We simply ask for everyone's patience until the situation is resolved in a favorable manor," Lindsay countered confidently.

"My neighbor said she had to wait almost thirty-five minutes for the elevator this morning and was late to work."

"Yeah, and I was stuck between the thirteenth and fourteenth floors for what seemed like a lifetime. Then, I was told I may have to call the fire department, because management refused to call the elevator company after hours due to the overtime billed."

"And when are you all going to repair the grates falling down in the smaller elevators? One fell over the weekend and hit my grandson in the head. Someone is going to end up getting hurt, and you all are going to have a hefty lawsuit on your hands." Audience members started to volunteer stories.

"Reptile Elevator assured me that the remaining three elevators are safe to ride. We have shut down one of the freight elevators until a part comes in from back order, " Lindsay responded.

"Ms. Waters, are you or owners prepared for a rent strike? Because that is what is getting ready to take place if we do not get any answers to this elevator situation," warned Mr. Wells.

"Obviously, we highly recommend you all not to participate in a rent strike. For risk of irreversible late fees and permanent blemishes on your rent record, it would not be beneficial to parties if a rent strike went into effect," Lindsay retorted.

"Is it true that each of the elevators has failed state inspections and does not display current certificates due to the owner's lack of responsiveness to bring elevators back up to code?" one audience member inquired.

"The state has recommended that we hire an elevator consultant that would help us in the redesign or upgrade of the elevators, yes—keeping in mind that the elevator operation is a shared responsibility. Do you realize how many times our maintenance team has replaced broken fluorescent light bulbs in the elevators? People continue to throw things down the elevator shafts, urinate in the elevators, break the push buttons, write on the doors, carve in the stainless-steel casing … I have been embarrassed by clients' questions about 'what type of people live here' due to the conditions of our elevators. Just this past weekend, Reptile technicians responded to an emergency call that a resident returning home intoxicated from a party dropped his apartment keys down the elevator shaft and was too inebriated to communicate such information to our courtesy officers," Lindsay read from an overtime invoice.

"I don't think it is the people who live here, but guests of the building that cause the majority of the damages," Mr. Wells observed his watch as he replied.

"Regardless of who the culprits are, it doesn't make the repairs and maintenance of the elevators any less expensive. Heaven knows I would rather better spend those dollars to fix the parking garage leaks or redecorate the lobby or this room even," Lindsay shot back.

After many conference calls and e-mails back and forth, owners finally signed off on a bid to refurbish elevator number four. It was one of two freight elevators in Castleton Towers that was in dire need of upgrading.

Katey faxed the approved proposal to Reptile's sales manager who scheduled the work seven days following the facsimile. The sales manager called Lindsay to confirm receipt of the signed bid and to offer his verbal recommendation that the elevator be taken off-line awaiting such repairs. Lindsay drafted an urgent memo to inform the building dwellers that the use of the elevator car would be suspended until further notice.

Problems and rumors of the rent strike persisted when elevator number two started skipping floors and opening midway between floors, soon after number four was taken off-line. This meant the building that housed over three thousand habitants now functioned with two working conveyors.

On Thursday, four days prior to scheduled repairs to commence, the maintenance supervisor released elevator number four to eliminate complaints during rush-hour building traffic. He planned to take it back off-line at 11:00 a.m. that morning, once most people were already at work.

At 8:15am, Mr. Francis called the elevator to the nineteenth floor so that he could retrieve his daily newspaper from the stands in front of the building. Upon stepping on the elevator floor, he pressed the lobby button as he had done for many, many years since his retirement.

Mr. Francis was a vibrant seventy-seven-year-old man. He ran two miles on his ProForm Crosswalk treadmill daily. His body looked that of a fifty something; however, his hands and neck told a different story. Even his face offered a more youthful number than reflected on his AARP card. Mr. Francis was a man of few words, but when asked, he would share the beauty secret behind eating plain oatmeal with blueberries every morning and his faithful patronage to Oil of Olay products.

Courtesy officers were startled at the raging crash that echoed through the lobby, as folks began to look around for signs of a ceiling caving or even worse an earthquake. No one was prepared to see the concrete floor buckled near the elevator shafts.

The elevator door was slightly ajar, displaying the crushed cab. The elevator ceiling, lights, and grates were barely inches from the car's floor.

"Jerome! Jerome! What's your twenty?" Katey's voice was in a panic over the two-way radio.

"I'm in route to the lobby from the third floor staircase … I heard it too!" Jerome responded in no way any calmer than Katey.

Lindsay took the radio from Katey and said, "Jerome, please confirm what the crash was so that I can call Keith. Over." Her demeanor was tranquil as she stood with eyes closed in prayer mode. Keith was one of the asset managers for Castleton.

Mrs. Lopez had just pushed the button after returning from the parking garage. She had left an important client's file on her kitchen counter and returned to the building to retrieve it. "I pushed the button in a frenzy, anxious to get back to the sixth floor … and this one came crashing down … I am so sorry," she apologized.

"Lindsay, elevator number four crashed to the lobby; however, there looks to be no one inside of it. I repeat, no one inside," Jerome responded to her request for information. He tried to console Mrs. Lopez to assure her the accident was in no way her fault, but she was overcome with an eerie feeling that something more was wrong.

An hour later, the lobby was crawling with engineers, supervisors, and consultants from Reptile Elevator, Castleton's ownership and management representatives. The city fire department also sent fire engineers to deem the elevator unsafe and to check the mechanical workings of the remaining three elevators.

One consultant from Reptile thought it best that the crushed cab be taken up to the thirteenth floor where all building systems were housed and ran, especially since no apartment homes were specked or built on thirteen due to architects' superstitions thirty years ago. After hours and hours of deliberation, engineers carefully and manually moved the pulverized cab twelve floors up.

"Oh my God!" Jerome screamed almost silently. "Someone is on that elevator. Call the fire department!" his voice escalated.

In less than ten minutes, sirens could be heard all over the building again. More firemen arrived with chiefs and more city officials. "Richard, how could this have been missed from this morning?" Chief Collins inquired as he ran aside the Reptile consultant who greeted the chief aside his SUV.

The fire department used the Jaws of Life to lift the elevator ceiling from the floor. One supervisor rushed to an opposite corner to regurgitate.

"Sweet Jesus." "Damn." "Oh my God," many sighed as the cab was elevated.

"Lindsay, close off all entries to the building's lobby. I don't want anyone entering or exiting until you hear my voice again, especially the media," Keith somberly commanded.

Firemen directed the emergency rescue team in with a gurney. All had agreed that the body should be propped up on the gurney with a neck brace on to appear simply injured. Building security personnel was heightened in an effort to eliminate media entrance. Residents gathered in streets adjacent to the building, since they were unable to occupy the very rooms they paid for.

Keith rode down to the first floor to advise Lindsay of the tragic news. He had photographed the deceased with his Motorola camera phone prior to the body being rolled out of the building. Lindsay dropped her head when she recognized the snapshot. "Please notify his next of kin only if you are absolutely certain of the identity. Offer our sincerest condolences and our cooperation for them to clear the contents of his apartment. Do not apologize; do not attempt to answer any questions. If necessary, direct them to our attorney's office in Boston."

Following his brief meeting with Lindsay, Keith called a huddle with all site leasing, maintenance, and managers to inform them of today's events. Questions fired off at him regarding the safety of the remaining elevators and if they should cancel appointments for the rest of the week or simply shut down for the day.

Instead, Keith advised them all to take lunch breaks while he decided if the office should close for the rest of the day. He assured the staff members that tomorrow needed to be business as usual and advised that they owed as much to the remaining building dwellers.

Days later, Lindsay e-mailed Keith for authorization to use the company credit card to send flowers to the funeral home. She had decided on a beautiful sympathy, standing spray that stood approximately sixty inches high and forty-eight inches tall on a green easel. Lindsay finished entering the pertinent contact information on the FTD.com screen, when an e-mail from Attorney Len Newman came across her screen:

To: Lindsay.Waters@propmgmt.com
From: Ruben.Newman@propmgmt.com
CC: Keith.Davids@propmgmt.com

Subject: Re: Approval for Flower Purchase

Lindsay,

While I think your heart is in the right place, I strongly suggest that you do not send flowers to the Francis family. It is the consensus of our legal department that though a sympathetic gesture, it would implicate guilt and/or liability.

Please feel free to contact me if you should have any further questions or concerns regarding the Francis case.

Ruben Newman, Esq.
Corporate Attorney

Months later, a second conciliation conference was scheduled at the law office of Ashcraft, Milgram, and Weaver. As details were explored and examined, it was discovered that the late Herbert Francis had never married, never had children, and both parents preceded him in death. However, soon after, litigation was brought on by his fourth cousin, Mimi. Investigations proved that Mr. Francis was estranged from his family because of his sexual orientation, and he had not spoken to Mimi or any other relative in over ten years. Cousin Mimi had only learned of his death and whereabouts from the evening news broadcast.

Mimi, now the plaintiff, was requesting $20 million for the loss of her family member, an amount that seemed preposterous to the corporate defense attorneys based on the distant relationship. Attorneys for Castleton Towers and Reptile Elevators all struggled with the reality that though Cousin Mimi was being unreasonable in her efforts, and they did not want this case heard by a jury or in any courtroom, the fact was that there were several requests made to repair the elevators prior to the fatal accident, to no avail. What the owners were trying to save in repair costs could possibly bankrupt them in litigation for failing to do so.

The judge in the conciliation conference was more concerned with the quality of life Herbert Francis had between the time the elevator was deemed unoccupied to discovery. Autopsy reports could not prove if death was instantaneous or if Mr. Francis suffered for several minutes prior to expiration.

The defense planned to continue the case, possibly dragging it on for years, for hopes that Cousin Mimi, at age seventy-four would not live long enough to see the case through. It just so happened that Cousin Mimi's attorney had pictured the same and pushed to have the case settled out of court. The brilliant female attorney out of UCLA was working on a contingency and could not run the risk.

Finally, the property owners and elevator company indubitably reached a settlement offer of $3.5 million, which they split 60/40, with Reptile writing the more sizable check for poor maintenance.

Castleton Towers went right on the market to be sold. It sat there for over three years prior to selling to a condo converter.

Chapter 5
(Dedicated to Rev. Gregory A. Simmons)

In all your ways acknowledge Him, and He shall direct your paths.
—Proverbs 3:6

Just as Josephine's feet began to hurt from what seemed to be a mile's walk from the parking lot, the usher opened the doors to the sanctuary. "Shh," the usher said as she held a white gloved finger up to her ruby red lips. Someone should have told her she had lipstick on her teeth, but why bother.

"Good morning. God is good. I said God is good all the time!" the minister repeated after a low response from the congregation.

"And all the time, God is good," they returned in unison.

"The topic of today's sermon is Empty Promises," he announced.

"Um," the congregations' murmurs fell over the sanctuary.

"If I had to choose a subtitle, it would be: There's Only One You Can Count On."

"All right." "Well!" susurrations continued from members of the congregation.

"Let me give you an example of an empty promise. Retailers have been known to do it since the beginning of time—the bait and switch. It's when a retailer would advertise for an appliance on sale to bait consumers to visit the store. Once shoppers would arrive, a salesman would say, 'I just sold the last one, but I have this other product over here …' bait and switch—an empty promise," the pastor paused acknowledging the whispers and head shaking in the pews.

"Another example of an empty promise is marriage," he said. He took steps back from the podium knowing in advance the response and sighs that would fall over the audience.

Josephine agreed with his summation of marriage, seeing that she had been divorced for seventeen years and counting. Her sons' father moved south for a better opportunity and was due to send for them once he set up housing and stability. "He must still be looking in the classifieds," Josephine joked once during a conversation in a bar.

"People stand before God and witnesses that they will love each other unconditionally, for better or for worse, in sickness and in health, but an alarming number of them have divorced and broken that promise to the other—an empty promise. Ladies and gentlemen, I come to tell you that there is only one in which you can trust to promise the truth—his name is Jesus Christ." A thunderous applause broke out while the minister took a sip of water.

"Church, even I have broken a promise or two," the pastor confessed. "Ask my wife; she would tell you."

Josephine looked over at the first lady of the church and smiled as she observed her shaking her head up and down agreeing with her husband.

The pastor continued, "Some of you may have had the best intentions, but somehow circumstances may hinder or alter your plans. I've seen many of you after Sunday service, and I would ask if you were coming back for the musical or other late afternoon events. And many of you have lied to my face, 'Yes, pastor, I'll be there.'" Laughter took over the sanctuary.

Josephine felt ashamed as she covered her face and chuckled. Just last week, she promised the pastor that she would return to attend the women's day banquet that evening, but didn't. Ironically, she had all intentions of returning to the church, but she had struggled with a flat tire in a grocery store parking lot. After a frustrating time with the tire and shoving out twenty bucks to a young passerby, she decided to ride her spare home.

"There's only one whose word you can lean on. God's word is the truth, and it will stand on its own!" his voice roared. "God's promise will stand the test of time."

Wearing a floral print dress and her hair pulled back in an asymmetrical style, Josephine sat frozen with her eyes fixated on the mural of Jesus on the stained-glass windows. The word "truth" stuck out like a pregnant woman's belly. She had come to church today looking for answers for a truth she would have to tell come Monday morning.

She was scheduled to have Friday off, for a long weekend, but, Friday night, she received a call from the maintenance supervisor, Ricardo. He called to warn her about her possibly being reprimanded or fired on Monday due to the day's events. Apparently, a hysterical sixteen-year-old girl entered the leasing office demanding that her door locks be changed immediately. She was offered a glass of water and tissue for her eyes by Veronica and Marsha, property manager and assistant manager, respectively.

Once calm, they learned that the young girl's name was Stephanie, and she lived in apartment 1904 with her mother, stepfather, and boyfriend. Veronica informed Stephanie that she was under age and would need her mother to authorize and pay a fee for the changing of locks. Stephanie went on to advise she and her mother had a huge fight after learning that her mother had slept with her seventeen-year-old boyfriend. Stephanie's mother was an ex addict and had lived on the street for ten years before getting clean.

Her mother did not meet the credit qualifications to lease an apartment, so she used her daughter's information during the application process and was approved. So, technically, Stephanie was the lease holder for the apartment. She screamed, "That bitch slept with my boyfriend so I put her out!"

Veronica explained that state laws required all contracts to be signed by legal adults, eighteen years or older, which meant the lease contract was null and void. Marsha pulled the lease file, which indicated that Stephanie and her family had lived in the apartment for nine months, and Stephanie verified her date of birth and social security number listed on the application.

"Wouldn't the credit check software pick up on the date of birth and decline the application?" Marsha asked.

"No, it was not set up to gauge the birth year, only the social security, driver's license, or state ID number for credit and criminal verification," Veronica answered. "The software relies on the property employee to catch the date of birth."

Veronica broke the news to Stephanie that she would have to non renew her lease in three months due to the newly discovered circumstances, but she assured her that Ricardo would come to her apartment within the hour to change the locks after her twenty-five-dollar payment had been received. Stephanie understood and paid the lock fee in cash. She thanked the managers for their time and apologized for the situation.

Ricardo had channel locks and cores in hand while exiting the elevator on the nineteenth floor. He knocked on the door, but there was no answer. He knocked a second time; the response was the same, so he stuck the pass key in the dead bolt lock. Before he could turn the key, a scary voice responded, "If you open that door, I will blow your ass to pieces."

Ricardo suspended all movement, removed the pass key, and ran toward the stair case. He rushed to the sixteenth floor, skipping stairs and almost falling twice to the elevator. He pushed the button profusely until a passenger elevator arrived taking him to the first floor management office. "Call ... the ... police!" Ricardo stammered out of breath.

"Now what?" Veronica questioned.

The police arrived in minutes. Residents milling about in the lobby began to question the reason for the officers' presence. After briefing the officers on what transpired, Ricardo volunteered to escort them to the nineteenth floor. However, he had no intentions of going near 1904 until it was yet unoccupied. Officers rammed the door only to discover three young men making counterfeit money and hanging the money on a clothes line that was strung on several lines in the living area. There were stacks and stacks of money on the sofa and floor. The dining room table resembled a military camp with fire power, including an AK-47, a street sweeper, several nine-millimeter glocks, forty-caliber hand guns, and two fully automatic MAC-10s.

There was one suspect brandishing a weapon near the balcony door wall. He looked to have armed himself shortly after Ricardo's initial knock at the door. Once the apartment door was forced open by officers, the suspect fired the first shot at a rookie officer entering first, who returned fire and fatally wounded the gun toter.

Veronica obviously revised the eviction paperwork from a nonrenewal to a three-day notice to vacate. Arrests were made of the remaining suspects, the locks were changed, and the lease file was audited immediately. New keys were not distributed to Stephanie or her mother, who were never seen or heard from again.

Ricardo went on to inform Josephine that Veronica was very upset to learn that she was the leasing agent that sold the apartment to Stephanie's mother and wondered if Josephine was involved with the moneymaking scam or not. Either way, this was the straw that broke the camel's back to Veronica, and she wanted Josephine terminated.

Josephine had never been so scared in her life. Being a single mother, she could not afford to lose her commissioned position, let alone medical benefits. In other words, she had lots to pray over in church that day.

Josephine snapped out of her trance just as he preached, "God is not dead! We serve a living God, and his name is Jesus. Jesus was crucified at Calvary. Three days later, he rose again with all power in his hands. He came in like a whirlwind … but he left like a whisper. All others who claimed to have the same power as our Lord and Savior are dead and in their graves. Confucius … is dead. Mohammed … is dead. Buddha, dead. All of their bodies may be resumed, and you will find them in their graves, but we serve a living God … Emmanuel! Hosanna! Go ahead … dig up his grave … I promise you it will come up empty. My God is alive, I tell ya!" he exclaimed.

The excitable congregation was in an uproar. Women were on their feet, dancing and shouting. Some had their arms outstretched as if Jesus Christ himself was reaching for them. Some spoke in tongues, while others had their skirts lifted and were dancing a jig.

"The doors to the church are open," he said. The pastor raised his right arm to welcome anyone who would walk down the aisle. Other ministers of the church stood, raised their arms, and walked to their designated areas to provide a welcoming coverage to those lost souls that would join the church.

"Won't you come?" the reverend called out. Josephine began to sob uncontrollably as she felt something or someone pulling her to the center aisle. She took the first lady's hand, felt a comforting group hug, and was whirled to a back office. There were deacons and church nurses in the room awaiting her arrival. They hugged Josephine and shook hands to welcome and congratulate her on saving her soul. A few other lost souls joined Josephine and the others in the pastor's quarters. Shortly after, the pastor and his wife came in to record the names of the individuals and lecture to them what it meant to give their lives to Christ.

The pastor asked all four individuals to give a testimony on what brought them to this stage in their life. One gentleman confessed that he had abused alcohol for over fifteen years, and it had caused him to lose so much: his job, wife, and family; he feared his life was next. Another woman admitted to being an adulterer and admitted that she was asking the Lord to take the desire from her to save her marriage. It approached Josephine's turn, and tears continued to flow down her cheeks. "I've never done anything right, my entire life. You've gotta admit, that takes skill," she said. She let out a nervous laugh, but no one else shared her humor. "I've lied, cheated, and stole my entire life. I'm forty-two years of age, and I'm tired. I'm just tired," Josephine sniffed. "I want better for my children," she finished.

The ministers all applauded the testimonies given and offered encouraging words along with a new Bible for the lost souls to begin reading. They were all dismissed.

As Josephine turned the lock to the door of her four-bedroom brick home, she remembered how quiet her ride home was. With the radio powered off, the only thing that spoke volumes was the thoughts in her head to not even show up at the property tomorrow—to simply call and resign over the phone.

"Thank you for calling Spring Hills; this is Randi. How may I help you?" An unfamiliar voice answered. Josephine was almost sure that Randi was from the local Temp Agency.

"Randi, you must be new there; I don't think we've met. Is Veronica in?" Josephine put on an act.

"Today is my first day, so I am sure we haven't met. I'm not sure how long my assignment is, but I look forward to meeting you. Veronica is in; may I tell her who is calling?" Randi asked politely.

"Just tell her Jo."

Chapter 6

Nine-tenths of wisdom is being wise in time. —Theodore Roosevelt

Quinci opened the door for her new client, "Welcome home," she said. The foyer was a raw-colored hardwood floor, with a coat closet just left of where Marla was standing. The closet door, like all other interior doors, was a white six-panel raised bifold on a chrome sliding track. Inside of the closet contained a half dozen of cedar hangers. The kitchen was to the right, and it had raw oak cabinets, brushed nickel hardware, and an artistic track lighting hanging from the ceiling. There was a black microwave over the stove, a dishwasher, frost-free refrigerator, and double stainless-steel sink. There were dish towels with a little French chef and coordinating pot holders.

As Marla did a 180-degree turn, she noticed the open breakfast bar with a dark cherry wood dining table on the other side. The sofa appeared custom made with chocolate brown floral print and turquoise accessory pillows. The ottoman was turquoise microsuede. Next to it were a floor lamp with three colored bulbs and a chrome magazine rack, which sat outside of two closed French doors.

"All that's missing is you," Quinci said, as she snapped into sales mode.

"I absolutely love it!" Marla admitted.

"Marla, you mentioned that you needed ample closet space—our apartment homes give you that. You also talked about your desire to paint the walls in warm earth tones. Colors with cool green and yellow undertones promote a more complacent and relaxing feeling. Can't you just picture yourself here?" Quinci closed the sale hard.

Marla was so excited about the closet space and view from the terrace; she sat in the model with a bottled water to complete an application to lease an apartment at Jaguar Towers. Quinci left her in the demonstration model to look around more while she processed her application and credit card.

During the interval, Marla walked toward the bedroom down the hall where a queen bed decorated with striped satin bedding. Behind it was a striped accent wall that looked much like wallpaper. Antique lamps on the night stands, with picture frames, shaggy accent rugs, and awesome black and white prints. The room resembled a successful HGTV project. There was one bath with a stand-up shower stall and plush linen.

She opened the doors to a mushroom painted room with a solid oak, L-shaped desk with a return. On top of the desk, there was a nineteen-inch flat screen monitor with a wireless mouse, wireless keyboard, and a unique desk lamp. In the north corner, there was a lime green plush chair with various vibrating options. A chocolate-colored chenille throw and a large screen TV were in front. Just then, Quinci returned with a sort of sober look on her face. Marla went on and on about how her grandmother's chest of drawers were going to fit perfectly in the master bedroom's corner. She described a set of circular mirrors she wanted to purchase at Target and …

"Marla, I've got some bad news," Quinci interrupted. "Your application was denied due to poor credit."

Quinci finally walked her unqualified client out the door and walked in on a conversation in progress in the leasing office, "Something we used to do at my old company that worked well was an 'all-in-one party,'" Robbie expressed.

"What is an all-in-one party?" Quinci asked.

"It's a way to draw neighbors closer together, a sort of networking scene in which participants would sell or demonstrate a skill, a service, a talent, or a product," Robbie said. Nelson, the property manager, thought it sounded like a splendid idea, one that would foster a more neighborly atmosphere, and it wouldn't cost a lot to put on. "Yes, because the tenants would bring their own products or props," Robbie added.

The planning stage began. Flyers filled the mail room, and corridors advising everyone to stay tuned for more exciting details. The staff agreed that it was best to host such an event on a Thursday evening. Mondays never produce the desired turnout—people are usually feeling the drag from returning to work after a weekend off. Tuesdays aren't a good idea—most are just bouncing back from Monday and now running errands in the evenings. Wednesdays are "hump days"—everyone is happy to have survived Monday and is looking forward to the weekend again. Thursdays just seem to be more relaxed—there's only one more day to go before the weekend. Friday through Sunday—forget about it. Weekends in the summer are reserved for social gatherings: weddings, cookouts, birthday parties, and bridal and baby showers.

Comfortable clothing was called for at the all-in-one party. "Bring your checkbook and an open mind," the flyer read. The posted sign-up sheets quickly filled with everyone from a yoga instructor to a Tupperware salesperson to an insurance agent to a life coach. There were six time slots offered from six to nine in the evening. Participants signed up in half-hour intervals.

First up was the yoga instructor, Mrs. Williams of 18B. She approached the center of the room wearing gray and pink leotards and coordinating leg warmers. "I know what you all are thinking. I'm not going to be rough on you, since this is our first date. Also with any exercise or physical exertion, you should always consult a physician prior to commencing any routine. Please center yourselves in your individual space keeping yourselves at arm's length from your neighbor. With shoulders externally rotated … I need you to inhale and bring your hands and arms up to reach for the sky." The breath was evident in the room.

"Inhale. Hold it for two, three, four, five, and exhale slowly while bringing your arms down by your sides, two, three, four, and five," she said. Mrs. Williams stretched the group while her assistant filled the room with easy listening music to a calm tone. She continued with abdominal and lower back stretches that she ensured would improve posture and increase flexibility. She instructed everyone to center themselves once again, this time in the akimbo position. "Speaking of flexibility, I want to clear up any premisconceived notions and inform you that you are sadly mistaken if you think yoga is all about bending, stretching, and breathing. That isn't even the half of it. Yoga is about a positive energy that you take with you long after class and into real life situations—rush-hour traffic, at work with your co-workers, at home with your children or spouse, better yet—in a room with your in-laws." The room erupted in laughter as the music suddenly changed from easy listening to Christian gospel.

With a soft, whispering voice, Mrs. Williams continued, "At this point, I am going to ask all of you who are able, to sit on the floor, curl into a ball, and meditate." She slowly took to the floor in the same fetal position. "No talking. No laughing. No coughing. Just close your eyes and meditate." A room of forty-five to fifty people all quietly reflecting does just that. After about five minutes, Mrs. Williams raised her head and said, "I'd like to thank you all for your participation and cooperation. Please give yourselves a round of applause." The room boiled in thunderous hand claps. "I'm not much of a salesperson, but I welcome each and every one of you to sign up for a trial membership at my 101 Main Street location in Rochester Hills, for more in-depth yoga training. Thank you," she said. Mrs. Williams collected her portable radio while her assistant walked the room with miniature bottles of ice cold water.

Robbie took center stage to thank Mrs. Williams for her presentation and encouraged audience members to attain one of her business cards and visit her in her Rochester Hills location. "Next up, we have Mya of 13A who is going to paint a picture for us through spoken word. Ladies and gentlemen, Mya," Robbie said. Robbie shuffled the three by five index cards she read from as a young, sassy twenty something approached the front of the room. Mya, wearing the lightest shade of blue eye contacts and a kinky, coily, wig was well received by the group. "This first piece is called, "No Watching My Weight," she said as the muffled sounds of giggles filled the room.

My man says I'm a dime piece, correctly curved. Thick. A ten;
While the rest of you chicks count calories and eat low carbs to remain thin.

*You thin girls, doing squats and sit ups, running on treadmills and
skipping meals for skinny thighs;*
*You're curious why I don't worry when he goes out clubbing with the
boys or works late—ask me why.*

It's because I suck him every day with a wet mouth—all tongue no teeth;
Every chance he gets—he's calling, texting, and speeding home to get to me.

*Running red lights and stop signs, imagining the great sex we'll have
that night;*
*While I'm soaking in the tub—Calgone take me away—hot water
shrinks it back tight.*

*You thin girls go through your man's wallet and pockets looking for
phone numbers—I've never been that type, but do what works for you;*
*I say to hell with Jenny, the lower beach, that stuff that killed Anna
Nicole, and damn weight watching too!*

Mya took a bow while the younger crowd members snapped their
fingers in the air. More conservative audience members hadn't recovered
from "sucks him every day."

"Talk about painting a picture—wow!" Robbie attempted to lighten
the mood. "Next up, Sam Wilkins of 20D giving financial advice. I
better listen carefully. Sam?" A round of applause was given.

"Uh, what a hard act to follow, Mya. No pun intended. Remind
me to obtain parental consent prior to the next function," Sam joked
as he set up pie charts and graphs on easels. His balding hairline and
pocket protector received more stares than the charts he displayed.
Mya, seated in the rearmost area of the room, lifted her glass to him
and smiled.

Sam gave sound advice on diversifying stock portfolios, money
market accounts, and 401K options. He stressed the importance of
resisting the desire to withdraw 401K funds, indicating that the tax
penalties are extremely harsh. "Do not allow this bailout to influence
you negatively, and please, please be cognizant of your FICO score—
knowing your credit history like the back of your hand is critical."

Sam also encouraged attendees to pay off and close department store credit cards due to the higher interest rates they carry and pay more than minimum balances on all others.

"Easier said than done," one guest recited.

Sam wrapped up his presentation and offered a Web site in which more stock tips were available. Leaving guests with food for thought, he said, "We've got to see around the corner—in respect to the economy—and anticipate some things so that we are proactive and not reactive."

Robbie thanked Sam for his expertise, "I am positive that Sam's tips will help everyone reap clear financial rewards, which, in turn, will help you all pay your rent on time … up next …" Robbie paused for laughter.

After several seconds, she introduced Yvette Cleveland, a motivational speaker and life coach consultant. Yvette received her Master's Degree from Harvard and doctorate from Howard University. She described herself as a precise, accurate, and meticulous individual—one who disliked making mistakes and showed grave concern with the details of her job and traveling assignments. "I start everyday by saying—today is going to be a fantastic day!"

She spoke a great deal about God and the universe. She shared her personal story and tied in her dreams and challenges, while offering encouragement and sound advice to the audience members. "It's important to keep a healthy balance between work, play, and family—not necessarily in that order," she preached.

She described her life as a child in an unstable household, "My father and I lived with my grandmother—his mother—because my mother ran off and left us. My father was a pimp and hustler, who was stabbed in the eye for dealing on the wrong territory."

Yvette went on to describe her bipolar mother who was addicted to psychotherapy drugs. She told a story of her sitting on her grandmother's porch combing her doll baby's hair when a gang member walked up the stairs and asked for Mrs. Cleveland. "Grandmaaaa! I yelled into the screened door never taking my eyes off this lout's hand. My grandmother appeared, wiping her hand on her apron. 'What chile!' I remember her saying. Once both of her feet were planted firmly on the porch, the gangster lifted up my grandmother's right hand to put in it my father's right eye."

A level of quiet that was unlike any pin-dropping moment fell over the room. Standing in two and three-quarter-inch stacked high heels, with a fair complexion and shoulder-length tousled, casual hair, Yvette talked about her failed marriage and how she raised two young boys on her own. "I married the high school football star. You know the type: handsome head of hair, kissable lips, cute face, and rock hard abs. Little did I know that the once-high-school-star athlete would wait until he was in his forties to become addicted to crack cocaine."

Several heads began to shake in the audience. "Yeah. I guess you could call me a life coach, because life sure happened to me," Yvette chuckled. "In life we're all dealt a different hand of cards. You play them the best you can—with skill, with strategy, with emotion. Win or lose, what matters the most is that you learn from the hand that was played."

Yvette combed the room looking for young adults, "The one thing I wish I had growing up was a wise person who could warn and get through to me of the struggles in life. Take the time now to further your education; read books and magazines that matter like *Forbes* and *Time*. Yes, I rose from the ashes, but had I known now back then, I would have walked around the fire and not through it." A round of applause filled the room. "Allow me to leave you with this Norwegian Proverb. It describes what the pencil maker said to all the pencils before he put them in a box to be sold."

> *First he told them, you're only as effective as the hands you are put in.*
> *Second, you will experience a painful sharpening.*
> *Third, you have the ability to correct your own mistakes by turning yourself upside down.*
> *Fourth, the most important thing about you is inside of you.*
> *Fifth, wherever you go, leave your mark.*
> *Last, but not least, even if you break, you can still write.*

It was a meaningful proverb that led to the plaudits of attendees. Yvette received a standing ovation as she took her seat. "Ladies and gentlemen, Dr. Yvette Cleveland," Robbie said, as she extended her hand in the direction of the life coach for an extended celebration for her presentation. "And if that doesn't work, remember that it takes one hundred muscles to frown and only three muscles to smile," Robbie said and paused for laughter. "I'd like to take this time to thank all of our participants tonight. We had no idea what to expect with our format, and you all have exceeded our wildest expectations—many, many kudos to you. I would also like to thank our fearless leader, Nelson, for allowing me to run with this. And last, but certainly not least, I'd like to thank each and every one of you, residents of Jaguar Towers, for attending with an open mind. Refreshments are being served immediately following the program, thank you for coming out, and good night."

Chapter 7

One that desires to excel should endeavor in those things that are in themselves most excellent. —Epictetus

"Things happen over time not over night. You have to be patient dear," Rebecca's mother offered sound advice. Rebecca called for some of her mother's animated words of encouragement after receiving yet another rejection letter from a prospective employer.

"I have a stack of rejection letters so tall, Erin could use them as a booster seat," she joked masking desperation. Rebecca, a free-spirited vegetarian, was also a licensed pilot, a certified engineer, and she received her doctorate from Michigan State University.

At age fifty-four, wearing voluminous wavy hair, she was an absolutely brilliant woman, but she was recently terminated from a firm for sexual harassment. "When I'm conversing with friends, I can be honest … I did it," Rebecca said candidly. She would go on to describe how she used her executive power to block the promotion of her office concubine.

Rebecca refused to heed the guidance of her best friend when revealing her sexual escapades with Felix, who was twelve years her senior. "Finally you're having a sex drought, and I'm having a bump in crop," Rebecca once bragged about her office romance shortly before relinquishing her six-figure salary and future pension.

Ms. Casey, Rebecca's mother, always suspected that her daughter's addiction to porn, one-night stands, and men in general was due to her father's absence early on. At the tender age of nine, Rebecca lost her father, Sergeant First Class Casey, while he was deployed overseas. Of course, commanding officers told a different story, but a weapons specialist very close to her father shared a more believable truth to the family.

He told the story of how a foreigner was begging near the military base in which their brigade was consistently stationed. An American military cook was washing dishes and discarding the leftovers in the alley behind the kitchen. Sergeant First Class Casey couldn't stand to see the food being scrapped when there was an obvious homeless and starving person in their radius. Sergeant First Class Casey graciously gave the pot of food to the beggar, who was extremely grateful. A sergeant major caught wind of such act of kindness and sent orders down to have Sergeant First Class Casey killed for his generous act of treason.

Two years prior, when Rebecca was seven, her father was injured in Korea. Ostensively, a little girl was on the side of a road in Korea selling bottles of soda to the soldiers. She had an innocent face and a polite gesture that melted the hearts of these trained American killers. Shortly, many were sick, and no one had linked the ill soldiers to be those that had purchased soda pop road side from the young Korean girl. Finally, one of the military doctors performed an x-ray exposing several small fragments of glass in the soldier's organs. It was soon discovered that terrorists were grinding up glass and adding it to the soda bottles.

Rebecca, who married once in her late twenties, fell in love and moved to New York with a law student who was gearing up to pass the bar. Rebecca was studying to be an engineer at the time that her promising prosecuting husband bought a condo in New York's Flat Iron District. Both soon learned that they were growing in different directions when Rebecca's husband tried to surprise her at a dinner party with a $30,000, mid-length Russian sable fur coat that she burned on the hibachi grill on the deck in front of an audience that same evening. Rebecca was an animal activist in her early college years, while her husband lived for the finer things in life.

In most instances, opposites attract, but Rebecca saw such an action as her husband not knowing her at all. Soon after her divorce, Rebecca took pause in seeking a new relationship and traveled the world by train. She spent the better part of her divorce settlement on a nine-month excursion from one end of the map to the next. Aside from a seven-day safari in South Africa, Rebecca primarily traveled the United States. An abundant amount of time was spent in the southeast rain forests in Alaska.

Rebecca was the second born of three siblings. Her mother along with other family members often attributed Rebecca's sometimes crass behavior to that of a middle child with middle child syndrome. What psychologists and other field doctors have suspected about middle born children is that they tend to be loners and have a pattern of failed relationships. It has also been suspected that the majority are very artistic and creative, and they have a tendency to start several projects but rarely finish them—hence, Rebecca's numerous degrees in a variety of educational realms. Another presumed characteristic of second born children is they tend to be under achievers, which in itself was definitely not the case with Rebecca.

Rebecca had gone on to accomplish several degrees and academic accolades, including a special tribute from PETA for a thesis she wrote on animal rights and her life as a vegetarian. After her fiftieth birthday, Rebecca was fixed up on a blind date by one of her best friends, Lisa, from Columbia University.

Lisa stood behind a gentleman in a 7-Eleven who was polite enough to allow her to take the spot in front of him. That kind gesture struck up a conversation, which prepared the opportunity for him to ask her out. "I'm happily married, though you would have never guessed by the absence of my wedding ring," Lisa said holding up her left hand. She smiled and turned back to the cashier to receive her change from her bottled water purchase. "However, if you are single … I have a friend that I would love to fix you up with," Lisa replied.

"If she is as attractive as you, by all means, pass my card on to her," the mystery man said with a smile and a business card in hand. His business card read, "Barry Scott, construction superintendent."

Rebecca had sworn off men and was dead set against blind dates, as she reached another milestone in her life. She was curious at the least and decided against her better judgment and called Barry. Being a public speaker and having an aggressive personality, Rebecca never felt as nervous as to when she initiated the phone call with Lisa standing next to her hanging on her every word. Barry's voice was soothing, and he acted as if he was anxiously awaiting her call, which put her at ease. The two agreed to meet at a nearby bistro for drinks and appetizers.

Rebecca arrived early to have the advantage of preparedness to walk out in case he was a total dork. However, she was pleasantly surprised. He was obviously physically fit, which she had suspected given his profession. He was clean shaven, tall with sandy brown hair, and spoke in a sexy baritone voice. He wore a corduroy blazer with a pair of boot-cut jeans, a button-up shirt, and boots. The two conversed for hours over appetizers and ended up back at Rebecca's place for a night cap. He talked a lot, which was comforting to Rebecca. She disliked having to romanticize her life to strangers so that they wouldn't think she was a freak—if the truth was revealed. Plus, she was a great listener and a great kisser, according to Barry.

One thing led to another, and the two ended up spending the night together—in the nude. Rebecca had a lot of self-esteem issues about her past and her upbringing, but all of her shyness went away whenever her clothes were off in the company of a man. The two saw each other as often as possible and even double dated with Lisa and her husband. Lisa was very assertive and used such occasions to toot her own horn over the love connection she birthed, against her husband's appetence.

The fall season was closing out, which gave Rebecca more excitement, because she knew that she and Barry would be spending a lot more time together—as he would be laid off for several weeks. Such time did permit itself, and the two were heavily involved until the incident. With Barry laid off, he was less frivolous with his money and often insinuated for Rebecca to fund an occasion or outing. Rebecca soon found herself writing checks to Barry's landlord and creditors.

One morning, Rebecca received the shock and disappointment of her life when she retrieved the mail from her box. Her alternate savings account was wiped out from over $3,600 to a negative $250. Clueless as to the culprit, Rebecca filed a police report and alerted the credit bureaus of the fraud. With an 800 FICO score, she could not risk being the victim of identity theft.

Turns out, Rebecca's perfidious lover was the culprit, withdrawing several thousand dollars from local ATMs after his crafty observance of Rebecca's pin number during one of their dates. After reviewing the images captured from the ATM camera, Rebecca recalled how Barry could have come to know her pin number. It was one night they chose to leave her car behind and take a taxi back to her place after having one too many drinks at a pub.

Rebecca refused to press charges, which infuriated her friend and reason for such a treacherous union, Lisa. Shortly after Rebecca's funds were replenished, so were the emptiness and lack of faith in love again.

The phone rang, "Is Rebecca Casey available?" a voice asked.

"This is. How may I help you?" Rebecca asked. It was a property management firm looking to interview her for a district manager position opening in Denver, Colorado.

"Greta Tressler from our firm sent an e-mail early this morning; however, I am calling to make your travel arrangements," the caller advised. Rebecca burst into tears of joy. During her nine-month excursion of the United States, she thoroughly enjoyed bike riding and hiking in Denver.

Her accommodations were in a four-star hotel in Colorado Springs where one of the management company's largest assets was built. At $2.95 per square foot, this high-rise community took pride in being one of the priciest and most sought after real estate in the multifamily market. As Rebecca prepared for her interview the following day, she took in great shopping, mountain climbing, and sightseeing in the Pikes Peak region.

The following Monday, Rebecca set out to interview with the lead stock holder and CEO along with the chief marketing director for the property management firm. She complimented the executives on achieving excellence in the multifamily residential industry and was honored to be considered for a position with their company.

"Please relax and have a seat," the CEO, Steven Cox, suggested.

"You'll be happy to know that we tend to have a more relaxed interview style than most Fortune 500 companies," offered CMD, Natasha Beasley. "Make no mistake, we are interviewing for a rather important six-figure salary position; however, applicants are pretty well screened prior to making it to this phase with our company," Natasha continued.

Steven Cox went on to explain to Rebecca that though they prided themselves on their eco-friendly construction projects and traditional architecture, the company was now moving in a new direction. "We are also interested in purchasing, constructing, and managing our own assets. Thus, we are looking for an individual with a creative clear vision that could help take this company to the next level," Cox said.

Natasha advised that she had several slides of properties to show Rebecca. As her first task, Rebecca was asked to recite a caption for each slide as if she was writing the marketing plan, request for proposal, or simply selling the management firm to a new client.

Natasha started the projector and revealed the first slide. "Tell me how you would pitch this property."

Rebecca prefaced this by saying, "You don't need me to tell you what a beautiful edifice you have on your hands here. What you and your affiliates have done to brand yourselves and dominate the market is nothing short of genius. In case I forget to tell you afterward, thank you for the opportunity to interview with you today."

She turned to the projected screen and said, "Whether you are retired or a top-notch executive, you will enjoy taking time to luxuriate in our spacious, architecturally unique floor plans. Admire breathtaking views from colossal floor-to-ceiling windows. Enjoy designer-selected color schemes and resplendent bathrooms with his-and-her sinks. Our high rise offers several well-appointed features such as a 20,000 square foot recreation center with a full-service athletic club as well as an on-site spa offering body treatments, massages, facials, and hydrotherapy."

Natasha nodded and said, "Impressive. How about this one ..." as she clicked the remote to the second slide.

"Uh, why don't we wrap it up here," Cox interrupted, giving Rebecca the feeling that maybe he was not impressed with her over-the-top antics.

"Actually," Rebecca punctuated. "May I return a question to you?" Rebecca asked, while sitting down in a chair, resembling the demeanor of a mob boss holding a cigar in his hand. "Who would you trust to manage your brand ... your gem ... your reputation? Would you leave it to some young hotshot fresh out of grad school, who's got a point to prove, but lacks the maturity? Or do you trust it with someone who's been around the block a few times and knows what bullshit waits around the corner?" Rebecca cleverly pointed out. "I have my real estate license in five states. Colorado will be my sixth. I am unwed and never bore a child, which means I am married to my job. Allow me to say that I look forward to golfing or hiking with both of you after I get your properties stabilized," Rebecca concluded.

"Ms. Casey, we thank you for your time this morning and wish you a safe trip back home," Cox fired back. Rebecca dropped her eyes and picked up her Coach briefcase from the floor beside her chair. "My executive administrative assistant, Sheila Griffis, will be sending your package information," Cox continued.

Rebecca's forehead wrinkled in confusion, "I don't understand—package information?"

Cox and Beasley stood and extended their right hands, "Yes, welcome to Cox Management Services."

Chapter 8

I never knew what real happiness was until I got married. And by then it was too late. —Max Kauffman

"Hi, we have a three o'clock with Dr. Tyner," a woman said.

"You must be Shelly Rucker and Phillip Rucker?" the receptionist asked. "Please complete the new patient form and return it on this clipboard to the desk. Dr. Tyner is recording notes from her last session and will be right with you," the receptionist instructed.

"Thank you," Mr. Rucker responded while taking the clipboard, as his wife had already walked away.

"You know, I don't have the best penmanship, would you mind doing the writing?" Phillip asked.

"Why should I? It is because of your extracurricular relationship that we are here in the first place," Shelly expressed. Phillip looked up at the desk with a nervous smile to see if the receptionist had heard the last few comments.

"Can we not do this? We're going into this first session with a negative mindset; it can't be healthy," Mr. Rucker tried to reason.

"Go to hell Phillip! Is that positive enough for you?" Mrs. Rucker exclaimed.

"You know what—screw it!" she continued, as she stood up to approach the receptionist's desk. "Excuse me, could you leave a note for Dr. Tyner that we are going to have to reschedule. It's too …"

"Mr. and Mrs. Rucker, thank you for coming. Please, right this way," The doctor interrupted just as Mrs. Rucker was attempting to reschedule.

The doctor advised that she understood their appointment was based on a referral by one of her other patients. "Yes, one of my good buddies, Chuck Henderson. He spoke highly of you," Phillip confirmed.

"Yes, and he also fucked around on his wife," Shelly retorted.

"Shelly, thank you for opening the floor. Why don't you start? Tell me what brings you both here?" Dr. Tyner encouraged.

"Excuse me if I come off extremely aggressive. I am not usually this bitchy," said Shelly.

"You said 'also.' Is that what prompted your visit today? Did Phil have an affair?" the psychologist asked.

"Correct. He has been carrying on with a woman I befriended—a woman I entrusted in my home, a woman that he screwed in my bed." Tears began to flow down Shelly's cheeks as Phillip adjusted several times in the microfiber chair he was sitting in.

The psychologist was sporting a dark red sort of wedding updo. "Phillip, you seem very uneasy and fidgety. Did you not expect us to delve right in during this first meeting?" the doctor asked.

Phillip answered saying that he really didn't know what to expect during their first session. What vexed him the most was his wife's tone. "I'm just altogether sick of her attitude," Phillip said.

"Really? How interesting of you to be so fed up," the doctor observed.

Shelly hit the sofa to confirm the doctor's last statement. "Ground rules folks; I am not taking sides—now or ever. I simply speak my mind and what I consider my truth. I invite you both to do the same. Speak candidly, speak freely, and speak only to me unless otherwise instructed. I have found in my twenty-three years of practice that people hear better when the most hurtful statement is not directed to them. Understood?" The couple responded to the doctor by nodding their heads.

Shelly spoke out, "You'll find, Dr. Tyner, that Phil's attitude is so arrogant at times, you would think it was me who spent a lot of time on my back over the past eighteen months."

"Uh-huh," the doctor said. She began taking notes again, as she did the first time Shelly made her "he also" comment. "Question, Phillip. Is the affair over?" the doctor queried while Shelly folded her arms as to say she would also like to hear the answer to that question. She swung her long, stringy locks over her shoulders while her right leg bounced nervously over the left.

Phillip cleared his throat and said, "I haven't seen that woman in over a month, nor slept with her or anyone else that I have been accused of sleeping with."

"Now we're getting somewhere," the doctor said. "What did she do for you that Shelly didn't?" she continued.

"Excuse me?" Phillip was taken off guard by the question.

"I'm sure you understood the question, but allow me to rephrase it. A spouse usually looks outside the home to find what they are missing or not receiving inside the home. Surely you've heard of the 80/20 rule. How did this other woman stimulate you? Was it mental, which is just as harmful to a marriage? Was it a physical stimulation—body language, flirting, aggression, or sex?" the doctor explained. Now it was Shelly who began to adjust in her seat.

"If I may be honest, it was more of the mental stimulation. She listened to me and seemed genuinely interested in my conversation. We talked about my hobbies …" Phillip responded.

"Which are?" the doctor interrupted.

"Well, I like to fish. I also like to build model cars, boats, and such. When we owned a house, the garage was my haven—away from the kids, away from my home office, away from my wife, even."

"What happened to your house?" the doctor questioned.

"Can I answer that?" Shelly asked while raising her hand as if she was in a classroom. "We had a beautiful home in a suburban subdivision. It was every woman's dream—a white picket fence, garden, deck, three-car garage, play space for the children—the whole nine yards. While Phillip worked, worked late and worked overtime, I was out spending the money. I shopped, and we took trips until we were forced to refinance ourselves into bankruptcy. We lost our house, moved into a small apartment downtown, Amour Terraces. How ironic, huh? My oldest daughter has not been able to forgive me since we lost our house. Isn't that what you would have told the doctor, Phillip?"

"Interesting," the psychologist said, as she took notes.

Shelly offered more, "I'm not too proud to admit my faults. I have a habit of being very controlling, very manipulative, and condescending. Yes, I am all of those things, but I am no adulterer."

"There she goes, playing the victim again," Phillip defended himself as he arose from his seat. He began to pace the back of the office with his hands in his khaki pant pockets.

"And how does that make you feel, Phillip?" the doctor examined.

"She forced me into this other woman's arms by being all those things she named—her manipulative ways, her condescending tones, her controlling personality, her constant attacks to my manhood," he resounded.

"Phillip, if I am hearing you correctly, this other woman made you feel like the head and not the tail. She gave you the control in all situations, primarily sexual situations, because there are not many opportunities outside of home life. She couldn't give you control over the kids. She could not allow you to control money, because I could image you wouldn't have joint accounts or much less talk finances with that type of third party. So she allowed you to dominate things like when you wanted to see her and how you wanted to be pleasured during intimacy. How am I doing so far?" the doctor checked for accuracy.

"You are right on. And if I am being honest with myself and my wife, those things are important to me, and those were the attributes this other woman possessed," Phillip admitted.

"Okay Phillip. But did I cause you to screw this woman in our house?" Shelly began to get defensive.

"Let's look at that, Shelly. You posed the question, so let's look at it together. By your own admission, you were a big problem in your marriage. You took away powers from your husband—powers that every man needs to have as head of the household. You, Shelly, got in your own way. Reading back in my notes, Shelly, you mentioned that you entrusted this woman in your home. How so?" the doctor surveyed.

"Well, we had just refinanced our home for the second time in an effort to lower our monthly debt. I thought it would be a great idea to hire someone to redecorate our home—a 3,200-square-foot project. Long story short, Phil spoke of a woman that did a 'superb job' decorating the office building in which he worked," Shelly said, as she gestured with air quotations during "superb job." "I asked that he invite her to brunch one Saturday so that she could see the house, the space, and such. I wouldn't say we became best friends, but this woman and I were fond of each other's tastes and levels of creativity. We shopped together for accessories she chose. I paid her, thanked her, and invited her back for future gatherings we hosted, but someone else invited her to our bed," Shelly finished.

"Interesting," the doctor commented. "Why don't we wrap up this first session here? Before leaving each session, I require couples to write down one thing—one word that describes your partner, one positive word that illustrates the reason you want to save your marriage. Unacceptable words would be children, money, convenience, etc. These words do not describe a person; they describe a circumstance," the doctor offered. "I am making a log of positive attributes and adjectives that describe each of you. Once you have written the word in the space provided, date that page, close your journals, and place them on the credenza near the door on your way out. Good evening to you both. You have three minutes," she said. The doctor turned off her recorder and stepped out of the consultation room.

Shelly returned to her downtown apartment home to cook dinner for the children, while Phillip retired to his buddy's house for the evening. The two thought it best that Phillip removed himself from the home in an effort to disrupt the children's lives as little as possible. In the meantime, Shelly was playing a psychologist's role for her friend, Naomi.

Naomi was a divorcee who had just reentered the dating scene. She met a gentleman by the name of Duane who she described as a hopeless romantic. Duane was an IT geek for a large automotive company who wrote Naomi poetry, bought her nice things, and wined and dined her. Since on her hiatus from men, Naomi found Duane to be very suspicious; however, she couldn't put her finger on what it was he could have been hiding. Duane, thirty-six, was a divorced single father of his twelve-year-old son. Naomi would sometimes spend the night with Duane where he would purchase a new negligee for her to wear and make mad, passionate love to her. He'd run a bubble bath for her and bathe her in the master bath suite. He was a great cook and prepared awesome candlelit meals for the two—always with champagne or her favorite Riesling wine.

After listening to an urgent voicemail left by Naomi, Shelly returned the call to get her mind off of her own marriage drama. "Girl, what took you so long to call me back?" Naomi asked.

"You know today was the first day of our marriage counseling," Shelly reminded her.

"I totally forgot. How was it?" Naomi asked with a concerned voice.

"Terrible. I don't want to talk about it right now ... what happened with you and Mr. Right?" Shelly switched gears.

Naomi described her last conversation with Shelly regarding the possibility that she was pregnant by Duane. Apparently, Naomi broke the news to Duane and was not pleased with his initial reaction. He tried to smooth things over by the end of that night by saying that he just needed time to think of the next best step. Naomi took matters into her own hands and stole a pre-signed blank check out of Duane's personal checkbook. "I wrote the check out for an odd amount so that he wouldn't suspect anything—$3,654. Girl, I paid $600 for the abortion last week and went shopping. I was calling to see if you wanted to go have dinner somewhere or I could come downtown, order in so that you wouldn't have to cook tonight!" Naomi had it all worked out.

Shelly was totally shocked by her girlfriend's news and suggested that they order in steak and crab legs from a local bar and grille downtown. "I'll put the kids to sleep after they eat, and you can tell me more. By that time, I'll be ready to discuss our counseling session ..." Shelly confirmed.

Days later, the phone in the apartment rang. "Courtney, don't hang up; it's daddy ... honey, it's good to hear your voice. I want you to know that none of this is your fault, nor has it anything to do with my love for you and your brother. Your dad is sick, okay ... I'm getting help right now, okay ... I just need you to work on forgiving me ..." Phillip begged.

"Whatever," she responded.

"No, Courtney. It's not whatever. I really need you right now, okay? Just because I'm not living there with you all right now doesn't mean that I don't still love you. I love you all so much … and I want to come home … it's just … it just has to be this way right now—temporarily. I hope you understand … I love you, Court," Phillip stammered.

"Yeah, yeah. Mom? Phone. It's Phillip!" Courtney yelled as she slammed the receiver on the kitchen breakfast bar.

"Hello?" Shelly said, after she picked up the phone.

"Hi Shelly. I was just checking—is there any way you could pick me up for our session this evening? I have a flat tire, and my spare is actually flat too. If you can't, I'll understand and find other means of transportation."

"Stop your whining, Phil; I'll honk the horn around 4:30. Look, I gotta go," she said. Shelly slammed the receiver on the cordless base.

"Courtney, honey, I'm going to drop your brother off at Aunt Mary Lou's on my way. I don't want you to have any company here until I return. Is that understood?" she asked.

"Yes, mom," Courtney answered with a devilish grin on her face. "Jax? Jax, sweetheart—mommy is gonna take you to auntie's, okay?" Shelly yelled out, as she instructed her son to grab his Spiderman pillow. "Courtney, I mean it—no boys," Shelly said with a firm voice.

"Okay," Courtney answered in an annoyed tone. As her mother and brother walked out the door, she picked up the phone and began to dial, "Turn your TV to the lobby channel. When you see my mom exit, come on up, okay?"

Courtney ran to the hall bath mirror. She let her hair down, and then she smoothed lip balm over her lips. Her long tresses resembled those of her mother. She smacked her lips as she twisted the top down on the strawberry-flavored balm. She dabbed a little of her mom's perfume behind her ears, then a little on her wrists, which she rubbed together. She skipped through the apartment, smiling as she went to unlock the door and pull out a bottle of Tequila from her dad's stash box. She set up two shot glasses, an ashtray, and a pack of off-brand cigarettes near the balcony bistro furniture set.

There was a light tap on the door, and then it opened. A teenage boy walked in with curly dark hair and framed glasses on. "Out here, Brian," she yelled from the balcony. He slid open the door only to find Courtney sitting in one of two chairs with her feet up on the balcony railing.

"You look great, babe," he said, as he leaned in for a kiss.

"So do you," she said.

"I brought two brews, want one?" he offered. She took one of the twenty-ounce bottles as he sat beside her in the second chair. At first, there was silence, except for the rush-hour traffic going on below. "Where was Jax going? To your aunt Mary's?" Brian asked in an attempt to break the silence.

"Yeah. My mom was picking up my dad for their therapy session tonight," Courtney answered.

"That's the first time in a long time that I've heard you call Mr. Rucker your dad," Brian observed.

"No, I didn't!" Courtney yelled.

"Yeah, you did," Brian reminded her.

"Yeah ... well ... I meant to say Phillip," she said. Courtney smirked as she stood up, leant over the balcony, and drank out of her bottle of beer held between her thumb and index finger. The silence was back.

"Hey, I didn't mean to upset you," Brian said, as he stood and joined her.

"You ever wonder where they're going?" Courtney asked.

"Who?" Brian asked, wondering.

"Them," she answered, pouring a swallow of beer down to the street level. "I love watching traffic from this level. I guess I've always loved it ... from any level—the moving cars. Imaging who the drivers are ... what they are thinking ... where they're going. Lame, huh?" she snickered.

"Not at all. Watching them does make you wonder," he said.

"Good afternoon. Phillip. Shelly. How are you? Come in and have a seat, please," Dr. Tyner said. "I want to start off today's discussion of moving day. You live separately now. How was that first day of separation?" the doctor continued.

Shelly spoke first, "As you know, Courtney has resented her father ever since my discovery of his affair."

"As expected. Remember, after we get to a certain point in our sessions, I will invite Courtney to join us. For now, let's talk about moving day. What was it like for you, Phillip?" the doctor asked.

He cleared his throat and said, "Well, it was no picnic; that's for sure. My wife and I agreed it was best for me to leave, with Jax in daycare downtown and Courtney enrolled in sports, it was obviously in the best interest that we did not disrupt the children's routine."

"Shelly, same question. How was moving day for you?" the doctor asked.

"It's funny, as badly as I wanted Phil out of my sight, as much as I thought I hated him at that moment … moving day was very painful for me. It was hard watching the children's reaction—watching Jax bring all of his toys and clothes out of his room and set them near his father's belongings near the front door. That was heartbreaking. Watching Courtney as she pouted and stormed the apartment trying her damnedest to seem emotionless—that was hard. But the most depressing, the most traumatic thing for me was the look on Phillip's face. The lonely and lost look he displayed was the most hurtful and caused the most pain for me. More so than the picture I get in my head when I think of him screwing that tramp in my home," Shelly said, as she began to cry.

"Interesting. Phillip, how does that make you feel to hear your wife say that it disgusted her more to see you hurting?" the doctor asked.

"To be honest, it makes me feel like there is hope," he answered back. "Shelly, what if I told you—that hurtful, depressing, and traumatic look was karma rearing its ugly head to Phillip? That lonely, empty feeling was reaped from the arrogance he displayed previously when he invited another woman into your lives. What do you say to that?"

"I say, well done, God," Shelly continued to cry as Phillip dropped his head into his hands, with elbows resting on his knees. "I mean … as I said, I felt sorry for him that day, but voicing that and hearing your response to that … I feel like right on. God doesn't like for his children to hurt, so when you hurt one of God's children, he will hurt you in return," Shelly finished.

"That's an interesting way to look at it. Phillip, any response to that?" The doctor asked.

"I guess I would have to agree in part with both of you. I remember the 'one up' feeling I would get juggling both women … both homes … both lives. I would feel this rush of power when I had to say, 'No, I can't see you today,' and she would just cower and ask when. The rush I felt when I would lie to Shelly and tell her I was working late and advise her not to wait up. I feel really bad right now, knowing that she believed me all those late nights," Phillip said, as he began sobbing himself.

"After your … dates with this other woman, what would you do Phillip?" the doctor asked.

"We basically never met or had a visit that did not end up with a sexual encounter. So afterward, I would shower and go home," Phillip answered. In the meantime, Shelly got out of her seat to walk over to the water cooler in the corner of the psychologist's office. She slowly grabbed a triangular cup from the dispenser, filled it halfway, and drank slowly all the while with her back to Dr. Tyner and her husband.

"So there you were at this woman's house, I presume?" The doctor assumed as Phillip nodded in affirmation.

"Feeling powerful, having your way sexually, then literally washing the other woman's stench off of you before coming home to be with your wife and family. Would you sometimes come home to be intimate with your wife immediately after your previous 'encounter' as you eloquently phrased it?" she asked.

"Sometimes," Phillip answered.

"And how does that make you feel, Shelly?"

"Sick to my stomach," she answered without even turning around. Phillip got up to retrieve a tissue out of a nearby box and walked to the corner in which his wife stood. Shelly snatched them out of his hands and pressed them over her eyes.

"Let's take a five-minute break. Excuse me," Dr. Tyner suggested as she headed for the exit door to the reception area. "Upon my return, be prepared to write your one-word characteristic in your journals and make note of your new assignment for this week."

Chapter 9

But without faith it is impossible to please Him, for he who comes to God must believe that He is, and that He is a rewarder of those who diligently seek Him. —Hebrews 11:6

It was the Monday after Labor Day weekend, and the manager bought breakfast for everyone in the office. Mrs. Goodman was dropping off her rent check for the following month, more than three weeks in advance, which was her normal practice. "I'm always afraid that I am going to be late. I swear I actually have nightmares about forgetting to pay my rent and coming home to find my belongings out on the street," she said. The entire office giggled as if to say, "We wish everyone shared in your fear."

"You just have to have faith, Francis that the Lord is going to speak to you every first of the month as a reminder to pay your rent. I wouldn't freak out about it like you do," the assistant property manager responded playfully.

"You're probably right, Shannon. I didn't realize how spiritual you were. What church do you go to?" she asked.

Everyone broke out into roaring laughter, "at home Baptist," the property manager, Brenda, divulged softly.

Another burst of laughter erupted while Shannon rolled her eyes. "I haven't exactly been to church—as in a building—in almost fifteen years, but the Lord knows my heart. He said that all I need is faith the size of a mustard seed, and he would bless me," Shannon answered the best way she knew how. "Besides, church is filled with a bunch of phony people, who try to be all in your business. Then, if you don't have that, you've got the deacons trying to sleep with the overdeveloped teenagers in the choir. And, on top of that, you have the preachers—or pimps in the pulpit as Michael Baisden calls them. They've got their fancy automobiles and big homes, while the members of their congregation are starving. I know what the Good Book says about tithing, but what is the purpose of me paying to get into Heaven as if it is some night club with a cover charge?"

Darnell moved from behind Shannon as she uttered her last sentence, "Lord, please don't accidentally strike me when you reach down to punish her."

Mrs. Goodman with a discerned look on her face asked, "Honey, what church hurt you? Yes, God knows your heart, and he says that we can have church where ever we are, because where we are God is … but God also wants our time … and our ten percent. We have to work as a team to build his temple and to build it so that it is pleasing to him. I'd like to invite you to my church." Mrs. Goodman ripped a neon colored sticky from a pad on Darnell's desk. "Here is my number and the name of my church. Google the address, and I surely hope to see you this weekend. Saturday is women's day, and, if you are interested in participating, we still need models for the fashion show. If not, it would be a blessing to just see you there on Sunday."

"I won't make any promises, but I thank you for the invite. You must think I am crazy, huh?" Shannon inquired.

"No, but I do think you are possibly bitter or misguided. Bless your heart, though." The two embraced and those standing by wished Mrs. Goodman a good day.

"I love Mrs. Goodman," Brenda confessed. "She is just the sweetest woman in the world, and she shoots straight from the hip. She is a God-fearing woman, but she doesn't take any mess. I remember a couple of years ago when she had a leak in her air-conditioning unit. She was very emotional and went off on me on the phone. Jackson and I rushed up to see how bad it was—the carpet was just wet in front of the AC unit. We soon realized she wasn't at all upset over the leak; it was the fact that she had just lost her husband, Mr. Goodman. What a good man he must have been!" Brenda continued, "She talked to Jackson and me for over forty-five minutes, when we were only planning to be up there for two to five minutes."

"She told us how Mr. Goodman was in the armed services, and, after JFK was killed, his tour of duty was up and he reenlisted for Korea against her better wishes. Mr. Goodman was a decorated officer with a Purple Heart and had suffered three heart attacks in a year-and-a-half time span. She recalled one evening at dinner with her sister-in-law asking Mr. Goodman if he had decided if he wanted to be buried in Arlington or not. She laughed at how ignorant his sister was in the fact that she was clueless as to what it meant to be buried in Arlington," Brenda evoked.

Mrs. Goodman described after Mr. Goodman's funeral how everyone had come back to the family house to eat and visit with her—a new widow. She shared with all of their family and friends the many, many shadow boxes and medals of honor that Mr. Goodman had collected during his army career. She described how all of their faces were in sheer shock while passing around the priceless memorabilia. Mrs. Goodman often attempted to bring some of those same pieces out during previous family reunions, social visits, birthday parties, but her husband would stop her saying that it would be like bragging, and no one would be interested in seeing them.

After learning of his death, a lot of his school buddies called to learn about his final arrangements. Mr. Goodman's sister advised everyone that he was going to be buried in Arlington. Most were absolutely shocked and oblivious to their old buddy's decorated status. One friend replied, "You can't just be buried at Arlington. You have to be cited and invited."

Finally, Sunday morning rolled around, and the assistant manager struggled with her decision to come up with a good excuse or illness and leave a message at Mrs. Goodman's apartment—knowing that she wouldn't be there. She wondered whether she should terminate her hiatus from church and show up in good faith, out of sheer respect after being invited by a very spiritual woman—a woman who she could truly adopt as a mentor. "What the hell," she thought. "Oops. Sorry Lord."

Shannon watched the clock as she slowly got dressed that morning. She had her usual cup of coffee—black with seven creams and six sugars. She knew she had the perfect cup of coffee when the steamy brew matched her light complexion. After stirring every cup, she would align the back of her hand with the brim to compare colors. "Here goes nothing."

After turning over the ignition, Barry White's voice blared from the factory stereo system. "Maybe not the most inspiring and appropriate music to listen to before church," she said to herself. "There's gotta be some gospel on one of these stations …" She laughed at herself as Marvin Winans crooned "All I Have to Give." In the year and a half she owned her Lexus, she couldn't remember a time when gospel music had played in the speakers, except a brief chorus heard when flipping back and forth from smooth jazz to R & B stations.

Shannon's palms sweated as she backed her vehicle out of her two-car attached garage. She thought of how proud her mother in heaven must be; knowing that after close to twenty years, her daughter was going back into the House of the Lord. The church parking lot was filled to capacity, so she parked in the overflow lot across the street. Shannon thought it was good to see church folk in their Sunday best, particularly the older women in their church hats.

She was greeted with a warm hug from many strangers handing out programs and fans with funeral home advertisements on them. The first thing she received was an envelope for tithing. She wondered if there would be a bookkeeper or auditor at the door checking pay stubs and W-2 forms as she had heard went on in a friend's church. She remembered her friend trying to justify the actions of the church staff members, "They have to verify income. It keeps cheapskates from balling up dollar bills and sneaking them in the basket."

The choir was already singing when Shelley entered the sanctuary. As she tried to find seating in the very back of the church, a very aggressive usher was motioning for her to sit in the front pews. Shannon shook her head harder as if to say, "No thanks," but the usher insisted and walked toward Shannon as if she was coming to grab her hand.

The preacher arrived from behind the scenes after a few song selections from the choir. Everyone rose in respect as he entered the sanctuary. Shannon felt embarrassed that she was a little late to stand. She wished she was paying closer attention to that side of the room, but no one looked to her as if she was wrong or out of sync.

The minister's voice was very demanding and godlike so Shannon's fears of nodding off to sleep diminished as she smiled and applauded at points in his sermon. His choice of topic and beginning seemed to be directed toward and personalized for Shannon: "It's Never Too Late, Jesus Waits." The minister's theme surrounded the theory that God has a prize for each and everyone. "You can't beat God's giving," he would often say. Along with, "What God has for you, can't no man take it away."

Shannon found herself applauding and agreeing a lot. At one point, she even thought that tears were filling her eyes, but none ever dropped. She closed her eyes as instructed by the minister and took in the story he told.

"I was in Los Angeles at a convention, and I suddenly remembered a story that my father, Bishop Charles, used to tell in his eulogies. He told a story about a father and son who had a wonderful bond and relationship. The son idolized his father, much like I did mine, and wanted to follow in every footstep his father took. As a child, this boy's father collected and built model cars—so did the boy. His father fell in love with and married his high school sweetheart—so did the boy. His father graduated from Michigan State University—so did the boy. In his early twenties, the now young man enlisted in the armed services—just as his father had done and at the same age. His plans were to serve a few years, get honorably discharged, and hired into General Motors or Ford Motor Company to continue in his passion for fine automobiles.

By the time he was fifty, the father and son duo had worked so hard and saved a lot of money over the years, they were able to build on a real life collection of their own fine automobiles—a 1964 Pontiac GTO, a 1957 Chevrolet Bel Air hard top, and a 1973 Ford Mustang two-door coupe.

One day, the father answered a knock at the door by one of his son's army buddies. There he stood in uniform, at attention, with his son's dog tags on a chain midair. The father sobbed uncontrollably in disbelief and denial over his son's death. The young man on the other side of the door assured him that his son died nobly. A few years went by, and the father himself soon died—most say of a broken heart. Now a widow and preceded in death by her son, the young man's mother decided to run an ad in the local newspaper to find one or several buyers for the collectible automobiles her husband and son had worked so hard to maintain. She hired a mediator to auction off the personal effects of her son and husband—gun and knife collections, car parts, magazines, and such. The proceeds were to be divided amongst worthy charities such as breast cancer foundations and advocates against drunk driving.

Many car collectors across the United States flew in for the grand unveiling of the collector vehicles. Some people showed up just to get a glimpse of such fine automobiles, but there were none in plain sight. People figured that the vehicles would be driven in by attractive models after all other artifacts were sold. Finally, all personal contents were auctioned off, and the last thing to bid on was a white, rusted 1989 Ford Escort. The once wife and mother came out to address the crowd and encouraged everyone to make a decision on a starting bid for the Ford Escort. The men were dumbfounded. Who would bid on such a clunker? There was a long pause until a middle-aged man from Locust Grove, Georgia, started the bid at $250. The crowd murmured as people tried to size the bidder up. "Is he drunk? It's a piece of junk. What happened to the '57 Bel Air, the '64 Pontiac GTO, or the '73 Ford Mustang?"

No other bids came in before the "going once, going twice, sold" edict came down, and the Georgian man was the new proud owner of a lemon, a 1989 Ford Escort. The wife was forever grateful to the southern man, she cried as she hugged him. She asked for him to write his home address on an index card when a man filled with testosterone began to shout from the crowd. The woman insisted that the mediator hand the aggressor the microphone so that he could voice his opinion.

He said, "Ma'am, please allow me to say that I am mighty sorry for your loss, and I extend my deepest condolences to you and your family. But I drove over thirty hours with a couple of buddies of mine, and we had every intention on bidding on and winning a couple of fine automobiles. Now, I'm sure that piece of junk Escort was maybe your son's first car after high school or college and holds great meaning to you, but we came for the '64 Pontiac Lemans with GTO option. The car I had in mind had a four-barrel carburetor, dual exhaust, and chromed valve covers. We were even more interested in the '57 Bel Air with its room and fuel efficiency; this vehicle would have never seen snow in my neck of the woods. And what about that '73 Ford Mustang you mentioned in your ad? Lee Iacocca was the best damn general manager Ford has ever seen, and, with his blessing, the most attractive Ford vehicle was built to last and to stand the test of time with its unitized platform-type frame and welded box-section side rails."

She smiled and expressed her sympathy back to him for his long drive. She asked him, "Sir, are you a holy man?" His eyebrows wrinkled as he struggled for an answer.

"I wouldn't say that I am a holy man, but I believe in God. What does that have to do with anything?"

"Well sir," she started. "If you were a holy man, you would know that all blessings are received from the Father by way of His Son. In the ad that I ran, I paid extra just to express the loving relationship my son shared with my husband, and, yes, I mentioned my husband's cars: the 1964 Pontiac GTO and the 1957 Chevy Bel Air and the 1973 Ford Mustang. But I also poured my heart out when explaining what my son's first car, the 1989 Ford Escort, meant to me and his father to gift it to him. So sir, because you and your friends did not care enough to see what that Escort meant to my son as a gift from his father and I to bid on it, you will leave here today the same way you came—empty handed. Unlike this holy man from Georgia who will be blessed when I ship all three vehicles to the address he indicated to me on this index card in my hand."

The Georgian man burst into tears as approximately 250 onlookers cheered for him as the proud new owner of four ... yes, four fine automobiles.

There was a thunderous applause from the congregation as the minister shouted, "Jesus sent me here today to tell at least 300 of you that what God has for you is for you."

Many shouted, "Hallelujah!" "Thank you, Jesus!"

Shannon soon found herself gravitating toward the alter. The man of God uttered seven final words and took his seat in the pulpit. "The doors of the church are open," he said.

Chapter 10

Be who you are and say what you feel, because those who mind don't matter and those who matter don't mind. —Dr. Seuss

The caterer was running late. The sound guys were having difficulty setting up. The concierge was on her way, and the photographer was annoying the hell out of Paige by following her around with his lens. *What else could go wrong today!* she thought.

"Paige, can you take line one? The driver is lost, and I have no sense of direction," Connie said, placing the caller on hold.

You have no sense period Paige thought to herself. "This is Paige. What are the cross streets to where you are now?" she picked up the receiver and asked while rolling her eyes. "Okay, what you wanna do is continue south on the beltway to I-66. From I-66, you want Route 50E, and the property will be down a quarter mile on your left. You'll see the red, white, and blue flags and balloons to guide you to the atrium."

The estate was a four-year-old, thirty-six-acre development in Virginia, called Trinity Bluffs at Fair Oaks Apartments. The acquisition combined sophistication and the convenience of suburban living, with lavish master baths, contemporary floor plans, sky garden, wireless lounge, modern architecture, designer features, and more. The property was minutes away from Dulles Airport and boasted an unadorned tag line: "Don't sacrifice style for simplicity—have it all at Trinity Bluffs at Fair Oaks."

The grounds were naturally, aesthetically pleasing, and amenities were designed to boast everything elegant and posh. Unfortunately, the property had never stabilized and began to be the worst asset in the owner's portfolio—a publicly held institution out of Seattle. After two and a half years of high turnover and low collections, the original owner sold the property to a public-funded organization out of Houston. The Texas company finally realized they bit off more than they could chew, and, within twelve months, sold the property to a condo converter from L. A. that saw that the homes were converted back to rentals and bought out all of the condo owners that had closed on their loan.

It is rumored that the mogul himself resided in a twenty-story, 4,500-square feet, apartment he built in 2005—relishing in excursions such as corporate meetings in Las Vegas via his private commercial jet. His frequent indulgences included Casa Fuente cigars, 120-minute spa treatments, and womanizing after hours. His residence was said to have impressive views of the Pacific Ocean, Santa Monica Mountains, and the skyline of Los Angeles. The home-based building raved amenities such as floor-to-ceiling windows, ceramic flooring, exposed architectural columns, a rooftop fitness center, and a clubroom along with his private helicopter pad.

Brad McLaughlin was the third generation of businessmen in his family. He chose a path more lucrative in today's society—real estate. Brad III purchased his first apartment building at the age of twenty-one, a twenty-six-unit fixer-upper in downtown Manhattan, while entering graduate school. That profitable flip gave him a taste that he would yearn for years to come.

Several diplomats, super delegates from the Democratic Party and Republican Party, and other government officials were among the attendees, along with executive board members of the city council, and many others would participate in exciting activities, including martinis and manicures. There was a limousine service that was going to take partygoers from the twenty-two-acre site to a host of night clubs in downtown D.C.

"Especially for you, we have crafted a superb menu of novel American cuisine—braised petite short ribs with horseradish whipped potatoes, warm sweet slaw, steamed broccoli with fried leeks, and a natural a jus sauce. We have pheasant cooked to perfection with spinach, pine nuts, and asiago cheese; steamed basmati rice with vermicelli; baby vegetables; and sherry supreme jus lie. We also have fried lobster tails with buttermilk whipped potatoes, stewed tomatoes with corn, steamed asparagus, and a Cajun red remoulade. Our signature salad is spinach and spring mix with bacon, button mushrooms, hard-boiled eggs, croutons, red onions, and a homemade raspberry vinaigrette dressing," Chris Pacini laundered a list. A round of applause erupted for Executive Chef Chris Pacini as he took small bows to the alluring crowd.

Set up in the rear of the great room were three one-room mock ups roped off as museum exhibits that displayed custom finishes and décor. One model was decorated with bagel-colored suede paint on the walls, stainless-steel Energy Star-qualified appliances with granite countertops, and gun-medal cabinetry. The microfiber sofa sat atop of stainless-steel leg posts with a wine-colored chenille blanket and pillows to accent. A thirty-two-inch flat screen television sat inside a noncumbersome armoire, while modern bar stools with a dragonfly pattern surrounded the granite countertop.

Another model exhibit demonstrated an even more energy efficient example with more Energy Star-rated appliances, light fixtures in the bathroom, central air-conditioning, windows, a Samsung high-definition television, an Apple computer, and a ceiling fan. With eggshell paint on the walls and polar white trim on the baseboards, chair molding and window sills, this display offered clean lines and a fresh look at the owners desire to be "green." Brad's ultimate goal was to earn the U.S. Environmental Protection Agency and U.S. Department of Energy's support by parading his efforts in saving money and energy and winning the Energy Star facility award for Trinity Bluffs.

With the constant turnover in management and maintenance, the property's reputation was a less desirable one with county and city officials alike. In an effort to improve the asset's image as a real-estate investment, taxpayer, community leader and the astonishing 63 percent occupancy, the asset managers recruited a young property manager from Boston. The property manager, Maliki Gretzki, held a Bachelor of Science degree in business administration from the University of New York and came with impeccable references and recommendations.

On Maliki's first day, he fired the entire maintenance staff and all office personnel with the exception of Paige Winehurst. Within six months, all apartments were turned over, redecorated, and ready to be leased; rents were raised 3.5 percent, and 100 percent had been collected; payables were all processed, and vendor checks were being cut; resident satisfaction had improved tremendously; and employee morale was way up.

Today was the first day most congressional leaders would have set foot on the grounds since the groundbreaking or grand opening event less than five years ago. What Maliki had done with the asset was nothing short of a miracle, and this was the day for him to shine in the eyes of his peers, the owners, political figures, and neighboring business owners.

The gala was a benefit being put on by a PR firm Maliki hired to aid in improving the image and reputation of Trinity Bluffs at Fair Oaks. The PR firm, Maynard and Wilson, partnered with a nonprofit organization to offer free housing to wounded soldiers that were returning to their families from Iraq and Afghanistan. Many of the soldiers were physically or mentally challenged and were often denied benefits from government programs. There were a total of twenty families that were moving into the high-rise community and seeing it for the first time in front of millions of TV viewers.

All of the top local and national news stations had RSVP'd to film the event, and the local newspapers and gazettes were also due to run a spread. Large corporations were invited to learn more about the charitable event and hopefully offer sizeable donations.

Limousines began to arrive, and important individuals ushered in and quickly filled the room. Many military branches came out to show support. Service men and women in uniform represented the air force, army, navy and coast guard branches; and countless others. A former secretary of defense along with mayors and city officials from around the United States took the podium to speak and thank the wounded soldiers for sacrificing their lives and limbs in an act of war so that others could walk in peace on earth. It was a very emotional event.

News anchorpersons were also outside filming the natural setting of the apartment community, and some even knocked on doors to interview existing residents—obviously to get a feel for the community in which the soldiers and their families were due to call home. One anchorman knocked on the door of Mrs. Dunn, a retired kindergarten teacher. She was eighty-one years of age and very feisty. "You don't look a day over sixty-five," the reporter told her.

"Well, I don't have any money—if that's what you're after," she said in a playful tone. The two shared a laugh, and the interview continued. He asked her about her life and what brought her here to Trinity Bluffs at Fair Oaks. She motioned for him to take a seat as she sat in a rocking chair near the window.

Mrs. Dunn described how she had retired from teaching shortly after her husband died. "He just dropped dead, one day in the yard while cutting the grass," she said, pointing to his photograph on the sofa table. "I thought I was strong enough to go back to work after James died. There I was sitting in front of a classroom during story time reading *Chicken Little* to the young people. I had a five-year-old little girl in my classroom start her menstruation. She was sitting in the circle listening to me read, and I noticed that the seat of her pants was red when she adjusted on the floor. I immediately called for an aide to watch my classroom, and I called the girl's mother. All the while, I was trying to shield the girl from any embarrassment among her peers. The mother rushed down to the school. Turns out, the mother was molested as a child and had contracted tuberculosis. She said doctors forewarned her that her child would menstruate extremely early." Mrs. Dunn looked the reporter straight in his eyes and said, "When I saw red at the seat of that little girl's pants, it was the same shade of red I saw when I found my husband dead in the yard of the home we owned. And I knew that was the same red James saw when he had nightmares about fighting in World War II."

The reporter grew very intrigued by Mrs. Dunn, having ties to the military through her husband. He asked, "So you must be pretty proud of what your landlord is doing to help our wounded soldiers coming home from the war. What are your thoughts of today's event?"

"No words can express how blessed these young soldiers are to have a second chance at life, to see their children grow up in front of them and not be a prayer that their mothers have to send up to keep them safe while they fight a war that they have no business fighting. Na' don't get me started on this whole war issue; you just take this check on over to that atrium, and you tell that Maliki that I think it's a wonderful thing that he is doing and God is going to bless him and everything that he touches from now on. I'm just glad to live in a community that has his touch. God bless you too young man, and have a good afternoon," she said. Mrs. Dunn got up to open the door for the reporter and his cameraman.

After she shut the door, he held up the $5,000 check she wrote and signed off, "This is Derek Russell on TV 20."

Over at the atrium Maliki was working the room and distributing business cards to local business owners and community leaders. He gave statements to several media sources, all surrounding questions on his intuitiveness to create such a worthy relationship with a nonprofit organization. "Mr. Gretkzi, can you define your intuition?" one reporter asked.

"I'm sorry, but I am going to have to answer your question with a question. Can anyone truly define or describe intuition? It's simply a subconscious way to make decisions and often the key to success. Much like my instinct, I trust my intuition. Now, if you'll excuse me …" Maliki humbly excused himself and started across the room.

He hoped no one asked about his background—his family background. Though they addressed him as Mister, one could clearly see his feminine mannerisms. People often stared or sized him up. His sexuality, though obvious, was still a mystery to most. With his dark hair filled with product and steel blue–gray eyes covered with the clearest contact lenses the optometrist market had to offer, he commanded a certain presence when he walked into a room.

He feared a male reporter would ask what line of work his father was in or where he grew up. His father was a project engineer for a prosperous construction company based in Cape Cod. His mother was a homemaker who died approximately ten years prior to his move to Virginia. His mother was a very soft-spoken woman, who catered to the men in her family and cared very little about her own well-being.

Though she didn't have to, she would go without so that her children would have more. Maliki was the youngest of seven siblings—five sisters and one brother. His parents did not plan to have more children after his brother was born, so you could say Maliki was a surprise.

At the tender age of fifteen, Maliki remembered the day his father came home to break the news to his wife that he was in love with someone else. It absolutely ripped the family apart, especially the girls in the household. Soon, it was discovered that their father's lover was of the same gender. Maliki's brother threatened to kill his father for breaking his mother's heart. During the family counseling sessions, the psychologist focused on the low self-esteem of Maliki's mother. "Often, if a person traffics in low self-esteem, you can trace it back to the source in their family. Nine times out of ten, it's generational."

Chapter 11

Speak only well of people and you need never whisper. —Unknown

During its culmination, The Athena was *the* place to be. Its antique Victorian structure gave it class, its yesteryear design gave it charm, and its time during the depression gave it property decline. The new owner told great stories about the property's history. From the famous Motown singers that couldn't pay their rent prior to their record deals and were evicted to the elected officials and judges that took part in adultery scandals—there was history at The Athena.

"If these walls could talk…" Art used to say. Before he purchased the building almost twenty years ago, the previous owners made several attempts to renovate the building. It was overran with roaches and bed bugs. The clientele left a lot to be desired—crack junkies, crack whores, you name it. The Athena was originally constructed of efficiency and one bedroom apartment homes in an effort to discriminate against people with children.

"The secretary was this ghetto woman from the local housing projects who sat at her desk all day with a flannel blanket wrapped around her shoulders complaining that she was cold. The maintenance supervisor was a lesbian woman that was more butch than any man walking the earth. She wore a low hair cut, bagging jeans and a tank under a flannel jacket," Art described to a business partner while touring the building. It came out that Martha, the maintenance woman, was committing fraud by ordering credit cards and personal checking accounts in the tenants' names unbeknownst to them. She lived in a free unit onsite and would wine and dine different women daily, pouring chardonnay in their glasses, providing the best marijuana in the Midwest and paying their bills with stolen checks.

Martha was thirty eight years of age and she had a son that was nineteen. Right around her son's eighteenth birthday, both he and Martha were imprisoned for check fraud and identity theft. What a gift it must have been to serve time with his mother!"

As Art continued to tour a business partner that had never laid eyes on the building, he gave more history on the last administration. "During the last attempt at renovations, the previous owners replaced all of the windows being careful to keep with the ornament window panes. They started on the second floor with a plan to work their way up to the twenty second floor which was the Penthouse level. Contractors installed carpet in seventy apartments from the second to the fifth floor. Painters completed sheet rock repairs and custom painted all corridors up to the twelfth floor. Shortly thereafter, plumbing risers failed and burst causing a massive leak from the tenth floor all the way down to the basement. The walls were soaked, the brand new carpet and padding were ruined and the owners gave up," Art concluded.

"Welcome to The Athena, My name is Jillian. May I offer you some champagne?" the leasing manager greeted a prospective resident entering the building.

"Champagne? I was only offered stale coffee and a cookie at the last place," the woman confessed; however, she passed on the glass of bubbly.

"We also offer artesian bottled water or gourmet tea. Please help yourself if you change your mind about anything, and I will return shortly with a key to a model home and a brochure for your personal tour."

Jillian was an ultra professional leasing manager. During the hiring process, her personality test results indicated that she was assertive, outgoing, intense, and an independent-minded individual. It went on to say she showed a good deal of work-related initiative and would be willing to go ahead and take action on her own with little or no direction or guidance from others.

When the property manager called her previous supervisor

for a character reference, he advised that Jillian was confident and charismatic in her relationships with customers. He also warned that Jillian preferred to be in control of situations and was willing to take risks in order to have such control.

After brief introductions and qualifying, Jillian opened the door for her wealthy client. She often associated her clients' monetary status by the size of their handbags and quality of shoes. "Mrs. Peterson, you mentioned the need for more closet space for your teenage daughters … allow me to introduce to you our penthouse loft." Jillian used the same dramatic delivery with each client's first tour of the well-appointed penthouse. Once the town's bread factory in midtown, the structure itself was converted back in the early 1990s to a posh and elegant living space for Detroit's aristocrats.

Jillian opened each walk-in closet and pantry cupboards for her client's viewing pleasure. All were constructed with trimmed six-panel raised doors and stainless-steel hardware. The walls were painted a bagel color with winter white trim baseboards and crown molding. The floor-to-ceiling windows offered a grand amount of natural lighting, which prompted Jillian to mention plant life and maintenance. "The loft encompasses 2,300 square feet, offers a spectacular view of the city's skyline, and commands respect as a twenty-two-story historic fixture," Jillian continued, as she opened the door to the sliding door and led her client to the terrace. Jillian began to point in the northeast direction to share a little history of other developments in the sky. When she turned to her left to check her client's level of attention, there was no one there.

"Mrs. Peterson?" she called out her name once more. Jillian exited the terrace and returned to the large bath with his-and-her pedestal sinks to check her client's whereabouts. "Mrs. Peterson, did I lose you?" Just then, she noticed the gorgeous Donald Pliner sling backs she complimented the woman on during their introductory period. Jillian walked over to the terrace and looked over the railing only to notice an intimate crowd forming around a young woman with the same curly tresses that resembled those that flowed down the back of her stylish client.

"Jill to Maxwell, come in Maxwell!" a wry voice came over the two-way radio. "Jill, Max is off-site at lunch. Are you still touring your client?" Rita inquired.

"Uh … I think I just lost her … literally," Jillian stammered.

Jill rushed to the leasing office to call for emergency assistance. She collapsed in the middle of the office after hanging up the phone. Down below, in the midst of the crowd, a reporter said, "Good afternoon. I'm Sandy Fischer with XXYZ News coming to you live from The Athena in downtown Detroit where apparently an unknown woman plunged To her death…"

Chapter 12

The Constitution gives each and every American the inalienable right to make a damn fool of themselves and ruin their lives if they so wish.
— Oliver Wendell Holmes

All of those long days and nights preparing for the ribbon cutting ceremony were finally paying off, Elizabeth thought to herself, as she perused the sundeck of the rooftop swimming pool of California Chateau—the newest high-rise development in Chicago's South Loop.

"Liz, the sky garden on the sixteenth floor was magnificent. What a beautiful piece of real estate. Thanks for having us here this afternoon," City Councilwoman Merriweather expressed.

"Thank you for filling in for the mayor. We are absolutely honored to have someone of your caliber assist us with our ribbon cutting this afternoon, councilwoman. May I offer you a drink?" Elizabeth asked.

"A Long Island iced tea would be wonderful," she whispered.

"Zoey, please fix the councilwoman your special tea," she winked and said, as she slipped the bartender a twenty-dollar bill.

It was time for the next group to see the model homes. In the eighth floor model, there was a spa theme. There were chocolate-covered strawberries on the granite counter top arranged in a stainless-steel fondue set. The kitchen sink was filled with lemons that really made the décor pop. The adjacent dining room displayed a pewter wrought-iron round table with coordinating chairs that flourished a refreshing butterfly pattern. Sid Dickens' plaques were showcased on the far wall. Expensive clocks and candle sconces were strategically placed throughout the living room area. The olive sofas with steel leg posts offered great reflection off mirror displays. The floor-to-ceiling windows gave the condominium a more lofty feeling.

"Oh, you thought of everything. Didn't you, Liz?" Diane gasped as she entered the master bedroom quarters. There was a masseuse table and a European massage therapist standing in the corner with his hands behind his back.

"Welcome to California Chateau. I am your personal masseuse, Rolf; please lie down," he said, extending his right hand to the president of the Chicago's Urban Development Association.

"Diane, go on. Enjoy five minutes with Mr. Magic Fingers, and we will come back to get you prior to heading down to the wireless lounge," she said. Elizabeth opened the door to the master bathroom. The bath mirror reflected her short hair cut that she wore in a wet look with product and finger-combed strokes.

It was a lavish bath with champagne-colored balloons filling the oval soaking tub. There was a pair of plush winter-white slippers in front of the tub with a matching robe draped over the door. Votive candles surrounded the tub, while Watercolors jazz tunes filled the vastness. A Conair diffusing hair dryer lay atop the marble vanity, while high-end Paul Mitchell products garnished the edges. Tennis balls permeated the bath sink—symbolizing the professional indoor court offered as an amenity to buyers on the ground level.

"Friends, welcome to Chicago's premiere high-rise and most prestigious address. We offer nothing less than contemporary floor plans, designer features, and modern architectures. From the floor-to-ceiling windows in your communal rooms to the molding accents, we are proud to be Chicago's finest condominium residence," Elizabeth started to describe.

"You will enjoy conveniences such as an underground parking garage and ground-level retail, including Morton's Steakhouse, Paul Mitchell's Salon, and Whole Foods grocer. Also offered are envious pleasures that include our sky garden on the sixteenth floor, Wi-Fi lounge, personal fitness studio, and a state-of-the-art movie theater just under our penthouse level," she continued.

"How many elevators are in the building?" Frank Palazzolo

inquired. Frank was a local business owner—a successful print and sign shop entrepreneur who had designed the monument sign for California Chateau. Frank moved to the United States after his father died in 1959. He married a young Italian woman in 1962, they raised five children—four boys and one girl—and relocated from Brooklyn to Chicago when their eldest son was eight. Frank was a brilliant artist who could duplicate any image almost without error. He started selling sketches, then drawings, and then paintings, and soon it all evolved into Signs by Paul, named for his son.

"There are five sets of elevators—two freight elevators for moving, two regular passenger cabs, and one lock-off for penthouse owners only," Elizabeth answered.

"Are we going to see one of those penthouses today?" another invitee inquired.

"Unfortunately, the architects only designed and built two penthouse plans, and both were presold prior to construction and occupied immediately after the certificate of occupancy was obtained," she said. Elizabeth opened the California walk-in closets in the second bedroom.

Diane finally joined the group who had crossed over the living area to the third and final bedroom, which was set up as a home office. "Diane, was your massage enjoyable?" Liz asked with a smile, almost knowing the answer to her own question.

"Magnificent! That little European boy made me feel as though I was cheating on my husband!" Diane shook her head with weakened knees while the tour group burst into laughter. Wearing a short dark-blonde bob, dark wash jeans with a cami underneath a red and white top, Diane fanned her face and blew out her cheeks. "I'm not kidding. You know my fiftieth birthday is coming up in August; I took a few of his business cards so that I can commission him for my event. It's going to be on our boat, you know," Diane bragged.

Her husband bought her a brand-new boat for their twenty-fifth wedding anniversary. She named it "Lady Di." It was a suede-colored Sea Ray, sixty-three-foot fiberglass express cruiser with twin inland 1,150-horsepower Detroit diesel engines. The deck boat was fully loaded with a Kenwood sports package audio system, including Sirius satellite radio. The master stateroom had a thirty-two-inch LCD flat screen and master bath with a granite four-person shower stall.

The wealthy and seemingly benevolent couple docked at Burnham Harbor on South Lake Shore Drive, which offered convenient distances between the homes of their grandchildren and work. Diane was an acknowledged gynecologist for a prominent hospital in Chicago, while Richard Millwork was a successful philanthropist. Mr. Millwork was responsible for raising over five million dollars for the oncology department. The couple, after a long battle with infertility, had one son who many say caused more heartaches in his teenage years than the miscarriages experienced by the power couple. Their son had been involved in everything from multiple DUIs and drug abuse to dropping out of college during his fourth year of medical school.

"Offering a profusion of opportunities to local business owners like yourselves, we would like to officially welcome all of you to California Chateau." Back on the rooftop, Robert Sokolowski reveled in his most promising real estate venture and raised his glass in a toast.

"Elizabeth and Caroline will continue the group excursions until 6:45 after which time I invite as many of you that will come to the Chicago Hilton ballroom for dancing, Las Vegas night gaming, and, of course, more cocktails. My drivers will transport the first seventy-five guests. All others will have to take their chances with breathalyzers and Chicago PD." Laughter broke out of the crowd as Robert returned the microphone to the disc jockey and recommenced mingling.

"Caroline, who is responsible for the decorating? These models are absolutely fabulous," one spectator inquired.

"Designers have all signed a nondisclosure agreement with Mr. Sokolowski, so, unfortunately, I am not at liberty to unfurl such information. I can, however, tell you that each fabric was custom made in France for California Chateau, and the designers are primarily based out of Boston and a few are from Montreal."

"Interesting," he said. They entered a one-bedroom plus den floor plan, which showcased live models in a corner of the living room sitting atop a red and white checkered picnic blanket, mimicking the feeding of grapes, cheese, and sips of wine to each other. The models were very careful to tarry in character, while the onlookers pointed and whispered, admiring the creativity of the theme.

On the kitchen counter, there was a romantic greeting card by Maya Angelou next to a bottle of chardonnay—Lewis Cellars 2002 Barcaglia Lane, Russian River Valley. The card was even signed, with a personal, handwritten poem at the bottom that read as follows:

> *P.S. I miss you, can't wait to see you. Tonight it's all about you;*
> *Music and mood, cooking and cuddling, a picnic—just for two.*

"I guess you're going to tell me that Edgar Allen Poe wrote this poem too, huh?" an observer exaggerated. There was laughter amongst the group.

"Actually, Mr. Sokolowski's wife, Mrs. Sokolowski, wrote it. She is a renowned literary author, essentially self-help books, but she also has a small collection of romantic poetry," Caroline counterclaimed.

The dual stainless-steel sink displayed a stainless vegetable strainer containing red cabbage, orange and yellow peppers, and organic green onions with a cucumber on the wooden chop board with two cuts. Contemporary jazz filled the suite, while satin eggplant curtains directed the room's design.

The tours continued until the daylight hours had subsided, and Robert Sokolowski could not help but recall his days as a schoolboy growing up in his parents' home in North Dakota. He grew up in a two-family flat in McClusky, North Dakota. In the upper flat his mother was a homemaker earning modest wages by ironing, cleaning, and sewing for posh political figures. The lower flat apartment was his father's office, and the shared basement was his father's laboratory for experimental animals. Robert grew up the youngest of six boys. The only girl his parents procreated was still born.

Just as the aristocrats of the grand opening began to sip from their champagne flutes, a fight broke out in the heated Jacuzzi approximately thirty feet from the guests. Two young women were spewing profanities and swinging like windmills at each other. There were two young men—assuming to be their significant others—snickering and moving in the opposite direction of the brawl. Within minutes, security personnel, who were off-duty Chicago policemen, rushed through the crowd that was forming around the women. One blonde's bikini top had been stripped in the back; however, her silicone breasts never dropped lower than her hanging top. The African-American girl's hair extensions were also drooping around the front of her bosom. What was once an elegantly stacked ponytail of human hair now looked to have been a horse's mane mauled from her head.

Later, it was discovered that the young women were strippers at a downtown gentleman's club. The blonde, otherwise known as Vanilla Cream, was a veteran dancer and took the other girl, Strawberry, in as a roommate and protégé. Strawberry was a runaway from Trinidad who had come to the United States when she was only fifteen. It was rumored that she was nicknamed Strawberry because of the many dents in her derriere.

"Ladies! Ladies! Have we had too much to drink this evening? Break it up, now!" It took four officers to break apart the grapple.

"First, she ate my apple fritter, and then she slept with my boyfriend!" the bronze-colored damsel shouted as she tried to break free from the two officers holding her back.

"You bitch! I did not eat your fritter, but Carl did eat me ... how do you like them apples?" she exclaimed. The pale temptress returned bouncing around as if she was in the ring of an HBO boxing match.

One of the elite guests leaned in to Diane and said, "Whether your mortgage is $400 or $4,000, whores need somewhere to live too."

Chapter 13

A hero is probably no braver than an ordinary person, but the hero is braver five minutes longer. —Michelangelo

"Sir, you're going to have to extinguish that cigarette and pour out the beer. There is no smoking or drinking in the common areas," the security guard told one of the lobby patrons.

"No problem, boss, I'm almost done," said the stranger. He took one last drag of his cigarette, dropped it to the stone tiled floor, and stepped on it to extinguish it. As he twisted his right ankle on tiptoe over the cigarette, he quickly chugged the remaining liquid in the twenty-two ounce bottle of beer.

Just then, three guys entered the grand lobby. "Good evening Mr. Bangoura. An overnight package arrived for you. Would you like to sign for it now or in the morning?" Security Officer Henderson asked.

Khalid looked down at his watch and observed that the time was approaching 1 am. "I'll take it now if you don't mind," he said, as he approached the guard's desk.

Just then, Khalid turned behind him only to notice his friend, Ted, conversing with the lobby stranger. Khalid removed his identification from his wallet, observing the concierge's package policy. His naturally dark skin made the gold tones of his class ring stand out more than usual.

Officer Henderson and Khalid had grown friendly during Khalid's comings and goings. During Super Bowl XL, Henderson and Khalid became sociable rivals boasting daily how either Pittsburgh or Seattle was going to whip the pants off the other. Having attended Michigan State University, Khalid had grown a soft spot for Jerome "The Bus" Bettis and often fantasized about Bettis winning a retiring Super Bowl at home.

Henderson, after admiring Khalid's brand-new leased vehicle—a grayish-blue Infiniti RXJ—purchased a Seahawks license plate frame for his opposition's vehicle. The two provoked good fun.

After issuing his John Hancock, Khalid gestured to his occupied buddy that he and his other friend were heading to his apartment.

He put the key in his door, and pressed his weight on the door while holding it open for his sidekick to enter. He removed the key, and the wind abruptly forced the door to slam. It swiftly unfastened with Khalid's friend, Ines, rushing in as if he was being chased. Before Khalid could react, four uninvited guests entered his apartment, including the beer-drinking stranger from moments ago.

"Whoa, whoa!" Khalid interjected. "Can I help you fellas with something?" he continued.

"Yeah, you can help me get my money," the beer drinker answered.

"Hey, I don't know what just happened, but I don't want any trouble," Khalid pleaded with both hands extended midair.

"Yeah. Well, we're a third-party collection agency for White Boy, and he wants his cheese or his brick back," an angry voice exclaimed from the group.

"I don't know anything about any money or White Boy, but I assure you we can discuss this like grown men once I bring Ines back out here," he said. Khalid walked slowly in the direction of the bedrooms off a long hall. Meanwhile, Khalid's second partner jumped out of the dining room window to escape harm.

As the glass shattered, it startled the group of four and prompted them to aggressively pursue Khalid. He fought them off one by one, while Ines cowered under the bed of Khalid's six-year-old daughter who visited every other weekend and summer.

His daughter was a product of Khalid's only biracial relationship, with Miranda. Miranda was completing her sophomore year in pediatrics when she and Khalid were introduced by a mutual friend at an MSU mixer. The two casually flirted, dated exclusively, and eventually grew very serious. The two had lengthy conversations about marrying after college. Khalid was in the United States on a student visa and planned to pursue a graphics engineer position with Ford Motor Company in Houston.

After sustaining a few hard hits from Khalid, three of the intruders ran toward the corridor and exited the building in pursuit of the friend that got away. Khalid was left to wrestle with the beer lover when finally he mustered up enough strength to force him out of the apartment door, immediately locking it behind him. Khalid slid down to the floor with his back pressed against the apartment door in exhaustion.

Soon, there was a knock on the door, "Security. Security. Open up Khalid," the knocker instructed. Khalid recognized Henderson's voice and reached over his head to unlock the door. He skimmed across the plush carpet allowing Henderson enough space to squeeze his way in.

"The police will arrive soon. What on earth is going on with those guys?" Henderson quizzed.

"I'm guessing ... a buddy of mine ... owes them money," Khalid huffed, as he gasped for air.

"The guy that was talking to them?" Henderson continued.

"Yeah, I assumed they knew each other ... I sure didn't see this coming," he said. Khalid began to pick himself up off the floor when he heard a second crash, much like the one heard earlier when his friend jumped through the glass. He looked up only to identify the same group of four had thrown his Weber grill through the patio glass door wall to once again gain entry to the apartment in pursuit of Ines. Khalid ran to his kitchen and picked up a large butcher knife from the dual stainless-steel sink. The aggressor of the four took a lunge toward Henderson with a glass stake he held with both hands above his head. He swung violently three times when his fourth swing was interrupted midair when a sharp edge sliced open the back of his shirt.

Ines finally ran out of the child's room toward the entry door, snatched it open, and hauled down the corridor.

Khalid exchanged blows and kicks with the remaining three intruders; before long, one reversed his entrance through the patio, while the two others laid on the carpeting, squirming or holding injuries.

The police arrived with guns drawn, based on the violent depiction Henderson had given over the telephone. They handcuffed Khalid immediately due to his demeanor standing over the bloody victims lying on the floor. "No! No!" Henderson yelled. "He's the owner of the apartment and the real victim." Partnered officers began to apprehend the wounded intruders.

Soon, a maintenance technician appeared in the doorway of apartment #113 along with the property manager, Natalie, who was outraged. "Who's going to pay for this damage? This accent wall was painted a few days ago! Look at this carpet!" she yelled while scanning the rooms for damages, totally disregarding the injured suspects at her feet.

Natalie had recently been promoted to property manager after she successfully led a three-person leasing team in Austin to lease up a 376-unit new construction project four months prior to the deadline. The owners were a publicly held investment firm who eventually sold the development to a condo converter and requested that Natalie stabilize an existing 844-unit, high-rise rehab building that had never reached an unfluctuating level of occupancy.

In January, Natalie was honored with a prestigious award at her company's holiday banquet in which she was awarded an all-expense-paid trip to Michigan for Super Bowl XL. The package included airfare for two, box suites at Ford Field, limousine transportation, and two nights at the Ritz Carlton in Dearborn. One of the construction superintendents personally threw in VIP tickets to Jerome Bettis' after party at a downtown Detroit establishment.

Khalid had been rattling off the nervous details of the incident when one of the rookie officers observed, "You don't have a scratch on you. Where's all of this blood stemming from?"

Henderson began to roll over the beer-drinking tough guy, exposing the lacerations to his back. "Ask him," he said.

The maintenance man, Jimmy, called in a glass vendor to secure the balcony to the first floor apartment. They measured the pane for manufacturing purposes and temporarily boarded up the door wall. Natalie offered Khalid the use of the on-site guest suite, but he refused. He said he refused to allow anyone to run him out of his home.

Khalid reminded her of an African warrior. "Strong. Resilient.

Fearless," Natalie described him to her fiancé as she returned to her penthouse apartment on the thirtieth floor. "Too bad. He'll be a homeless warrior come tomorrow," she said, as she removed her slippers and hopped back into bed.

The next day came and the phone rang, "It's a great day at Almeda Park Towers; this is Justin, and I can help you," the leasing agent answered. "Mr. Bangoura? How … how may I help you this evening?" Justin stuttered while motioning for Natalie to stay in close proximity, thinking that Khalid might ask to speak with her.

"I'm sorry. I am not at liberty to answer that. If I may take a message for the property manager, I will ensure she returns your call tomorrow." Justin moved the receiver farther away from his right ear. "Mr. Bangoura, unfortunately, the office is closing within the next twenty minutes, and Natalie has already …" Justin stalled until Natalie snatched the receiver from his hand.

"Hi. Khalid? How may I assist you?" Natalie cross-examined him after snatching the phone from Justin. "Sure. The document you are reading is a thirty-day notice to vacate due to breach of lease. The commotion in your apartment home early this morning violated approximately four of our community policies and, unfortunately, warranted eviction proceedings to commence," Natalie replied to his demand for an explanation. "How do we know you were not affiliated with the suspects? The damage to your apartment is extensive and expensive; who do you suppose is going to pay for it?" she asked. Natalie sat and crossed her right leg over the top of her left, while twirling the phone cord running to the receiver.

"As stated in the notification you have in hand, Khalid, you will have thirty days to vacate your apartment home and Almeda Park altogether. On the thirty-first day, I will enter your apartment to verify your residency. If at that time you are still occupying the apartment, I will file what's called a holdover motion with our attorney's office at which point a court date will be scheduled. In court, you and your attorney will have the opportunity to share your testimony to the judge, and our attorney will offer testimony on why you should be evicted," she said, now holding the receiver between her left shoulder and left ear. "Mr. Bangoura? Mr. Bangoura? I have yet to raise my tone with you. If you refuse to be professional and dignified, I will end the conversation. Mr. Bangoura, my boss does not pay me enough to sustain verbal abuse," Natalie pleaded. "Your mother is a cunt!" she yelled. Her pleading quickly turned into a lash back as she slammed the phone on the cradle.

Chapter 14

(First Person)

It was a scenario in which the pond was shrinking and all the fish were nervous. —Unknown

The property in which I adored was being sold. It was a beautiful 198-unit Farmington Hills community with fifteen two-story buildings, lush landscaping, character, and class—a buyer's dream. The funny thing is it was an unsolicited offer to purchase. The owners were out of New York—a public investment firm. The asset manager was a tough and intelligent woman that respected and rewarded hard work and dedication.

My career there started out after my management company had taken over the property from a competing property management firm. During the due diligence process, it was obvious that the community lacked preventative maintenance, capital investments, and just simple tender love and care. We took possession on the first day of the month in the fall—a day when the foliage couldn't have been better. Upon our arrival, the previous management team had stripped the walls of all of their marketing material—a common practice; stolen all office supplies—to be expected; and torn all of the blinds off the windows; and turned over all desks—an unprofessional tactic, but whatever.

We presented an attractive salary package to the maintenance supervisor to stay on board with us. It was funny, because the former property manager declined our offer; however, she continued to reside on-site for thirty to sixty days after we took over. I was a fairly new employee with this Dallas-based management company, and, quite frankly, I had reservations about the offer to transition into a role at an older, stabilized community. But the regional manager sold me, saying that my quick adoption of the company's mission statement and policies and procedures made me a more qualified candidate than anyone outside the company. As you can image, I bought into his bullshit.

The apartment community I was transitioning from was a brand-new gorgeous town house community in the historic Ford Estate campus. That property was still in lease up, which meant sales commissions were enticing and plentiful (sigh). Nonetheless, my only experience was in brand-new lease-up communities—even with my previous employer. By the way, I failed to mention that the same regional manager stole me from their competition. He walked into the community and posed as a client relocating from out of state to the area. I had an above-average closing ratio of 45 percent at the time when the industry standard was 33 percent. I remember describing how accommodating the gourmet kitchen was since he revealed his passion for cooking, when he cornered me and offered me an assistant management position and his business card for an immediate interview.

My property manager at the time was a thief and possibly schizophrenic, so I took swift action in following up with the regional manager. We met in the lobby of a four-star hotel, I wowed him in the interview, he wowed me with an introduction to a larger firm with national presence, and the rest is history.

I have a very rare set of core characteristics and like to think that I cultivate professionalism. On my first day, I awaited the arrival of my new property manager only to learn that though the company had paid for her move to the area, she made other plans and turned down the position moments after she was due on-site. I worked with sedulousness in implementing the company's creed, policies, procedures, and brand on the stabilized asset. I was too new to be considered for the property management role; thus, I waited patiently as the regional manager made other offers to tenured employees in other states.

Finally, a Drew Carey look-alike showed up with a moving truck and his inexperience to run the $17 million acquisition. We got along great—at first. He had a free-spirited personality and a great sense of humor. It wasn't until he would insist that the maintenance men take turns shaving his back that I had an issue with him. After he learned what a work horse I was and how I was not easily distracted, he would roll into work at 1 p.m. and roll out at 4 p.m. "You don't mind, do you? Put yourself down for some overtime, and I'll approve it," he would often try to bribe me. The final straw was when he seduced a bisexual male resident and talked him into terminating his lease agreement early to move in with him. Because of cutbacks in the industry, free rent was no longer a luxury or benefit offered by owners, but managers received more than a 50 percent discount—no deposits, no application fees, and no credit checks—pretty sweet deal.

No one thought much of the roommate situation, until our monthly meetings would turn into hilarious stories involving the purchase of small rodent, the use of an empty paper towel roll, and the property manager's buttocks. Now that he was out of the closet, the maintenance men were really uncomfortable shaving his back—duh!

Long story shortened, his days were numbered until they finally ran out. It was months before a new property manager was secured; in the meantime, I staffed the property seven days per week, until I finally received authorization to hire a temporary employee from a local staffing company. Guess what? He was also gay and often performed in drag queen shows all across the metropolitan area. That was not the issue—every girl likes to associate with gay men; it's the best girl talk in town! As my gay friend would say, "I talk. You talk. We talk girrrrrrl talk!" The problem was not only was he a performer, but he was also a thief. He stole several identities from our wealthy and elderly clients and was charged with identity theft before it was even popular.

The new manager showed up. Finally … Woo hoo! I'm thinking. She was mature, nice, and very knowledgeable. Finally, there was someone I could learn from for the next opportunity when a property manager's position opened up. She taught me a lot … when she was there. She was consistently sick with gout, measles, chicken pox, food poisoning, unexplained viruses, you name it! Ugh! As my favorite boss told me once, "You must be present to win."

Her resume reflected a seasoned management professional. She was married, unable to bear children, and owned a home approximately 40 miles away from the community. This often gave her more excuses not to be present at work, especially when my husband and I moved on-site. If the Midwest snow storms didn't keep her home, the power outages and inability to remove her vehicle from her garage did. By this time, the owners were not happy with the management company's turnover. The writing was now on the wall for the young female regional manager that I was just building a rapport with.

I began feeling discouraged and updated my resume to possibly move on or rehire with my previous company. My regional manager announced that she was leaving the company to try her hand as an entrepreneur. She begged me to "hang in there" and get some more training under my belt. She gave me a business management test to see if I was promotable prior to her departure, but there were reservations. She told me that the new regional manager sounded like a really nice person and came with a wealth of knowledge of multifamily residential, and, in another twelve months, she could assure me that I would manage my own site.

The vice president did not want to make the decision to fire the absent property manager without the new regional manager meeting her and trying to get a feel for her. The VP did, however; approve a permanent, part-time assistant for me. This new part-time candidate was phenomenal. She owned her own business and came with a wealth of sales experience—mainly car sales. One Sunday afternoon, I was out front sweeping up cigarette butts when a Range Rover pulled up with two attractive Caucasian gay males exiting the vehicle. I greeted them and welcomed them to tour the community with my new salesperson. Afterward, it looked as if they enjoyed their tour, and I was hoping to see them back again, soon.

As luck would have it, the Caucasian gay male with the dark hair and Burberry scarf on was my new regional manager! He posed as a client a day before introducing himself to get a feel for the Farmington Hills staff. He soon mentioned how impressed he was to see me shoveling debris out front and the warm greeting he received. "Honey, if I was a prospect, I would have loved to rent an apartment at your community," he complimented. After about one and a half to two weeks, the regional manager returned to my community, meeting with the property manager and me. He announced that he was promoting me to the property manager's position and moving her to my original site—the brand new lease up, which after much turnover itself still hadn't stabilized. I was elated! Finally, there was someone who had recognized my efforts and would assist me in the only area in which I showed the most weakness—owner's reports.

I did not have much experience preparing variance reports and communicating with owners on a daily, weekly, monthly, or quarterly basis. I checked e-mails frequently as a primary communication vehicle. I did, however, have complete autonomy with creative marketing resources and familiarity of the area, which, once again, made me the best candidate for the position.

I took immediate ownership in the property—raising rents, hosting weekly staff meetings, and networking with chamber of commerce and apartment association organizations—with total support from the new regional manager, who was an absolute scholar and I truly adored. In our lunch meetings, he complimented my designer handbags and shoes, and I complimented him on his luxury sports vehicles and designer ties, suits, wool coats, you name it! It was a dream come true and a match made in heaven.

By this time, I had been at the community for three years and had never met the asset manager or owner representatives. During a new budget presentation in Chicago and New York, the regional manager invited the controller out to see the asset and get a better understanding of the capital dollars he was requesting. He wowed her, I wowed him, and we received every dime of capital dollars we asked for! This ranged from exterior building improvements to chimney repairs to $2.5 million in unit renovations, which included stainless-steel appliances, granite-like countertops, new cabinetry, six-panel raised doors, two-tone custom paint, chair and crown molding, nickel hardware, and nickel lighting upgrades.

I mean, this new regional manager had showed an unprecedented sense of urgency in getting things up, running, and stabilized quickly. I was impressed. I am still impressed. By this time, he was building a great Midwest team. Because of his sales and management ability, he had increased the company's management portfolio from two properties to seven—in a short period of time. There was talk of the necessity of a satellite office in our metro area. My Farmington Hills community was now an award-winning real estate acquisition.

Because of an ash disease attacking the mature trees on the property, it was necessary for us to cut down over one hundred trees, which left a bare curb appeal. However, those one hundred plus trees were swiftly replaced with approximately sixty-five beautiful trees. The community was performing at a remarkable pace, which allowed me more time to work off-site—in the community doing volunteer work to raise funds for the Muscular Dystrophy Foundation. I was locked in a mock jail cell with great food and beverages and my rolodex.

On Saturdays, I participated with the local chamber of commerce to sell raffle tickets on a busy thoroughfare. Tickets were fifty to one hundred dollars each, and prizes ranged from spa getaways to brand-new GM Corvettes. I remember being the only black female working the event one Saturday morning. Folks were out shopping, running post office errands, and having brunch, and there I was in some tight white slacks and a bright top with high heels pulling older white men off the street to purchase these raffle tickets. Originally, the organizer had sent out an e-mail to several chamber members asking for each of us to fill one slot on one of three days—a Friday, Saturday, or Sunday. However, I was asked to return the following day after my two-hour shift had expired, and I had sold a record $4,500 in ticket sales. My God-sister used to tease me. "It wasn't your sales ability that did it ... it was those damn tight white pants you were wearing," she said.

Then, the unthinkable occurred. The vice presidency changed hands, and the new vice president was apparently homophobic. He consistently made wise cracks at the regional manager's choice of shoe color and even went as far as to inquire if he wore makeup. It was obnoxious, ridiculous, and offensive. Finally, after coming off like a bull in a china store during a construction meeting with the asset manager, who adored the regional manager and me, the vice president demoted the regional manager to site level as a property manager. I remember crying like a baby when that happened. I found myself in a state of darkness, because he was the only regional manager that believed in my ability based on a first impression. He believed enough to give me the chance and the tools to succeed.

By this time, I had been awarded five prestigious awards annually from the management company for multiple categories: positive attitude, top sales, consistently scoring in high ranges on shopping reports, overall professionalism, and positive attitude again. The former regional manager was now out performing me on every level at my original town house community: rent collections, occupancy, leasing trends, bottom line budget numbers, and so forth. It was a fun and annoying competition! He was heartbroken over the demotion and promised to give the company six solid months before asking for his "old job back" or pursuing a corporate career outside of the company.

Six months came and went and so did the regional/property manager. I was devastated. The vice president and new regional manager made it their mission to "keep me happy." They knew that the former manager would land a worthy position elsewhere and try to recruit me, which he did—on several occasions, but I was not for sale. Aside from the basis of his departure, I was extremely happy with the management company as a whole.

My new goal became to train and groom leasing professionals into assistant managers and finally into property managers. I had a great time with that and had some success. One failure came when I hired this man—let's call him "Charles"—to fill an assistant manager position. My perfect candidate was someone outside of the industry, because I was tired of investing my time training and reversing bad habits and instilling people with my sales, marketing, customer service, and management style. So I decided on Charles who had a used car salesman look about him, but he was very charming, very articulate, and simply interviewed well. Unbeknownst to me, Charles had difficulty taking direction from a woman, working for a woman, and being second in command. He challenged me on every angle. This is not a bad thing in itself, but know what you're talking about before you do so. Needless to say, he didn't make it past his ninety-day introductory period.

The maintenance men teased me for months after Charles' termination. When I think back on it, it was pretty funny. I had cooked this huge breakfast in the clubhouse kitchen that morning—a potatoes and sausage medley packed with green peppers and onions, crisp bacon, scrambled eggs with cheese, waffles with pecan syrup, fresh fruit, orange juice, and coffee. We could barely work on such a full stomach. Just before the end of his shift, the axe was lowered for Charles. Ahhh, the good ole days!

Finally, I began to get bored. Unchallenged. Stale. Mundane. At that point, the company began flying me all across the country to train new managers and new salespeople, and I began to see the company in a whole new light.

Just as I began to get too comfortable, I received the most shocking news in my life—my favorite, plush suburban community was for sale. Owners received an unsolicited offer from a condo converter, and, poof, my job was in limbo.

I felt like it was midnight, and someone had just turned down the gas. Fearing the unknown, I received immediate comfort from the vice president, regional manager, and marketing director that a position was coming available at a downtown high-rise location that desperately needed my help. From what I was told, my former assistant manager—turned promoted property manager—had been on somewhat of a power trip for the past twelve months and botched up the business plan our management company outlined for that property.

In the end, I worked closely with the asset manager and the purchasing company to finalize the sale. I was awarded a large bonus for doing so and made a graceful, professional transition, all the while being propositioned by the purchasing company to stay on with their organization. No thanks.

I still have family members that reside in this community today. I visit them and the property frequently. It is still the most amazing asset in that suburban area, but condo sales are extremely slow, so it is apparent that the condo community is still renewing and leasing rental apartments.

Chapter 15

Creative minds have always been known to survive any kind of bad training, bad experiences. —Anna Freud

Offering a level of luxury and comfort that is rarely combined with such transparency, I introduce to you, The Sullivan. Owned by Geiman Realty Investors with Jeffrey Geiman at the helm, The Sullivan was built with you in mind. Jeffrey incorporated a multifamily portfolio based on specific anomalies and opportunities. Geiman Realty Investors' acquisitions range from value added to stable to more aggressive and tactical opportunities. Geiman purchased The Sullivan in the late 1980s and completed major renovations, including new kitchens, bath vanities, tiled flooring, exterior painting, irrigation, new roofs, resurfaced parking lots, and improvements to common-area amenities in the mid 1990s.

Wining the TOBY award for two consecutive years, Geiman was nervous about the staffing issues at The Sullivan. The TOBY award recognizes excellence in building management and overall operations on a local, regional, and international level. The building is evaluated based on professional management, physical appearance, maintenance, and the effectiveness of the community's positive image and ability to maintain an eco-friendly business. In an effort to improve the overall maintenance aspect, the management firm was charged with recruiting a qualified chief engineer for the buildings. The regional manager ran a classified ad on Craig's List that read as follows:

Have you ever been described by a former or current supervisor as ethical, dependable, calm, proficient, decisive, bright, skillful, intuitive, refreshing, passionate, thorough, resourceful, determined, receptive, trustworthy, diligent, intelligent, self-reliant, purposeful, respectful, analytical, with a positive attitude? If so, e-mail your resume along with one other adjective that describes you to msrussell@e-mail.com.

It was three months of interviewing unqualified, under skilled, and inexperienced candidates when the perfect applicant finally walked through the door—Martin Schuler, a forty-nine-year-old seasoned engineer from Akron, Ohio. During the three-phase interview process, it was learned that he actually managed the maintenance team at The Sullivan in his early twenties while under a different ownership and management firm. Martin started out as an apprentice and over time worked up the ladder as chief engineer of the buildings. "Why did you leave The Sullivan?" Barbara Russell, the regional manager, asked.

"Back then, I was younger, working seventy-plus hours per week. My wife had just had our youngest son, and she basically gave me the ultimatum— your family or your job," Martin began to explain. "I chose my family and ended up taking a job with her father as a painter. So I've always been connected to the industry one way or another," Martin concluded.

"Tell us about your experience in Chicago," the property manager, Jon instructed while reviewing Martin's resume during the interview.

"There's not much to tell. Chicago, as you know, is a union town. So I took a job as a chief engineer with a condominium association downtown. It was the same building that Oprah Winfrey approached about a unit and was denied by the association for whatever reason; so she purchased the entire building next door to it. We laid carpet, performed carpentry, everything. I had a six-guy crew working under me; life was good," Martin confessed.

"What made you leave Chicago?" Barbara inquired.

"My wife and I were in the middle of a divorce. The company I'd worked for promoted me to regional director of maintenance over five properties while they were in the process of firing this other guy. He was placed on administrative leave while an investigation was pending against him. The union fought for him, he got his job back, and the rest is history. My old site had already replaced me, so I was laid off," he said. Martin adjusted in his chair. "Look, I'm the right guy for this job and these buildings. I absolutely love what you have done with the place with the renovations. I ran into Brett outside in the parking lot; man was it good to see him. I hired that guy almost twenty years ago, and he hasn't aged a bit. I'm going to be turning fifty next year—reaching another milestone in my life—and, basically, I want my feet planted for retirement," Martin said, as he wiped the perspiration from his brow.

"I've got to be honest with you, Martin, I have some reservations about the way you have jumped jobs in the past. We are looking for a long-term hire. Your resume doesn't tell me the type of manager you are, and that's another difficult situation. I'm running into a lot of guys with the skill set we are looking for, physical knowledge of life safety equipment and building mechanics, but none that possess the right amount of managerial skills. With that said, you are the best candidate that I have run across in over ninety days," Barbara said frankly.

"Jon, Ms. Russell, I know that you two don't know me well, but trust me, you can stop looking; the right guy is sitting right here in front of you." Martin's thumb was pointing back at him.

"I like the fact that your personality test says that you are a precise and meticulous individual. It describes you as a person who is quite concerned with the details of your job assignment and one who hates to make mistakes. I could tell from your initial interview that your general approach is a conservative one. You prefer to gather all the facts and data prior to making a decision," Barb shared.

"Interesting. What else did the test reveal?" Martin asked.

"It says that you are systematic, methodical, and disciplined in your work approach. You tend to follow the rules closely and work more efficiently in structured and unambiguous situations. In other words, you are a terrific problem solver," Barbara continued.

Barbara asked Martin to excuse her and Jon while they deliberated over the decision. Martin stepped out to have a cigarette and return a call from his cell phone. "What I didn't tell him," Barbara started to tell Jon, "is that the report also red flagged some other personality traits. It indicated that he is sensitive and easily defensive and emotional when criticized. He avoids antagonistic situations and stresses when he makes a mistake or doesn't have enough time to organize everything." Jon expressed that with all said, he was willing to take a chance on Martin. However, the ultimate decision rested with Barb.

After several minutes, the concierge clerk called him back into the manager's office. Martin extinguished his cigarette and ended his call abruptly. After reentering Jon's office, Barbara extended her hand, "Welcome back to The Sullivan; don't let me down."

Martin firmly shook Barbara's hand and then Jon's. "You won't be sorry," he said with joy in his eyes. Jon explained that they were ready to make an offer contingent upon Martin's successful completion of a criminal background check and drug test. "Piece of cake. I have no problems with that," Martin assured them.

"So you don't foresee any problems passing both checks and starting immediately thereafter?" Barbara asked, and Martin assured them once again.

The three bid each other a good weekend as Ms. Russell sent an e-mail from her Blackberry informing the owners that she just extended an offer for $75,000 with a $5,000 signing bonus to the new chief engineer, Martin Schuler. Jon caught Barb before she got in her BMW i35 to advise her that he received a settlement confirmation from their liability carrier advising that Hollie Kesselring accepted a $195,000 settlement against her $400,000 lawsuit.

"Really? What was the claim on that one?" Barbara asked, drawing a blank.

"You wanna phone a friend or buy a vowel?" Jon joked. "How could you forget? This was the woman who claimed that she slipped and fell in a wet stairwell of the sixth floor in Building II."

"Oh … Oh … now I remember," Barb recalled. The resident, Hollie, alleged that an "unknown liquid substance" resembled dried blood at first glance, but it turned out to be spilled fruit juice. She claimed to have hit her head on the concrete step; however, she remained conscious. Hollie used her cell phone to dial an ambulance and was transported to the nearest emergency room. Hollie was treated and released after three days and surgery. Ultimately, Hollie was diagnosed with a fractured sacrum and suffered from diplopia and bitemporal headaches. The court transcripts were closed, but it was rumored that Ms. Kesselring incurred $46,853.10 in special medical damages and lost wages of $3,525.01. The initial settlement demand was $400,000—clearly exceeding out-of-pocked damages by close to $350,000.

"Apparently, there's another lawsuit that was recently brought forth involving an automobile accident that occurred on the property approximately three years ago. The former tenant is suing for $275,000, saying that our maintenance team failed to properly salt the grounds, which resulted in her sliding on ice and crashing her 1992 vintage Jaguar into a wall. The attorney's summation stated that the former tenant's medical bills are mounting after her initial surgery to repair the broken pedicle screw in her neck."

Barbara hunched her shoulders, smiled, and said, "Never a dull moment." Jon agreed and shook his head in disbelief.

Wednesday morning rolled around, and Jon was copied on an e-mail to Barbara Russell from the Human Resources Department. The e-mail specified that Martin's criminal history was flagged. The department was asking that he elaborate and explain the derogatory information found. A lump formed in Jon's throat as he read along. He calmed himself out of a panic and decided to just call Martin. "Are you in the process of having anything expunged from your record?" he tried to hint. Martin promised to march down to the courthouse the following morning and meet with Jon immediately thereafter. "Damn! I hope this guy comes through," Barb expressed to Jon. "The owners are on my back about filling this vacant position."

Thursday morning arrived, and Martin Schuler walked in Jon's office at 11 a.m. with a court document that showed he was charged with theft—valued at less than $500. Jon's eyes widened.

"Let me explain," Martin started. He described how six years prior, his son had stolen a $44 costume jewelry bracelet for his mother's birthday by dropping the bracelet in the bag that Martin was carrying. Martin was obviously apprehended near the store's sensor detector and hauled off to the county jail. "I'm telling you the God's honest truth. This has never come up during any other background check I have taken. I was charged with a misdemeanor due to the amount, so I did not lie on your application, which clearly asked if I had ever been convicted of a felony," Martin pleaded.

"Unfortunately, I have zero input on this decision. My best advice to you is to put in writing exactly what you just told me, and I will fax it along with the court document to HR. We'll go from there," Jon advised.

Martin dropped his face into his cupped hands and wiped the sweat from his forehead. "I'm not a thief. I hope you believe that," Martin claimed.

Jon cracked a small smile and left Martin to his writing assignment. Jon called HR from another office to give a heads up on the documents being faxed. "I think it's best for me to tell you, we do not hire anyone with any form of theft in their past—regardless of the dollar amount," the voice from the other end of the phone replied. *Gulp.*

Chapter 16

This world isn't kind to small things. —Unknown

Hank—raised on the west side of Detroit during the Depression—grew up, moved out, enlisted in the army, and was now raising a family of his own in Detroit's west side neighborhood. Married with two children, he worked odd jobs to support his family.

They rented a two-family flat—upper story, with a small yard, great neighbors, and big dreams. After an honorable discharge, Hank set off for a postal position. It was very common back in those days for military personnel to have first dibs on government employment opportunities. However, because of a blood disease—sickle cell anemia—and a consistent blood-alcohol level, Hank was never considered for the postal carrier position. At the time, the children were four and seven when an apartment opened up in a four-unit building two doors down from Hank's mother.

Hank's mother, Vera—about 5'1" and 280 pounds with freckles—was raising two of her other grandchildren at the time. One was a boy, and one was a girl—who was really not her son's biological daughter, but no one treated Francis like a stepchild. Like most teenage girls, Francis became rebellious and disobedient over time. Once, she ran up Vera's telephone bill to well over $500. Back in the 1980s, even a $100 telephone bill was outrageous, and most households needed to make "arrangements" to pay it. It was soon discovered that Francis was accepting collect calls from her boyfriends in jail, along with dialing

1-900 numbers to listen to vulgar sexual exploits. It wasn't until Francis began to steal money from her grandparents that her irrational behavior became a problem.

One Thursday afternoon, Vera was in the one bath in the 1945 built, brick three-bedroom colonial home, which included a full basement. Vera was finishing a bath preparing for her four o'clock to midnight shift. As she exited the bathroom to iron her stark white uniform scrubs, Vera left her nightgown and brassiere in the bathroom along with the change purse she kept tucked into her 44DD bosom. Francis—who was outside the door dancing and hopping from one leg to the other—rushed in to use the facilities. In such time, Francis found the perfect opportunity to steal a $10 bill out of Vera's change purse.

At 3:30 p.m., Vera started up her Park Avenue Buick, which was parked in the driveway. This was part of her daily routine—preheating the vehicle and defrosting the windshield before driving off into town. As she picked up her half pack of Virginia Slim cigarettes, Vera tucked the pack in her change purse only to notice that her fuel and lunch money was missing. She searched profusely and pulled everyone in the household into the search. Suddenly, it dawned on her. "Francis! Get down here right now!" she demanded.

"Ma'am?" Francis yelled downstairs, masking her guilt. Fair-skinned and a little on the heavy side herself, Francis' footsteps started down the staircase,

"Where is my $10 bill?" Vera interrogated. Francis appeared oblivious to the money in which Vera spoke of and volunteered to join in on the search.

Grandpa Frank covered the plastic trait in his throat, "Girl, you better not have taken money from your grandmother's purse—as hard as she works to feed you and clothe you since your sorry-ass daddy can't!"

Francis helped in the search, looking between book pages, under lamps, sofas, and the coffee table. Her choice of impossible places pointed the guilty finger in her direction. "I am going back to the bathroom where I last left my change purse. If that $10 bill is not in that bathroom, you better call your dad or Jesus himself to keep me from strangling you," Vera said out of anger, as she gathered her coffee and work bag for her ride to work.

Francis raced up the stairs as if she was attempting to look in the bathroom. "I found it, Grandma!" she yelled down from the bath. "It was under the tub." Vera was so upset she could spit.

Frank was very disappointed and called his son, Jimmy, on the phone to advise of the day's events. "You better get yourself together and get a place for your children to be with you before your mother kills Francis. Teddy is not a problem, but that Francis …"

Years went by, and more and more things became messy and missing. Once, Francis was even sent home early from school for stealing a bottle of White Out from typing class and sniffing it during algebra. There was another instance when Francis was expelled from school for getting into a fight with a bully in Teddy's special education class. It was during Francis' senior year, so the principal felt merciful and allowed her to finish out the year at the same high school, but she was not permitted to walk the stage.

Prior to graduation, the grandparents sat Francis down to serve an ultimatum, saying, "Either you get enrolled into community college, or you get a job to support yourself, or you get out. Those are your choices." Francis did not qualify for financial aid due to Frank's pension and Vera's salary, so she chose to get a job at a fast-food restaurant nearby. "Okay. You will be responsible for your separate phone line, transportation to and from work, and $40 per month for food, room, and board." The grandparents continued to lay down a foundation of responsibility for the troubled eighteen-year-old.

Francis held down a job for about two months before she was terminated for her cash drawer coming up short. But, somehow, she found an alternate source of income in a drug dealing boyfriend they called Blaze. Blaze was twenty years of age, drove a $20,000 car, and had jewelry draped around his neck and wrist. "What's wrong with that damn boy? He can't get out of the car and ring the bell like most respectable young men?" Vera would say after being annoyed by Blaze honking the horn for Francis to run out of the house before their dates.

"Oh, Grandma, you're so old-fashioned," Francis would respond. Frank was getting to be so ill by this point that he spoke less and less.

Suddenly, there was a family rumor that Francis had slipped and fell in a fast-food chain's vestibule and sued for $100,000. Francis bragged to a cousin, who in turn told her mother, who then called Vera to confirm. Francis denied such claim and was later condemned when confirmation of a $40,000 settlement document arrived in the mail one morning. Vera opened and read the mail, but she chose to reseal it and leave it for Francis as a test. Francis became more and more interested in the mailbox thereafter, racing Vera to the box daily. Vera suspected when the check came, because Francis stayed out overnight several nights in a row. She never offered a dime to Vera and griped about her required $40 rent, "I hardly eat or stay here anymore; I don't think it's fair that I have to pay you a whole $40," Francis challenged one day.

"As a matter of fact, you don't. When I return home from work tonight, I want you and all of your belongings out of my house, and leave your key on the kitchen table, understood?" Vera made her point clear.

Vera was hurt and disappointed over Francis' actions. It wasn't about the money; it was the principle in which she felt no gratitude to offer any to Frank and Vera—after all they had done. That night when Vera got home, Francis was gone all right, so were the living room and kitchen curtains off the window. Frank was almost bedridden by this time and could not have observed Francis' exit.

Later that week, the Lord called Frank home and Vera was forced into an early retirement. Family members traveled from all over to be by Vera's side. Her no-good son, Jimmy, even surfaced and attended his father's funeral. He wasn't sober, but he was in attendance. At the repass dinner, Vera confided in her relatives about the stress and disappointment Francis put her through. Hank, Vera's other son, had heard first hand of Francis' antics and was very put off by her presence in Vera's home with other family members—acting as if everything was hunky dory.

However, Hank was having drama of his own at home. His alcoholism had deemed him unemployed for five consecutive years. He was very angry and consistently abused his wife—physically and emotionally. By this time, Hank's homosexual brother-in-law had disclosed to his older daughter that Hank was not her biological father.

This explained why she was treated differently from her younger sister, Patty. After a broken nose, a head print in her bedroom wall and being held at gun point for more than three hours, Hank's wife finally left him. "That good-for-nothing wife of yours, always kicking you when you're down," Vera consoled her son. She had the hardest time finding fault in any of her four sons.

Meanwhile, Patty; her only sister, Jade; and her mother, Paris, were living happily ever after in a rented home on the same street as Vera's house. This was for convenience and so that Patty could see her father every day; she was absolutely a daddy's girl.

By the age of eighteen, Patty had graduated from high school and had become pregnant. Her mother was furious and said, "You want your father to beat my ass, don't you! He is not going to take this out on you; he is going to blame me!" Paris feared. She forced Patty into having an abortion, which infuriated Patty's high school sweetheart, Dean. Patty and her mother did not see eye-to-eye after that point, and, she vowed that as soon as she healed, she and Dean would get a place of their own. At the time, Patty was an assistant manager of a chicken shack, while Dean worked as a street mechanic.

A shocking phone call came from a local emergency room. Hank had recently secured a position as a security patrol guard who'd wrapped himself around a telephone pole in the vehicle from drinking on the job. Doctors phoned Paris, since she was legally still married to Hank. Unfortunately, Hank had not cleared his ninety-day probationary period with his employer; thus, he did not have medical insurance of his own. Doctors were calling for Paris to immediately taxi to the hospital and authorize surgery to save Hank's life. "After all that man has put me through, God wants me to do the right thing by my daughter," Paris cried on her knees, as she struggled with the pain and feelings she had for Hank. "He has found a way to pull himself back into my life, once again," she said, as she continued to cry.

Paris signed the necessary paperwork that authorized a life-saving surgery for Hank who had broken his neck, right arm, and both legs. Nurses advised he had a blood-alcohol level higher than four times the legal limit. Hank was a vegetable during the early stages of treatment. But soon, with physical therapy, medicine and God's grace, he was released from the hospital to his mother's home in a hospital bed. Hank wore a halo screwed into his temples and shoulder and was fed by a tube for several months. Though she lived in close proximity, Paris visited in person only once per month, but she called Vera often to check the status of his recovery. Patty continued to be devastated by her father's condition and was by his side often.

Soon, Patty was expecting yet another child. In less than a year's time from her previous abortion, Patty and Dean had chosen to keep this baby. Her mother was so depressed, but she didn't have the strength for anger and wished the two well. Patty moved to a suburban community where she rented a government subsidized apartment for her baby, Dean, and herself. To ensure a lower monthly payment, Dean was not listed as an occupant or leaseholder on the contract. After delivery, Patty was moved to the top of the waiting list for Section 8 housing when Hank's half sister learned of the happenings with the family, including his accident.

The apartment community was a midrise, C grade development with a predominately white demographic. Hank was on the road to a full recovery, walking with a slight limp and a new appreciation for life. He worked odd jobs to support his only daughter and granddaughter and soon met and fell in love with several women—one at a time. He and Paris were finally somewhat civil and talked about finalizing their separation with a divorce decree. Paris had definitely moved on with her dating life, but held on to her physical fear of being in the same room with Hank, whose intimidating demeanor continued long after his accident and recovery.

Hank did not care for Patty's boyfriend, Dean, and he made it known to everyone, including Patty and Dean. "What is *that boy* doing to help you with this baby?" he would often ask. By this time, Hank was married to a woman who had three daughters from a previous relationship and immediately insisted on carrying another child for Hank. Family rumors concluded that he had gotten an older woman he dated pregnant, trying for a son; however, she miscarried. Yvonne, Hank's new wife, was now expecting, and everyone had their fingers crossed for a healthy baby boy.

Christmas was very profitable for Patty as she played on her father's guilt for having a new family. He gave Patty everything from baby furniture, kitchen appliances, money, and cars to keep her happy and knowing that she was his number one girl in the whole entire world. "Don't you ever let me see that boy driving this car," Hank warned the year he bought the car. It was a used, navy-colored Ford—and such was the same year Hank's violent streak resurfaced. Living in the lap of Section 8 luxury, Dean had invited several family members to room with he and Patty in their two-bedroom apartment.

One night, Dean and his brother, Mason, went to a bar in the city. Dean was driving home drunk, hit a tree, and totaled Patty's car. Her father was furious and so was she. Dean made up some lame story on how he was driving completely sober and was t-boned by a drunk driver who was also speeding. Patty didn't believe that story for one minute, but she tried to sell it to her father. "You're on your own," Hank warned again. "I can't do anything else for you, while you have that boy in your house. If the baby needs something, let me know, but you are on your own."

Another turn of events came when Dean and his little brother were caught stealing in a large chain store. Dean's little brother was caught on closed-circuit camera tucking a $3.75 notebook into his jacket for school. Because of his age, Dean was charged with a misdemeanor for conspiracy of theft and ordered to pay restitution and court costs totaling $250. That's one expensive notebook! Once again, Hank was disappointed in Patty, who was the only working parent in the home at the time and struggled to pay the $250 to keep Dean out of jail.

One summer later, it was discovered that Dean was unfaithful to Patty with a girl who lived in the same complex, except, she wasn't a single parent receiving government subsidy for herself and her child. Turns out she was a fourteen-year-old child, for which her mother received government subsidy to support. Apparently, this little girl's mother read her diary about her young daughter's sexual encounters with Dean, found out where he lived, and confronted her daughter, who alleged rape. Dean was arrested and serviced by a public defender who advised that though the sexual encounters were all consensual, Dean engaged in such encounter with an underage teen, which constituted rape. Dean plead guilty to a lesser charge and served less than one year in jail. Once again, Hank was disappointed.

While this story circulated to family members, more rumors returned about Francis who was on her fourth frivolous lawsuit and had collected more than $250,000 over time. This time, Francis was suspected for insurance fraud, as she asked to temporarily move back to Vera's home since hers had burned down in a fire. Vera obliged as she struggled with her new Christianity. Pieces of the puzzle were put together when Vera's daughter in Georgia was forced out of her apartment home due to an electrical fire from a faulty wire. Luckily, she had renter's insurance that covered her temporary stay in a hotel and cash settlement on lost personal contents. According to Vera's daughter in Georgia, Francis called her one night out of the blue asking for details on her settlement claim.

There, she was pacing the floor each day prior to the mailman depositing mail in the box. It wasn't long before she received a $175,000 insurance settlement and disappeared for a long time. Relatives would joke, "She only resurfaces when the money has run out—somehow she's more humble when she's broke."

As time elapsed, Hank's sickle cell disease kept him down and extremely ill. He was in and out of the hospital and constantly changing jobs, this time due to his blood illness. Patty grew more and more afraid that her father would leave her soon. She recalled her grandmother telling her once that doctors forecasted that Hank would not live to see age thirty-five due to the sickle cell anemia. He was now forty-seven, and she was afraid. Hank did the responsible thing and initiated a life insurance policy for himself—one that would take care of his family in his absence.

Hank died a year later. Patty was absolutely devastated and nearly fainted in the hospital corridor when doctors pronounced the news. More bad news would strike when it was discovered that the several hundred thousand dollar life insurance policy was voided due to Hank's deception on the medical history portion of the application. His blood disease was definitely preexisting; however, he checked "no." This left a monetary strain on the family to pay cash for his burial. His new wife was not gainfully employed. She came from a very poor background; thus, there was no one to borrow from. Francis even chipped in to the tune of $60 for the spray that would lie atop his casket. An estimated half of million dollars has passed through her hands ... and sixty dollars was all she could spare to assist with her uncle's burial. Talk about mismanaging money.

Vera was in her late sixties, early seventies at this point and on a fixed income. So it was left up to Patty, who worked extremely hard to beg, borrow, and steal—so to speak—to bury her father. Patty collaborated with her older sister, who was not Hank's daughter. She wrote the obituary, coordinated an arrangement of photos, and spent the night in Kinko's making colored paper copies of the obituaries to be passed out at the funeral. The grieving family formed an assembly line the morning of the funeral to organize and crease the pages of Hank's obituary. In the end, the family couldn't afford a headstone, but they buried him nonetheless. Rest in Peace.

Chapter 17

Loving is not just looking at each other, it's looking in the same direction. —Antoine de Saint-Exupery

Terry called in to say she would need to take four hours of time from her vacation bank to tend to the 'baby-daddy drama' she was experiencing. From the lengthy voicemail she left Venice, the property manager, drama was an understatement. She described going to the hairdresser at 7 a.m. that morning in hopes to be made over and in the office for her 10 a.m. to 7 p.m. shift. Terry was separated from her husband, Ray, for the umpteenth time, and both children were living with her in a two-bedroom apartment in the building in which she worked.

The youngest child, four-year-old Aisha, was born for Ray, while the teenager, thirteen-year-old Sheena, was born for Terry's second husband, Phillip. Phillip was remarried to a woman who could not bear children and thus did not want his biological children in their lives as a constant reminder. "You would think the sawed-off bitch would want to experience the pitter patter of little feet from a child that has the same DNA as her husband, regardless," Terry would often comment. Phillip graciously paid child support and asked that he not be contacted for any other support, including bonding, rapport building, and disciplinary purposes.

Venice understood; for one, she and Terry were also friends outside of work, and she was Aisha's godmother. She called Terry's cell phone to see if she needed a ride from the beauty shop. "Hey girl. No, he didn't take the car out of the parking lot," Venice reiterated after listening to her voice message.

Terry described how she was sitting in the chair with hot curlers frying her hair when she noticed her champagne-colored Chrysler 300C drive out of the parking lot. Before she could hop out of the chair, her text message ring tone alerted. "You don't pay the note on this damn thing, so why should you drive it!" Ray's text read.

Terry hit the call button on her pink Motorola Razor, "You stupid son of a bitch! We had an agreement that you would stay in the house, and I would keep the car. I'm still paying the fuckin' mortgage on the house, while you allow your mother and father's lazy asses to lay in it!"

Ray charged back, "Like I said, the car is in my name, and I am not going to continue to pay for something that I can't drive. Have the asshole you are sucking buy you a car."

"As a matter of fact, I will," Terry slammed her flip phone shut and broke out in an angry cry.

Back at the office, Venice was interrupted by a crying tenant, "Let me call you back; better yet, I will just see you when you get here."

The resident was a small Indonesian woman; she looked to be about fifty-five years of age in a small 4'9" frame. "I need to speak to a manager … about bugs. Bugs that eating me up all night," she said.

The first thought that came to Venice's mind was bedbugs. She'd hoped the community was not experiencing another outbreak. She struggled with the idea of inviting the woman in her office and spraying the chair and the office down once the woman left or sit in the vacant office next to her that belonged to her leasing manager, Martha. "Let's have a seat in Martha's office to discuss this," she responded with a smirk.

The woman went on and on about how bedbugs and mice have taken over her 400-square foot studio apartment. "I don't have much money so my mattress … is on the floor, and the mice have eaten through the bottom of my mattress. It has holes in it, and I am not happy in that apartment. I like to transfer to a different one," she said.

"Ms. Shah, unfortunately, we do not transfer residents with an infestation due to the risk of spreading and affecting more apartments," Venice tried to explain sympathetically. "What I can do is schedule our pest control company to set traps to try to catch the mice. You mentioned something about being bit at night ..." Ms. Shah described how little bugs have been biting her at night and the blood stains on the wall of her one-room apartment home.

If you were like most people and thought bedbugs were a myth, they are real. Bedbugs are small nocturnal insects that feed off the blood of humans. So after your mom would tuck you in at night and say, "Don't let the bedbugs bite," she meant it.

Aside from the bedbugs biting Ms. Shah and leaving their secretions on her bedroom walls, mice were also taking over her apartment. She described a time when she turned on the kitchen light and saw three of them on her countertop. She knew she first had a problem when she found the droppings near the stove and under the kitchen cabinet. Ms. Shah was very old-fashioned and felt that if she had reported the infestation nine months back, she may have been evicted. It wasn't until her mother was in town visiting from the old country that she gained the courage to report the issue to the management office.

Venice retrieved the bedbug preparation letter to give to Ms. Shah and said, "The pest control company requires that you make the following preparations: launder all linens in hot water three times, move all furniture three feet away from the walls, throw away any mattresses with holes in it, and so forth. It is all outlined for you in this letter. I will give you a call with the date of the initial treatment."

Venice handed Ms. Shah a tissue as she walked her out of the management office, "Everything will work out just fine. I'm sure that the matter wouldn't be as urgent had you brought it to our attention sooner."

Just as Venice pushed the elevator button to escort Ms. Shah on, Terry walked off. Her face was frowned, her demeanor was rushed, but her hair was flawless! Venice bid Ms. Shah a good day and ran after Terry, "At least your hair looks fabulous," she said to make light of the mood.

"Shut up!" Terry responded, as she tried to hold back a smile. "Girl, I am so mad I could spit. Can you believe him?" she asked.

"Actually, I can." Just then, Terry's cell phone rang; it was her mother, Belinda. "Are you sitting down?" Belinda asked.

"I am now, what's up?"

Belinda asked Terry if she remembered when she was a little girl and Belinda told her that she got pregnant at age fifteen. Belinda's mother was a devout Baptist and did not believe in premarital sex, fornication, and definitely not teen pregnancy. "You are going to have this baby, give it up for adoption, and not shame this family ever again," Belinda's mother told her. Prior to the bump in Belinda's belly showing, her mother sent her off to a transition home in Grand Rapids. It was a facility for teen mothers, staffed with midwives to take the baby at birth and connect with adoptive parents that were ready and willing.

The father of Belinda's baby was a drug pusher, twelve years her senior. During the seven months that Belinda was away, neighbors would ask about her well-being, while Belinda's mother would tell a white lie, saying, "She's away at boarding school for a semester … she'll be home soon." Belinda was calling to tell Terry, who was thirty-two at the time of the call that the adoption agency called her grandfather's house looking for a Belinda McMillan— her maiden name. Terry's grandfather gave the social worker Belinda's cell phone who called to advise that Belinda's daughter Monique had been trying to reunite with her after thirty-eight years. With butterflies in her stomach, Belinda panicked and asked the social worker if she could call her back. "Don't be afraid to be honest," the social worker started. "There are no strings attached and no requirements here. You do not have to accept her call or her reaching out to you. You do, however, need to let me know as soon as possible so that I can figure out what I want to tell Monique."

"I really don't know what to say, but I will call you back one way or the other," Belinda retorted. The hundred butterflies surmounted to one thousand in her belly. She recalled all of those old suppressed memories of her mother looking down on Belinda during her early pregnancy and the idea that no one in the household spoke of the pregnancy and adoption ever again.

"Up to her deathbed, my mother never spoke of it again; it was as if it had never happened," Belinda continued. Tears rolled down Terry's eyes as she struggled with her emotions. At thirty-two years of age, could she really be jealous of another woman—another woman entering her and her mother's life as the oldest child when she had been such all of these years? As fun loving as her mother was, did she have enough love to go around? Would her new sister be prettier than her? Terry was speechless.

It was a time when Belinda was struggling with her own self-esteem, settling for intimate moments with men who did not belong to her. She struggled with her faith as she remained a big part of "the world." As she remained in limbo between gainful employment and a lay off, between a downtown apartment and living with one of her children, this may not be the right time to introduce herself to someone to whom she gave life. Many questions arose about the reunion. Belinda thought, *Will she hate me? How will I answer the "why" question?* Finally, Belinda called the social worker back to authorize her to release her cellular phone number to Monique.

"Wow. Call me later, and tell me what happens. I gotta get back to work," Terry said abruptly.

"What was that about?" Venice inquired.

"The story of my life. I don't know whether I'm coming or going—whether to kiss the kids or kick the dog ..." Terry rattled on.

Monique called shortly after receiving the phone number. It was a beautiful reunion. The new mother and daughter duo talked on the phone for hours. After thirty-eight years, Monique even had the wrong impression and remembrance about her biological father, who turned out not to be the man she grew up with. Turns out, Monique's foster father led her to believe that he was her biological father—a former pimp who had turned out her missing mother. "He lied to me?" she asked. Monique was speechless, as she learned the true fate of her biological father.

After spending hours and days on the telephone and Internet exchanging photos, Monique organized a trip to Detroit to finally meet her mother and siblings for the first time ever. It was an emotional reunion at the airport. It was like looking in a mirror. "That's a story beautiful enough for the Oprah show," a friend of Belinda's boasted. Soon after, the jealousy began. Terry was very standoffish and rude for most of Monique's trip.

Mother and daughter were together for the first time. They had the same habits, addictions, taste in men ... it was so bizarre exploring each other and memory lane. Monique thoroughly enjoyed her long weekend, and the two cried as hard in departures as they had done previously in arrivals. After spending hours, days, and months on the telephone and e-mail and laughing, crying and confessing, Monique decided to arrange for her mother to visit her in D.C. before the holidays.

As luck would have it, Belinda had a good friend who had just taken a job in Washington, D.C. She would be killing two birds with one stone by visiting. Her friend had already made a trip to Detroit to meet Monique during one of her vacations. The three spent a whole day together—reminiscing, drinking Patron, eating Caribbean food, and discussing an opportunity Karen had for Belinda to also take a job in D.C. paying $10,000 more than her current salary, plus bonuses. It was another emotional milestone in the new mother and daughter relationship. To have her mother in the same city was a dream come true. The three clinked glasses, shed tears, and tried to make a pact that would bring the three of them together finally and forever.

Karen stopped interviewing, waiting for Belinda to make a final decision once she returned home to Detroit. Days and days went by, but no word from Belinda. An e-mail hit Karen's inbox: *Any news from mom? Has she officially accepted the position?* What was Karen to do? To say? She knew that Belinda struggled with the decision to move from her hometown. It was a place she had known for over fifty years. D.C. metro was scary. Yes, salaries were higher, but so were food prices and the overall cost of living. Housing in Maryland was surcharged over rental rates in Michigan. However, Monique's perspective was understandable: Belinda had lived her entire life in Michigan. It was time for Belinda to finally be a mother to Monique after years and years of being with Terry full time.

Belinda finally called Karen to decline the position. Her next call was to Monique to explain her decision. It was difficult to accept, but no hard feelings were going to stand in the way of the mother and daughter team. They went on with life as usual, talking on the phone every day and e-mailing every chance they got.

More months went by, and Belinda came down with a brutal cold. She had a nasty cough that landed her in the hospital and off work for days. "Girl, I'm so sick—I can't stand the taste of a cigarette or a joint," she told her girlfriend, Karen. After more tests in the hospital, Belinda was diagnosed with lung cancer and was ordered to take chemotherapy after her bout with radiation. The news was devastating. Belinda's health took a turn for the worse, after weeks of being out of work, sleeping constantly, no appetite, hair loss, and loss of bone marrow and the ability and agility to stand, bathe, and live on her own.

Something went from a hopeful defeat to defeated and hopeless, when doctors revealed that Belinda was originally diagnosed with Stage 4 lung cancer. The team of doctors were extremely concerned with silent and obvious strokes becoming a part of the equation. "We can't treat the cancer because of the strokes, and we can't treat the strokes because of the cancer. The best thing for you to do is to begin making burial arrangements," the doctor told her. The words from one doctor in a private consultation room stung like a 120-volt shock.

No, no, no. This couldn't be what God intended when he brought us together, Monique thought.

This is all happening too fast, Terry thought. Thank God that she joined the church and confessed with her mouth that she was saved, and Jesus died for her sins.

Her soul will rest in eternity in Heaven, was all that Karen could think.

Terry, who had lost her job, became the responsible one and made all of the funeral arrangements. "She has three to four months—tops," the doctor's recommendations started to come down as tears began to fall. Belinda wasn't eating, drinking. She could barely swallow her medicine.

"She has four days to live," another doctor announced. The doctor's forecasts had changed abruptly within a matter of days. The pastor of her church visited her in the hospital and prayed over her soul. Karen flew in from D.C. metro to spend one day in the hospital praying and talking to Belinda and offering support to the family.

Within days, she was gone—from a flawed childhood to married life, from married with children to divorced, from divorced to single city, from single city to adoption reunion, from adoption reunion to illness, from illness to death, and from death, ascending to Heaven.

Rest in peace, B. D.

Chapter 18

It's the good girls who keep diaries; the bad girls never have the time.
—Tallulah Bankhead

Welcome to the Palladian located in the beautiful, lush, and quaint city of Naperville, Illinois. The Palladian is a privately held investment property owned by Mr. Harry Van Syckle of Fargo, North Dakota. Mr. Van Syckle was the chief financial officer of a mortgage banking entity prior to venturing out on a $75 million multifamily investment opportunity of his own. He earned his Bachelor of Science degree in accounting from Illinois State University and is a member of several local and national apartment associations.

Prior to transitioning from rural upbringings to a big city banker, Harry was victimized, as a child, in an abusive and dysfunctional household. His mother was a homemaker, and his father was a vacuum repair salesman. Harry's father was also an alcoholic and often physically abused Mrs. Van Syckle.

As a child, the fights between Mr. and Mrs. Van Syckle grew more and more frequent, forcing Harry to take sides. He recalled thinking to himself, *If mom would only be a better housekeeper, dad wouldn't be so angry.* Mrs. Van Syckle enjoyed and spent most of her day preserving jams, working in the yard, and crocheting. By the time Harry was a teenager, he grew to hate his father. Often times, Harry would run to his mother's defense when his father would hit her. As Harry became of age and size, his father would then turn his frustrations to Harry. Once, at age fourteen, Harry dialed 911 for help after fighting for some time with his father and seeing his mother helpless and sobbing.

Police officers responded to the domestic violence call and wanted to help Harry, but Mrs. Van Syckle sent the officers away. "It's just a little misunderstanding, officer, between father and son," she would say, concealing the situation. Harry saw no way out of his situation and resented his mother's weakness. He poured himself into his books and accepted a scholarship at the Illinois State University nine months after his mother died of a brain aneurysm. Harry grew very distant from his family, keeping in close contact with only one cousin—Raymond.

Raymond was also a product of his environment. By the time he was nineteen, he had five DUIs in three states: Iowa, Wyoming, and North Dakota. Raymond's last DUI was awarded when he decided to take off on his brother's four wheeler after finishing off a twelve pack. His license was suspended, and he could not get insured with any of the major insurance companies in the Midwest.

During Harry's sophomore year, Raymond petitioned that he would sober up, enroll in college, and he and Harry could become roommates. Harry reveled at the idea of having someone other than strangers to talk to daily about his family life. He thought Raymond would understand better and not pass judgment, seeing that his home life wasn't rosy either. One day, Harry allowed Raymond to drive his vehicle and loaned him the money to have his driving rights reinstated at the DMV.

Raymond waited patiently in the lobby for his number to be called. He paid his reinstatement fees and was advised of the requirements necessary to lift such restrictions, which included not operating a motor vehicle until he successfully completed one hundred community service hours. However, upon entering the parking lot to get back into Harry's vehicle he'd borrowed, Raymond was arrested by a sheriff that observed him making his transaction at the window inside. It probably wasn't a wise idea to drive himself to the DMV on a restricted license.

The Palladian, a high-rise building, was managed by Mrs. Carrie Knox of Austin, Texas. Born of Dutch and African-American ancestors, Carrie graduated magna cum laude from Texas A & M University fifteen years ago and still found the need to brag on her dual Master's Degree in Business Science and Education. She had long hair tightly curled, green eyes, and wore a darker shade of red lipstick to give prominence to her naturally full lips. Married with no children, Carrie was known by her colleagues and subordinates as a narcissistic creature with a God complex. She had the highest staff turnover in the Van Syckle portfolio. She hired only young, single woman without children due to the lack of outside commitments.

Carrie would show up to team meetings and conference calls late. Once, the Palladian was hosting a budget prep meeting in September. Most hosting properties would use petty cash to purchase bagels, coffee, and juice—not Carrie. She hired a caterer to serve fresh omelets, two choices of breakfast meat, freshly squeezed orange juice, gourmet coffee, and an assortment of pastries. She also demanded that caterers served on fine china and real silverware—no plastic or paper.

Carrie's set schedule was 8 a.m. to 5 p.m., Monday through Friday. Most times, she would stroll in from noon to 5 p.m. or 11 a.m. to 4 p.m. On one occasion, she interrupted a conference call concerning a system conversion approximately thirty-five minutes into it. After her assistant, Keisha, covered for her throughout the entire call, Carrie barged in the office, "Please pardon me if you have already covered this, but I have a question about ..." And, of course, the question involved a section that had already been covered.

On Keisha's first day on the job after accepting the position, Carrie told her, "One thing to remember about me—I am right 98 percent of the time. For the remaining 2 percent, you better be prepared to prove me wrong." During the holiday season, Keisha, along with the leasing and maintenance staff members, was invited to Carrie's home in Hyde Park. They were surprised at the humble personality of Carrie's husband of ten years, Kenneth Knox. Kenneth was a famed jazz musician from upper Manhattan, who also came from a wealthy background.

Carrie had a gorgeous home—a $750,000 five-bedroom, four-bath vintage condo in Hyde Park. Her holiday décor was just as elaborate as one could imagine the style resemblance of Oprah Winfrey or Martha Stewart. With her solarium, a Juliette balcony, high-end Sub-Zero appliances, elegant hardwood floors and no children to scuff them up, one could say that Carrie had married into a lovely home!

The entire staff remembered a much gentler, kinder Carrie during the holiday party. Most would agree that it was necessary for one's home personality to differ from that of a business or work personality, but she took the cake. She was very accommodating and domestic that evening. The hired caterers kept all the guests' glasses full and consistently circulated tasty appetizers. The menu contained lobster medallions wrapped in bacon and served with fontina cheese sauce; six-ounce filet mignon with a Cabernet demi-glace served with lyonnaise potatoes; herb-marinated grilled lamb chops served with wild rice, and, for dessert, pecan rum bread pudding served with rum raisin ice cream. "Oh, but on December 26th, she converted back to Carrie, the bitch!" Keisha recalled.

Unlike most multifamily investors, Harry was more of a hands-on investor. He visited the asset quarterly to keep the staff stoked, and he gave out crisp one-hundred dollar bills when he observed someone doing a great job. He rewarded and encouraged hard work and dedication. He wouldn't just meet with the property manager; he would ask the housekeeper or the groundsmen to accompany him on a property tour. "Tell me Virgil, if you had a blank checkbook, what would you spend and change about the property?" was his favorite question to ask. Everyone respected him, because he was genuine and cared. He remembered their children's names, pet's names, and who had kids in college.

During a property tour, Harry and Gordon, the porter, were greeted in the elevator by Taylor Saxon or as she preferred to be called, "Glitter." She was sobbing with mascara running down both cheeks and holding an oversized Coach handbag and a wad of cash. She was also hitting the sides of the elevator while pacing back and forth. "Whoa, what's the matter honey?" Harry asked, while offering his handkerchief.

"I hate this place," she yelled. "The bailiffs are at my door right now ... evicting me ... and I've got all the money right here in my hand," she stuttered.

"Okay. Why don't you calm down, and Gordon and I will help you get to the bottom of your situation?" he asked. Harry continued to charm, while Gordon had his hands covering his face trying not to reveal his laughter. Harry allowed the elevator to stop on its original floor, and then he followed Glitter to the management office on the first floor. Carrie cringed when she spotted Harry escorting a hysterical Glitter in her office. Prior to his arrival, Carrie asked her leasing consultant, Carmen, to escort the bailiffs to apartment number 1313 for the eviction process to be completed.

Carmen was a sultry, leggy, and attractive African-American woman with almond-shaped eyes and full lips that she kept moisturized with MAC cosmetic lip gloss. She was very well endowed, with a small waist and an apple-shaped bottom. Carmen was a very private person and did not form any clicks in the building; however, she was extremely friendly with the men that resided in the building.

While in Carrie's office, Glitter went on and on about how she thought Carmen was setting her up. She described an occurrence during the holiday season in which she claimed Carmen had a ménage a trois with Glitter and her boyfriend after having quite a few drinks at a local bar. Glitter confessed that they met by coincidence in the nearby bar. Carmen came in alone and was spotted in the VIP section being seduced by several men. Supposedly, Carmen was wearing a bright white tank top that illuminated in the bar's neon fluorescent lights and gave her double D breasts just the light they needed. The tank was short and revealed a diamond-studded belly ring. She also wore white horse-riding pants with fire-engine red knee-length leather boots with a four-inch stacked heel and a Santa hat. "Fitting the description of a ho, ho, ho!" said Glitter.

Carmen smoked cigars all night while sitting on laps of different guys in the VIP section. According to Glitter, she didn't discriminate. There were guys that were obvious drug dealers and thugs; private businessmen; ordinary or good-looking men; and confident, heterosexual black men. Glitter and her boyfriend were sitting at the bar ordering shots of 1800 Gold when Carmen observed them. She sent a round of Patron along with a message through one of the barmaids—"Happy Holidays." The barmaid pointed up in Carmen's direction, and the three raised their glasses and said, "Cheers."

Glitter went on to say during those thirty minutes before last call, Carmen came down to join them at the bar. It was a packed house so Ricky, Glitter's boyfriend, rose to offer his seat to Carmen. In his standing position, he probably had a better view of her breasts. The group was buzzed and very flirtatious. The conversation went from holiday shopping to family gatherings to preferred sexual positions. The next thing she knew, Carmen was stroking Glitter's hair, kissing her hand, and complimenting her—all which teased Ricky. He was so turned on by the girls winking and giggling at the rise in his pants.

All three lived in the same apartment building, so they split a taxi after closing and went back to Carmen's loft for more shots of Patron. According to Glitter, Carmen was the aggressor, never allowing their glasses to become empty and constantly tugging at Glitter's pants begging her to take them off. Carmen turned on a provocative CD and begged Glitter to striptease with her for Ricky.

Lap dance after lap dance and drink after drink, one thing led to another, and the night ended with a rolled joint, a western omelet, and mimosas the next morning. The now-sober group swore to keep the event a secret—Carmen being the aggressor on that topic as well. "Guys, I can't afford to lose my job over this. I like you both and think the world of you both, but this can't happen again, nor can it be spoken of again," Carmen pressured.

All was fine, until Glitter learned that Carmen and Ricky had both hooked up behind her back one night when she worked late at her club. "Glitter" was Taylor's stage name—she was an exotic dancer at a gentlemen's lounge near the airport. Glitter and Ricky fought the night of discovery, and neighbors called the cops after the fight spilled into the hallways. Glitter admitted to calling Carmen several times via cell phone and threatening to tell her boss, Carrie, but she never did.

"So let me get this straight, Glitter. You think that your eviction today is due to Carmen's attempt to retaliate against you?" Carrie asked.

"Right," Glitter answered.

"Let me help you out with that. No. Your eviction today is due to the four thousand dollar balance owing on your rental account," she said.

"Okay, fine, but I've got the money right here," Glitter poured the contents of her handbag onto Carrie's desk and attempted to straighten the crumbled bills. It was paper currency that had been God knows where on her body. "This is not necessary. I cannot accept any money from you at this stage, and I suggest you use these bills to get yourself a U-Haul truck to retrieve all of your items on the thoroughfare," Carrie said.

"Screw you!" Glitter yelled, as she stormed out of Carrie's office.

Meanwhile, Harry was impressed by Carrie's demeanor and business savvy decision. "Tell me something, Carrie, would you have accepted the money if I weren't sitting here?" he asked.

"Harry, you have known me for some time now. I am the same bitch regardless—with or without supervision. Strippers, prostitutes, exotic dancers, or whatever they prefer to be called, their income is unwieldy. Had I accepted her cash today, she would be late paying next month's rent. So, to answer your question to a moral certainty, no."

Chapter 19

One way to make sure crime doesn't pay would be to let the government run it. —Ronald Reagan

Harold slowed the wheels to the golf cart to almost a complete stop while carrying his clients from building to building on a leasing tour. They were a successful and wealthy couple from Princeton, New Jersey. It was after he observed six police cruisers and an ambulance in front of building 15 that he heard the frantic cry of Tammy Reynolds of 1501. Tammy moved in several months back with her boyfriend, who preferred to be called Smoke, born Terrance Webb.

Harold actually was the salesperson who sold them the apartment, though Terrance refused to complete an application because of the required criminal and credit background check. Though it was company policy to process applications for all individuals over the age of eighteen, Terrance flipped a one-hundred-dollar casino chip in Harold's hand, and, poof, such policy went out the door.

Terrance bought, sold, and distributed marijuana for a living. This little-known fact may have been unsuspecting to you, with a street name like Smoke, but it was true. In a neighborhood where biracial couples were rarely seen, Tammy and Terrance stuck out like a sore thumb. Both were very flashy in his and hers eight-cylinder automobiles, diamond pendant charms hanging twenty plus inches from his neck, and oversized Juicy Couture purses slung across her shoulder.

They entertained often. While driving through the community, their guests chose to share their bass-filled music with the entire apartment complex. Terrance and Tammy were a young couple in their early to mid twenties. Everyone partied when they were in their twenties. But these two also fought a lot, which is what Harold was thinking happened here. Terrance hung his head low and tried to shield his face from the media reporters that had shown up. Tammy was screaming bloody murder as she was being transported on a stretcher by EMTs.

Later, it was learned that she was brutally beaten, sodomized with a nine-millimeter gun, and subject to over thirty cigarette burns on her buttocks. Apparently, Terrance had entrusted her with a duffel bag containing $40,000 in cash. Instead of going straight home as she had done so well in the past, she decided to stop by one of her brother's home and was allegedly robbed by two of his friends while showing off the bag full of money in the trunk.

Neighbors claimed they heard Tammy sobbing uncontrollably for more than three days, but they assumed the young couple would cool down in a day or so—as they had done so many times in the past. It was reported that Terrance yelled constantly, "You gave my fucking money to your brother and his friends … didn't you? Are you sleeping with one of his friends … is that it? I want my money …" He pounded against the adjoining walls. It was concluded that Tammy's caterwauling was the reflex result of the multiple cigarette burns to her buttocks.

Terrance's family members described him as a much more collected guy in the courtroom. Some say he just snapped. Want to hear something interesting? That couple from New Jersey rented the apartment Harold showed them on that same afternoon. It was a hard sell, but they simple asked Harold for a summary of different unusual or criminal events that had taken place in the past year or so. "It says on the back of the application that residents can request to review criminal activity and/or unusual events that have taken place in the community for the past twenty-four months. Is that true?" the gentleman asked.

"That is absolutely true," Harold reassured them, which gave the woman more optimism in his sales ability and community knowledge.

"If it's okay with you, when we pull back up in front of the clubhouse, we can all sit down in the conference room with a freshly baked cookie and cup of gourmet coffee. That way, you can take your time reading, and we won't be in the way of other future clients or residents stopping in with rent checks," he said. Harold was a seasoned leasing agent and carried himself with so much confidence that people trusted him and felt very comfortable in his care.

The couple fired away questions at Harold immediately after opening the binder, "Look, I'm not going to read these reports word for word. Do you know what each incident is about?" Mr. VanBuren asked.

"Sure. Let's see; that one happened when one of our contracted painters stole a random check out of a tenant's checkbook and cashed the $450 check," Harold explained. The couple's eyebrows rose. "It was an isolated incident, and he paid the money back the very next week. Though it was hardly acceptable, the painter did pay back the money, which was the only way the tenant new that her checks had been stolen. He was contracted to complete some drywall repairs in her kitchen and obviously wandered through her apartment into the master bedroom and took a check from the middle of her checkbook. She spoke to my property manager and showed her a copy of the thank you card and note inside that read, 'I need $450 for my sister in El Salvador to have surgery—I very sorry.' The note was signed, Mr. Latino."

"What about this one?" Mr. VanBuren's obviously younger woman asked.

"This occurred in March. One of our residents, a school teacher, assaulted her student's parent and turned herself in to one of two courtesy officers living on-site. The educator is a fifteen-year veteran school teacher for Allegheny County Schools—kindergarten level. From my understanding, it was nap time when the teacher had to counsel a whiny student the day before. This little boy sulked uncharacteristically and crawled up in the teacher's lap. Naturally, she asked what was wrong with him and why the tears. He cried explaining that his mother didn't love him anymore. The teacher basically asked what had brought him to that conclusion. The toddler sobbed saying that his mother usually allowed him to sleep with her in her bed, but since she had a new boyfriend, she was making her son grow accustomed to sleeping in his own bed. The teacher counseled the boy advising that his mother obviously loved him very much, and she just wanted him to grow up to be big and strong. Shortly thereafter, the boy cried and rocked himself to sleep in the arms of his teacher. Ms. Griffin felt that she was not getting through to the lad so she sent a note home to his mother. The next day after their parent-teacher conference, the mother was very gracious, compassionate, and thankful to Ms. Griffin for her comforting words. The next morning, the little boy showed up at school with what looked to be his mother's handprint across his cheek. The print hurt to the touch, and he was obviously sworn to secrecy, because he would not elaborate on what happened to his face. That same afternoon when his mother arrived to pick him up, Ms. Griffin, the teacher, slapped stars into the mother's eyes," he explained.

"Wow, how do you keep up with this stuff?" the blonde bombshell asked.

"What I am not involved with first hand, I read thoroughly from this binder. I like to be informed, especially to offer an intelligent summary for clients such as yourselves who for great reason are concerned with the type of people that live around you," he said.

"I hope we aren't taking too much of your time; it's just that with me being a pilot, I am away from home a lot. I want to make sure that my future wife is safe and secure at night, because all she does is shop during the day," Mr. VanBuren said, trying to lighten the mood.

"I totally understand; say no more. Do you have questions about any others?" Harold took back control of the conversation.

"Yes, this report looks a little thick, what happened here?" the pilot inquired.

"Ahhhh … the nursing home incident," Harold started. "That was actually pretty sad." He went on to explain how the former management regime had signed a five-year lease on a three-bedroom unit for a franchised nursing facility to house six elderly patients. The apartment had been modified to accommodate the six elderly patients and even offered an office area for non-network doctors to write prescriptions, exams, and so forth. A licensed geriatric nurse, Vicki, was in charge of overseeing the daily care and needs of Ms. Gruich a ninety-three-year-old woman with dementia. Ms. Gruich was widowed and was preceded in death by all but one of her children—her youngest son, Ryan.

It was the policy of the nursing home that family members could take the patients out for the day; however, all must be returned by 9 p.m. daily. Ryan, fifty-one and single, was very attentive to his mother and was on-site six days per week to take her out to local parks to feed the ducks, out to dinner at different restaurants, and to visit friends of the family. It was observed by Nurse Vicki that each time Ms. Gruich would return from her visits with her son, she had a body odor that resembled the smell of sex. After squinting and making such claim during an undercover visit from a state health inspector, Vicki was interrogated and asked to assist licensed inspectors and doctors in a rape-kit examination of Ms. Gruich.

After taking Vicki's statement, police had visited the home of Ryan Gruich to arrest him. He pleaded innocent during the entire ordeal and was later exonerated when the ordered rape-kit proved that Ms. Gruich was not being sexually assaulted and was simply a victim of old age and unpleasant body odors. These odors were attributed to hasty sponge baths that did not include the cleaning of crevices in sagging skin.

Harold went on to explain how every person familiar with the sexual assault claim against Ryan surrounding his mother was relieved to learn the truth and outcome of the situation. Ms. Gruich died shortly after the conclusion of the crucible. Ryan eventually sued the nursing home, which settled out of court for several million dollars causing the business to eventually fold.

"Okay, last question, and you don't have to go into as much detail as you have been, but what is this a photograph of ... it's hard to make out," Blondie asked while turning the pages upside down to view.

"It's funny how everyone has the same reaction to this photo—by turning the book around as if looking at the picture right side up would make more sense," Harold confessed. "This is an occupied apartment home that we stumbled upon. Apparently, the apartment was rented by the girlfriends of two notorious gang members who were contracted to clean the office buildings off of I-80. The girls were obviously bringing home shredded documents from the office buildings and trying to piece credit card statements and other financial documents together for their own personal gain. By the time our maintenance crew had discovered the scam, the girls had covered a half of dozen walls in the unit with shredded pieces of their puzzle. It was the most bizarre thing. So as you can see, there is no apartment community more exciting than this one. Should I write you a receipt for your deposit and first month's rent?" he asked.

Chapter 20

(In First Person)

If you find it in your heart to care for somebody else, you will have succeeded. —Dr. Maya Angelou

I can be pretty mean at times. I am a big enough person to admit it. As a child, I was very timid, very shy, soft spoken even. But, as I came of age and began going through the trials and tribulations of dating and building a life with my husband, he sparked the fire in my attitude. That spark ignited the inner bitch in me. Something about dating a city boy will take your tenderness away—take away your quietness. I am convinced he is to blame for my no-nonsense behavior. Tupac said he got his game from a woman. I guess I got mine from a man.

I had just started a new position, but, by the end of the week, it felt as if I had been in that role my whole life. One Sunday afternoon, I stopped by my new office with my grandmother after church service. I was excited about my new downtown office overlooking the city skyline and wanted my grandmother to see my new location prior to my start date. While she admired the view, I had planned on drafting my "to do list" for the next day.

Upon entering my office, I heard voices and cheering from a television. It sounded as if someone was watching a basketball game in *my* office. Sure enough, there he was: tall, dark, and handsome—my new assistant, Christopher Morton. There were sports memorabilia on the walls, a desktop stereo system playing gospel music, family pictures, and a shiny new name plate that read: 'Mr. Christopher Morton.' I thought to myself, *Did I get off on the wrong floor?*

"Hi, Chris? We met a few months back at the company's holiday party. I'm Kia and this is my grandmother, Mrs. Velma Frier." My grandmother and I shook his hand simultaneously as I asked what he was doing in my office. The look on his face said a thousand words, when in actuality he only said two, "Your office?"

"Yes, I'm starting tomorrow morning at this location due to the sale of the Farmington Hills location. Didn't Jake tell you?" I questioned though I already knew the answer. I've been told I have this discerning instinct when it comes to judging a person's character.

Jake was our spineless regional director. He advised me that he had interviewed Christopher for the management position; however, he felt Christopher was a little too green for the position. Thus, he suggested that he work under the wing of a seasoned property manager (me) for six months to a year to improve his marketability. "I would appreciate it very much if you moved your personal items into the smaller office outside while I make some notes for tomorrow's meeting," I said politely but stern. Christopher inquired about tomorrow's meeting agenda as he began clearing all his masculine things. I don't think he was interested in the meeting's agenda; more or less, he was making small talk to mask his embarrassment.

I took out my Blackberry and began e-mailing Jake to ask why he hadn't made the announcement to the existing staff of my arrival. I explained to Christopher that the meeting was an opportunity for me to meet the staff of twenty and communicate my expectations of each one. "The strength in our human capital should work to our advantage in making Chesapeake Towers number one in our company's portfolio," I wanted to express a clear message to Christopher that I am not here to paint my nails or twirl my hair.

I remembered when Jake hired Christopher seven months ago. Christopher had been a tenant of the building with his mother, Evangelist Stephanie Morton. Mrs. Morton was a divorcee who had managed to put Christopher through college while holding down two jobs to maintain a downtown penthouse-style apartment, car payments, and so forth. Christopher was a football All-American at U

146

of D and was also known to come home for mom's cooking and to have his dirty clothes laundered by guess who—his mother. Yes, he was a mamma's boy, and it was even rumored that his mother scheduled and was present during the interview process. Get off the tit already!

Just then, the Mary J. Blige ring tone sounded on my Blackberry indicating Jake's timely response. Jake's e-mail basically said he was planning an introductory celebration in the morning. He ended his lengthy e-mail asking if he could bring me a frappuccino or Earl Grey tea in the morning. *Don't try to butter me up now, you snake*, was the thought in my head. Nevertheless, I chose to respond with a simple: "Neither. Thanks though."

I assume he was referring to me as the seasoned manager with the wing to coddle Christopher with. This was the second "project" Jake had given me. The first was a young Caucasian girl by the name of Margaret from Indianapolis, Indiana. Similar scenario, the property had sold to a local developer who was going to tear it down to build a new cooperative asset as part of a state-funded program. Jake called me thirty minutes earlier to tell me that he had set up an interview for me to meet Margaret Vancourt who had drove in the snow from Indiana to Michigan just to meet me. "She's a little rough around the edges, but I have seen you mold superstars out of lumps of clay," he said. "Just think of the positive influence you can bring to this young girl's career," Jake continued, as he sensed my irritation. He went on to describe a trashy Jerry Springer scene for me to envision Margaret's background. The moment I visualized the trailer park setting, he warned me that would be the same visual I would have upon laying eyes on Margaret.

Moments later, a monstrosity of a vehicle—a 1988 Ford Tempo with the bumper, muffler, and fender hanging—drove up to my luxury apartment community with a bit of smoke under the hood. I could hear it loud and clear while sitting at my desk as if I was sitting in the parking lot. I politely met her at the door and asked her to move her vehicle around back where the maintenance tool shed was housed. For however many minutes she could sustain my interview questions, I didn't want to run the risk of losing a qualified client who might be turned off by the stereotype of people that lived here based on Margaret's parked car.

I held the door open as a 5'4" frame walked through with stringy, greasy hair flowing from an off-white skull cap. *Rough around the edge, my ass, where did Jake get this ghetto white girl from?* I say off-white in hopes that it was a color issue and not a cleanliness issue. I extended my hand while making a mental note to douse them in hand sanitizer, "You must be Margaret ... I'm Kia," I said. I had hoped she couldn't sense my trepidation.

One of my sales agents offered Margaret a warm cup of coffee from the Starbuck's coffee station in the clubroom kitchen. I asked her a series of interview questions and observed her hands as she cupped the coffee mug. To have such a small frame, her hands were those of an adult male employed in a steel mill. She did not impress upon me at all. Just as I offered to walk her back to the door and promise to call her after interviewing other candidates for the assistant's position, she stopped me in my tracks and said, "Jake also told me you would help me pick out an available one-bedroom apartment. Should we do that now? I have some stuff in my car that I would like to put in a closet." I was stunned. I radioed maintenance personnel to escort her to two available apartments while I called Jake out of his meeting.

"You must be kidding, right? Am I being punk'd?" I asked. Jake was extremely apologetic; he tried to spin it by saying I would save more money in the payroll category by hiring an inexperienced assistant manager, because I could start her at a $30,000 salary versus the industry standard of $45,000.

"Jake, she is a housekeeper/porter—going from scrubbing toilets to managing them. I don't get it. Does she have something on you? Are you screwing her or what?" I asked. Jake knew that I shot from the hip, said the first things that came to mind, and reflected afterwards.

"I just see ... I see potential in her that only you can bring out, Kia. Just do this ... for me," he begged.

Meanwhile, I was finalizing plans for the second annual holiday party for the tenants, and I had a meeting scheduled with caterers in under twenty minutes. I called Irving on his Nextel and asked to speak to Margaret to welcome her to the team and inform her of tomorrow's festivities. She replied that she didn't have any formal clothes and had planned to drive back to Indianapolis the next day to bring the last of her "stuff" in her car. I first tried to picture how it was possible for an adult to move all of their prized possessions in two carloads from out of state. Then, I considered the source and advised that she get a hot bath and a good night's sleep tonight, because all tenant parties have a mandatory attendance by employees, and, since she was now on my payroll, she was required to attend.

I had invited family members and friends to serve as fillers in the clubroom and to enjoy free food and spirits. Caterers served whiting, roast beef, and baked chicken with red potatoes, mashed potatoes, green beans, corn, garden salad, and a host of desserts. There was an eight-foot Christmas tree near the fireplace with scratch-off lottery tickets valued at a dollar each clipped in between the Martha Stewart holiday décor. Beautifully decorated gift bags lined the opposite side of the fireplace where gift cards in ascending denominations were housed to serve as raffle gifts. The grand prize was a mall gift certificate for $250. In another corner of the clubroom, a uniformed bartender served cocktails and beers to ticket holders. In the next room a fortune teller read palms for tips.

Margaret's awkwardness was highly evident, and she stuck out like a sore thumb. I put on my best hostess hat and attempted to introduce her to all the partygoers. My sister pulled me to the side and said, "She must be the swan you were telling me about. Girrrrl, you've got your hands full!" It took everything in me to hold back a thunderous laugh, while "Silent Night" played in the background. Margaret's holiday attire included some black slacks that looked as though she removed them from her front pocket and put them on. She wore a pair of red, Dorothy-in-Kansas patent leather shoes that were a little run over and another off-white sweater. Her greasy hair was twisted in a bun, which actually made you notice her eyes—a bright sea blue.

The next morning, Jake sent his regrets via e-mail for missing my Christmas party. He also asked how Margaret was meshing with the team and tenants. I responded with a simple, "She is somewhat of a people person ... we're taking off a couple of hours today. I need to take her shopping."

"Good. Just expense it. Thanks for keeping an open mind; have a great time," he said.

I drove Margaret to Sears in the Seven Mile Crossing Shopping Center. She thanked me during the drive to the store, and we hadn't shopped for anything yet. "Thank you for taking me under your wing,

I know this must be hard for you. You have so many other important things you could be doing," she humbly expressed.

"More important? What could be more important than my new assistant?" I forced myself to say, as she lit up like the Christmas tree from the clubroom.

I walked the aisles in the misses department, coaching her on the importance of basic colors to build a wardrobe—buying one pair of quality slacks, a skirt, two blazers, and a variety of tops and blouses to mix and match. I selected a basic black pump and asked her to try it on. She stumbled and staggered in half inch heels as I verbally guided her down the aisle finally walking a straight line. "Can I see this in a nine?" a customer asked.

"I'm sorry. I don't work here," I answered.

"Oh, I just assumed …" the woman said, as she pointed to Margaret stumbling down the aisle ways. I laughed and assured the woman that it was a long story.

After watching *pretty woman* try on several varieties of clothes in the dressing room, I paid for her items, and we headed over to a fast-food restaurant. Sitting across from her at a small table, I couldn't help notice her hands as she devoured the bacon burger she was eating. Her hands were monstrous, damn near manly. "So where do you see yourself in five years? I mean, what are your long-term plans?" I couldn't help but ask.

"Well," she started. "My ultimate goal is to become a truck driver …" A small amount of lettuce spilled out of my mouth as I was caught off guard. "Are you okay?" she asked with concern. *You're asking me?* I thought to myself.

"Go on. Pardon me, go on," I said. And on she went explaining to me how her mother was a local artist in a small town near Indianapolis, and her father managed an insurance agency also in Indiana. Margaret described how her mother had taught her to draw, sketch, and paint and that she was pretty good at it, but her real passion was to be on the road, driving cross-country in an eighteen-wheeler truck. I guess property management in a multifamily residential industry would be a stepping stone into truck driving … right?

As time went on, I began feeling as though Margaret just wasn't getting it. I even sent her to a company-sponsored training seminar for four days thinking that maybe I was biased, and my opinion of her was getting in the way of my teaching and coaching. On the second day, I got a call from the trainer, Michelle Canton. "Okay, this girl is as dumb as the sidewalk. Where did she come from?" were her exact words to me. She described how Margaret continuously stared at her with wooden eyes and how Margaret had broken down crying during the lunch break saying that she "couldn't do this, it was too hard."

Michelle had a great deal of influence with our senior vice president, and, after listening to me vent for forty-five minutes over how Margaret was pawned on me as a "project" and her lacking interview and professional skills, another decision was made to transfer her from our posh Farmington Hills location to Dearborn. I felt bad and relieved at the same time. I wished I was a fly on the wall to observe the conversation between the senior vice president and Jake. It was only a matter of days when Jake invited me out to lunch to apologize for promising Margaret the position prior to consulting with me. He was very humble and apologetic; it was scary. That night, I called my mentor to tell her about my lunch date with Jake. Her thoughts were that the senior vice president and other upper management personnel showed a valued opinion of me and my work and didn't think my aggravation with Margaret was worth the risk of me leaving the company. Thus, they removed the road block.

I remember following up with Jake shortly after Margaret's removal, and he raved at how well she was performing and grasping at the Dearborn location and the value she brought to the team there. Surprisingly, I was happy for her and felt that I gave up on her too fast. I felt guilty and much like a failure. "Good for her," I remember saying. I couldn't help but recall one particular sales call she had taken where the woman was looking for a one-bedroom apartment with a fireplace and a den for a home-based office. Margaret stumbled and stuttered throughout the conversation. She showed no signs of confidence in the product she was selling, nor herself. She constantly put the woman on hold while she ran to ask the other leasing consultants questions about the list of apartments she had in front of her. Good for her.

Several months had gone by, and our region's quarterly performance meeting was approaching. None of the properties had budgeted for hosting such meeting, and most were performing poorly due to the devastating affects of 9/11 so we had a tight budget to work with. Instead of purchasing food or veggie trays, I decided to design and build the trays by hand. I bought deli meats, exotic cheeses, and breads from Costco and sprang for desserts and cases of pop and bottled water at the warehouse too. I was looking forward to seeing Margaret. How she would walk in the auditorium in her two-inch stacked heels with her head held high. Maybe she would win an award for top sales of the quarter or most improved rookie.

All employees began to fill the room. Most people were hugging or slapping five—excited about seeing each other since the company's holiday party mid December last year. I scanned the room several times over, but I did not see Margaret. Jake was running late as usual, so I delegated the filling of solo cups with punch and moved to set up the power point projector for the presentation. I noticed Karen, the property manager in Dearborn, so I motioned for her to come up to the front of the room. Her cell phone was glued to her ear as usual. I giggled as I pictured something that Jake had told me six months prior about Karen. He said she was so obsessed with that phone that once he was reprimanding her about making so many personal phone calls at work, and, while he was writing her up, she had both arms extended below her knees while sitting in a chair, text messaging.

"Karen, where's Margaret?" I whispered while she continued to talk on the phone. "Let me call you back," she ended her call and had a look on her face that was worth just as much as a picture—a thousand words.

"You haven't heard about Margaret? That cunt screwed me and Jake over," she said. Her words were harsh and piercing, and I was hanging on each one of them with my eyes wide shut.

Because Margaret could not afford the high rents in Dearborn, Jake authorized her to live in one of the one-bedroom model homes for six months rent free until she saved up enough money to pay rent. That was the first mistake. The owners had just spent $100,000 upgrading all of the model homes to improve the quality of traffic coming through the doors. According to Karen, the asset manager was flying in for the International Auto Show at Cobo Hall and wanted to tour all one-bedroom-style vacant and model floor plans. The property had sold out of two–bedroom homes, but continued to have a stock of one-bedroom homes. We all know how loss of revenue due to vacancy affects the bottom line—net operating income.

Chad, the asset manager, was flying in one Thursday, renting a car at the airport, walking apartments upon arriving at the site, and meeting with Karen and Jake to discuss a plan of attack during a lunch meeting. Upon entering the one-bedroom model floor plan, there were beer bottles all over the apartment, stains on the carpet, and the $500 bed linen looked as if wolves had been raised on it. There were pubic hairs throughout the bathtub and hair extensions and wigs all over the bathroom sink and toilet cover. The refrigerator was dirty, and the stove top and countertops looked as though no one lived there for years. There were gnats swarming around a pot of food on the stove, and the garbage aroma filled the kitchen and hallway. Seemingly, Margaret had requested a ten-day vacation saying that she was planning a drive home to Indiana for a spell.

The maintenance supervisor swore he saw her picking up prostitutes on Michigan Avenue. My mouth was wide open from the shock, but I finally had to laugh when Karen described how the asset manager tripped over a two-and-a-half-foot, two-way dildo in the middle of the living room, picked it up with his bare hands, and asked, "What on God's green earth is this?"

I hated to find such pleasure in Karen's sorrowful situation, but, I told ya so!

Chapter 21

It's always helpful to learn from your mistakes because then your mistakes seem worthwhile. —Franklin P. Jones

By the end of the third quarter, most of the apartment communities in the company's portfolio were performing at their peak—raising rents, experiencing high occupancy, and collecting 95 percent or better monthly revenue—life was great. The owners of the different acquisitions agreed to treat the employees and their family members on an all-expense-paid day at the park. Being centrally located in the Midwest, all employees decided on Cedar Pointe in Sandusky, Ohio. The regional managers decided that renting a couple of charter buses would be a little pricier, but, compared to DUI fines, the extra three grand appeared well worth it.

All residents were notified a week in advance of the office closings, and three maintenance men volunteered to stay behind, on call in case an emergency occurred on any of the sites. Thursday prior to the off-site excursion, the annual awards ceremony was held at the Ritz Carlton. It was a semiformal gala that property management industry vendors sponsored in an attempt to network with different management companies and drum up more business for themselves.

One of the largest apartment advertising magazines sprang for the open bar tab. There were the usual house liquors with the unexotic alcohol, but there was plenty of beer and wine. A landscape company paid the food bill, and a maintenance supply company paid for the ballroom reservation. A law firm that specialized in landlord–tenant litigation paid for the trophies and awards. The management company paid to have a Casino Night vendor come in. After dinner was served, all of the tables with white linen cloths were broken down and stacked in a room. Out came the poker tables, blackjack, three-card Monte, craps, and good ole Texas Hold 'em. Employees were playing with real poker chips, but, instead of money, total winnings qualified for a number of raffle tickets and prizes.

Aaron Jr. was awarded the 100 Grand Award for achieving over one hundred leases in twelve months; he had leased 156 apartments. Aaron, at age twenty-two, was the Midwest's superstar; being promoted from security guard to file clerk to leasing agent, he was a proven performer and had a promising future. Raquel won Rookie of the Year for her solid performance as a newcomer to the industry. Orlando won Trainer of the Year for the diligence he showed traveling across the country training new employees, sometimes at a moment's notice. Caroline was awarded the Attitude to Have Award, and Remy won Maintenance Person of the Year for the exterior painting and brick repairs he performed on his property—on his own time and without charging overtime. Not to mention he saved the property almost a quarter of a million dollars in doing so.

Aaron was cornered by a vice president, asking if he was satisfied with his current position and hinted that a management position was coming available in Atlanta. Aaron was a shoe-in for as long as he was willing to relocate. Aaron was very moved and honored that he was approached and considered, but declined the offer, because his girlfriend was expecting a child in a couple of months.

There was a thirty-minute intermission between the distributions of the awards. All employees were encouraged to refresh the alcohol in their glasses, use the facilities, and return to their chairs to enjoy dessert and a brief overview of the company's performance along with words of wisdom by Rick Stansbury.

Rick was an eloquent speaker. He told a story of his mother who grew up on the third floor of a dilapidated building and attended public school in New York. Rick's mother was a renowned balletoriographer. She studied classical ballet in Switzerland under a masterful professional ballet dancer, Rocco De Argento, who was also known for backpacking and smuggling Bibles into neighboring countries. As an adolescent, she wrote with her left hand and was often teased by other children.

"My mother told this story often about being a lefty in Ms. Hollingsworth class," he started. While taking great notes and writing with her left hand, Rick's mother would get whacked across her knuckles by the likes of Ms. Hollingsworth's yardstick. A young Stansbury would attempt to switch hands as the social studies teacher walked rows in the classroom with the yardstick held behind her back. However, she struggled with completing her work and for the best grades when she would attempt to use her right hand.

Mrs. Elaine Stansbury was extremely conscious about her grades and suffered a great deal of anxiety over the consistent D's she scored in Ms. Hollingsworth's class. Otherwise a straight A student, Mrs. Stansbury's mother insisted that she attend after-school studies to improve her grade. When the extra effort proved to fail, her parents insisted that she see a psychologist over the anxiety of the one subject. The psychologist prescribed gum to the young Stansbury to aide in what he suspected was a nervous condition. The doctor believed that chewing gum kept the brain stimulated and offered a better focus on any task at hand.

One night at the dinner table, Rick's grandfather asked Elaine to explain her consistent failing of the social studies subject. She finally confessed that she understood the subject perfectly and was able to accurately recite important historical facts. She went on to also describe why she wasn't able to get her work completed in a timely manner. Elaine enacted how her teacher would whack her knuckles each time she was caught with the pencil in her left hand.

Her father, a man of few words said nothing, yet he chose to appear in class the following day with his arms folded standing in his 6'3" stature. Elaine's father followed behind the school's principal as he apologized to the students for interrupting the classroom.

With a thick mustache and frowned eyebrows, the principal asked the teacher, Ms. Hollingsworth, which hand she wrote with. Naturally, she advised and raised her manicured right hand. Just then, the principal forced her to the blackboard with chalk in her left hand, instructing her to inscribe her full name for the class. It was an obviously impossible task. Regardless of how hard Ms. Hollingsworth tried, she could not legibly write out her full name. Rick's mother felt sorry for her teacher and began to sink down in her chair during the charades at the chalkboard. Though she sympathized, she also realized that she had felt her last yardstick—at least in Ms. Hollingsworth's class.

"Can't do it, can you?" the principal reprimanded. "As long as you work for Park Hill School District, you will never scold a child for the hand in which they write." The principal's exit was just as dramatic as his entrance, with Elaine's father following closely behind.

"In other words folks, no one can force your hand at doing what you do on an everyday basis. Selling, repairing, building, managing … it's all gotta come from within. And, by the judge of the faces in this room today and the remaining awards to be handed out, you all are doing a remarkable job at playing the hand you were dealt—thank you, and keep up the great work," he said. At that moment, Rick lifted his glass as to say cheers, and a thunderous applause filled the room. "Speaking of playing the hand you were dealt, let's get back to these awards so that I can win some money on that Texas Hold 'em table." The cheers and applause continued.

In total, there were fifty-five award recipients. They were all phenomenal individuals and very deserving of their recognition. Along with a beautiful statue to display in their work space or at home, each winner received a crisp one-hundred-dollar bill and a gift certificate to an airline for a free roundtrip anywhere that the airline traveled in the United States.

After a night of drinking, dancing and crapping out, everyone made it back to their homes for a good night's sleep in anticipation of Friday's day at the park. It was great to see individuals engaged with their families at the theme park. It seemed many had a better understanding of their peers once they were observed with their children and/or significant others. Everyone loaded the buses and headed for Ohio. Parents brought along all kinds of board games and coloring books to keep the children occupied on the road trip. Most were cracking jokes and making fun—hardly watching the DVD movie that was playing at the time.

Janet's cell phone rang. It was Max, the maintenance supervisor, calling to report that the DEA was on-site and just raided a town house. Apparently, a CI living in building four had been working with the DEA to bring down a crystal meth manufacturer in apartment 603. The apartment was a three-bedroom with two-and-a-half baths and a two-car attached garage. Drug enforcement agents took a ram to the front entry door; however, the drug pushers had bolted steel rods in the foyer area, blocking the front entrance for this type of entry. A road block like this offered the drug sellers extra time to react and possibly flush drugs down the toilet.

Janet, the property manager, covered one ear with her index finger while she pressed her Motorola phone onto her opposite ear, struggling to hear the details from Max. He went on to describe how drug agents recovered drug paraphernalia including a respirator mask, a 5,000–millileter round bottom boiling flask, thermometer holders, Erlenmeyer flasks, and retort and recovery flasks. There was over seventy-five pounds of marijuana in storage totes in the garage. Agents also recovered $400,000 in cash in the trunk of a Mercedes Benz E-class vehicle.

It seemed as if agents were waiting around for the Child Protective Unit to show up to take a three-year-old boy into custody. The toddler was sleeping in the third bedroom of the home, which was customized as a playroom for the son of the head chemist and his girlfriend, who were both arrested along with three other drug dealers. A wire tap proved that the dealers were on their way out of town to make a drop. The confidential informant relayed information surrounding a white Cadillac Escalade that was suspected of having packs of money inside the rubber tires and leather seats. The Escalade was driven by one of the drug operation henchmen, who was a major suspect in the bust.

Janet so wanted to stop the bus and head back to her property, but, in essence, there was nothing she could do to be of any assistance aside from completing an incident report and forwarding it to the corporate office. Janet walked slowly to the back of the bus while balancing her extended arms with the bumps in the road to transmit the information to a district manager. Aaron overheard the conversation and suddenly became very private when talking on his cell phone that rang several times thereafter.

Janet attempted to put it out of her mind, as instructed. There was simply nothing she could do even if she was not on the bus.

After closing down the theme park, the employees and family

members boarded the charter buses and headed back to their respective vehicles and drove home. On Monday morning, Janet dialed the detective's number from the business card left behind after the drug bust. He was very adamant about not speaking to her while she was in her office and instructed her to meet him outside the clubhouse, and they could speak inside his vehicle. The detective was on-site in minutes and looked very frustrated as Janet approached the vehicle.

"You tell that fucking Aaron I ought to arrest his ass and bring him up on charges for obstruction of justice!" he yelled and rubbed his head in disgust.

"What does Aaron have to do with this?" Janet asked, throwing her hands up in desperation.

"We have him on wire tap calling Mad Dogg to warn him about the bust on unit 603. My agents were this close to finally closing in on Mad Dogg, aka Devin Grady. That little asshole has compromised this entire investigation and his freedom. When you see him, tell him I'm looking for him," he said.

Janet exited the vehicle and called Max on the two-way radio. "Could you go to Aaron's apartment and tell him I need to meet with him—now?" She kept a cool demeanor as to not alarm Max, which, in turn, would alarm Aaron.

Janet sent a simple message via Blackberry to her immediate supervisor, Tony. "Our golden boy is tarnished—call me." In that instant, Janet recalled a resident sitting poolside a couple of months back, telling her that "Aaron was 'not all that,' and he should be watched more closely."

When Janet questioned Aaron about it, he had a quick response, "She is just jealous, because she heard that my girlfriend was pregnant, and she and I were fooling around." Aaron went on to say that he had met the resident at a strip club near the airport where she danced. He had no idea that she was a resident until one day he saw her lying topless in a chaise lounge by the pool.

Janet fought with the idea of calling this young lady, fearing that she might get an exaggerated truth because of her possible bitterness. She sat at her desk with her office door shut and called anyway. What Janet discovered from the phone call was beyond anything she could ever imagine. As the tone rang on the other end of the receiver, Janet wondered to herself, *What is the real story with this bright, promising, and twenty-two-year-young man? Does he have a secret? How or does this drug bust have anything to do with his sudden flashiness—treating staff members to lunch everyday—wearing $400 pairs of slacks—improved grooming practices? Had he fooled …?"*

A voice answered on the other end. "Uh … hello. Yes, may I speak with Mya George?" Janet snapped out of her trance.

Janet reminded Mya about their poolside conversation months back and asked if she could elaborate on what she was trying to accomplish by warning her. Mya went on to explain how she had met Aaron at a club. She was very forthright with her profession and made absolutely no apologies for it. Mya advised that she referred a couple of clients, not friends, to the apartment community—mainly to receive the $500 referral bonus offered.

"I'll do almost anything to make money," she admitted. Mya claimed that one of her clients thanked her for "the hookup" and said he rented an apartment from Aaron. By "hookup," Mya assumed her client was referring to the one-month-free rent incentive going on at the time. However, he was actually referring to the fact that Aaron had sold him keys to a vacant apartment for $2,000 so that he could grow marijuana and put up one of his "baby's mammas."

"Look around you, Janet. Haven't you noticed a drastic change in your clientele? When I first moved here two years ago, I was the second person to occupy my unit, and there was barely a tan face in the crowd at the pool. I didn't mind it, but then I started hearing that the management here was racist and were denying all the black applicants that would apply. So I started referring everyone I knew—at school, because I am studying to be a nurse at the community college; at work; and at church. I have received $1,500 in referral bonuses so far and had hoped that my referrals were making the difference, but you and I both know three new people moving into this complex does not account for the pool crowd resembling the likes of the Cabrini-Green projects."

Her words were piercing. Janet could not help but think that she was partially to blame for Aaron's actions. She would have to do some quick thinking and fast. The next morning, Janet turned in her two-week resignation, advising that she simply needed to take some time off work and reevaluate her personal life. It came as a total shock to everyone. The senior vice president, Rick Stansbury, called her personally to see if there was any way he could change her mind, but there was not. He assured her that her position would be available and waiting for her if she had changed her mind. He said the property ran so well that it didn't need a full-time manager.

"With Max heading your maintenance department over there and Aaron leading the sales team, I think I will just ask Tony to work out of that office in duo positions—regional manager and property manager. Janet, you take the time off you need, and give me a call when you are ready for your seat back," he said. She thanked Rick for his offer.

At the time, Tony worked out of his home and had mixed feelings about being back on-site. Tony had been with the company eight years and had worked his way up the ladder from a lifeguard to a regional manager. He was a part-time life guard for a third-party contract company and studied information systems technology at Penn State. After graduation, he received the first job he applied for with the management company in their IT department. After three years in IT, he decided that he wanted to groom into a managerial role so, he accepted a pay cut and an assistant manager's position on a property in Naperville. From there, he was awarded his own site, and he had been a property manager for two years and then finally a regional manager. Tony was very laid back, shutting down the offices early during major sporting events and even showing up on-site to take the staff drinking during lunch hours.

After about one week, Janet couldn't stand to look at Aaron, and he was none the wiser. She called in sick and used up her week's vacation during her notice period.

Tony quickly got adapted to the property. He ordered a Sub-Zero freezer for the maintenance shop to house his cold beers. He threw a cookout the eve of his first day and invited the staff to his and his fiancée's home in Park Heights. The staff at Hines Town Center now consisted of six males and one girl, so Tony tried to be as sensitive to her needs as possible. His fiancé made margaritas with cute umbrellas for the two of them to drink, while the guys shoved down beers and shots of Yager.

Back at the office, Tony no longer found it necessary to wear suits; he would show up in jeans and tennis shoes. He'd have a case of beer under his desk, having to garnish his mouth with peppermints if an irate resident demanded to see a manager. In the meantime, he and Aaron were like bosom buddies, inseparable.

When holiday season approached, Aaron's girlfriend was close to delivering the baby. He and Tony would leave the office at noon, claiming to have to shop for baby's clothes and accessories. Aaron and girlfriend had a coed baby shower, and Tony offered to host it at his home and even purchased large gifts: a bassinet and crib combo set, the mattress and a designer car seat. Their relationship was totally inappropriate and had drawn a wedge through the on-site staff.

One day, Max was asked to help out at a downtown property that was undergoing major renovations. He jumped at the opportunity. While there, Max shared several stories involving Tony and Aaron with his fellow maintenance colleagues, and they were shocked to say the least. Jackson, the lead maintenance person for the downtown property, was the most interested in the details and posed a lot of questions.

That evening after dinner, Jackson picked up the telephone to call Janet, saying, "Janet, how are you? Happy holidays to you and your family; this is Jackson." The two talked and talked, catching up on old times. "Do I have a Christmas gift for you!" he teased. Janet probed and probed but could not get Jackson to open up about the surprise Christmas gift he had for her.

Weeks later, the International Auto Show was unveiling new vehicles in Motor City. Aaron, being a car fanatic, asked Tony if the properties could shut down the office early one Wednesday afternoon to attend the auto show. Everyone knew what Aaron wanted; Tony wanted it as well. So the offices closed, and employees enjoyed an afternoon among celebrities and local politicians.

Tony received an obviously disturbing phone call during one of the group huddles. He walked out of the showroom for more conversational privacy. Tony returned to the room, still a bit shaken by his last phone call, to ask if anyone of the employees had called the corporate office to lodge a complaint against him. The employees all shook their heads in horizontal motion and were astonished by his line of questioning.

Attitudes had changed drastically as the outing came to an abrupt end. Tony called one of his property managers and asked that she inquire if any of her employees had rooted any complaints or issues where he was concerned. The inquisitive manager queried the purpose behind the question and if it was related to the mysterious phone call he received earlier. Trusting in her, Tony advised that the call was from Rick Stansbury advising that an anonymous e-mail came into the corporate office characterizing illegal activity taking place at a sister property. "We will be doing a full investigation, and, so help me God, you better not be involved or implicated in this," Stansbury warned.

Tony was obviously perplexed over Stansbury's caveat, not to mention the fact that there was a manager's meeting in Chicago in two days, and he was to sit in a boardroom meeting with Stansbury. Tony laid spooned next to his female counterpart in bed that night. She caressed his hair and tried to assure him that everything would be okay, but he would have to change his lackadaisical work ethic and become a strong manager again. *That's it*, Tony thought to himself. *I am being too nice.* Tony had authorized a holiday party for the residents at one of the properties and made it mandatory for employees to attend with their families. Tony attended as well, and he made an announcement that he and bride-to-be, Tina, were expecting a baby.

Aaron proposed a toast to the unborn child and the happy couple, and everyone wished them well. Tony and Aaron were inseparable at the social gathering and sneaked off often to snort coke during the store runs for more alcohol. After about three hours of drinking, Tina was growing very annoyed with Tony's inappropriate conversation and intoxicated behavior. She tried to get him to leave several times by complaining to be nauseous and tired, but he always offered to arrange for a ride home for her instead of accompanying her. Finally, Tina was able to get Tony out of his seat and in the foyer area of the clubroom. "Honey, let's go. Let's go now. You are drunk, and you are embarrassing yourself and me. You and Aaron have had way too much to drink … you're not eating … Let's go," she said.

"You don't tell me what the hell to do or when the hell to leave. I have four people in that room waiting to take you home; just leave," Tony slurred and pointed at a group of employees that had their coats on and car keys in hand.

Suddenly, the bickering escalated, and the two were physically fighting in the foyer area. Some maintenance men and male residents ran over to the couple to break the fight up, but most were too afraid to hold Tina, as she was warning them all not to touch her. As they carried Tony to the chair he was sitting in, Tina ran behind him and bit a plug into his back. "You bitch!" he yelled prior to falling on the floor and on top of two residents. She was crying and stormed outside without a coat. One of the managers ran after her with a jacket and her purse, hoping she would go home.

That night, Tony crashed on Aaron's couch, and, the next day, he had to take Tony to the airport for his board meeting in Chicago. Tony arranged for an earlier flight so that he would have enough time to stop by Yorktown Mall for a suit. He tried to go home to get a change of clothes but was refused by Tina and greeted by two Park Heights police officers after neighbors observed Tony banging on the front door.

Tony returned home from Chicago on a Friday afternoon. He and Tina decided to give love another chance and have a quiet weekend at home without outside influences. Aaron called and texted several times, but Tony did not respond.

Monday was back to business. Rick Stansbury called the downtown property to ask the property manager to meet him at the Dearborn location. "Do not tell any of your staff members where you are going, and do not call Tony to advise you are coming," he instructed.

She didn't ask any questions, except herself. *Did that mean that Rick Stansbury is in town?*

She wanted to call Tony so bad to alert him that Rick was in town, but her better judgment won the toss-up.

She arrived to the site at a quarter to three to see Rick sitting in an economy-size rental car. The two exited their vehicles and entered the leasing office. Tony looked like death warmed over as he exited the men's room, tucking his shirt into his pants. "What are you two doing here?" he asked with a nervous smile.

"We're here to see you. Let's talk in your office," Rick said. "Why are you wearing jeans in a business office?" Rick continued.

"I was actually going to e-mail you to advise I am using a personal day today, but I had been having difficulty logging into the database today," Tony countered.

"Oh, I had your access suspended at 5:30 this morning," Rick said, as he looked around the office noticing its disarray.

"Why would you do something like that?" Tony inquired.

"Because I am here to terminate you today," Rick said with a smile on his face.

Rick went on to explain why he was being terminated. He explained how illegal and conflicting activity was happening on-site, by the hands of an employee that reported directly to Tony. Stansbury described how Aaron was earning countless accolades when he should be locked up in prison. "The drug dealers buying vacant unit keys from your star pupil. Drug enforcement agents having Aaron on wire tap giving up confidential information and putting an informant's life in jeopardy. Aaron's mother occupying a unit free of charge, showing $12,000 in delinquent rent and no court proceedings commenced to ensure her eviction. Residents terminating their lease early and paying small penalties directly to Aaron and not the property. The property damage being done to these drug units, without any security deposits on file to help recoup some of the loss. The drunken episodes you have had in front of paying tenants. The fact that you look like you are high right now. Should I go on?" Rick asked.

"Okay, first of all I did not know that woman was Aaron's mother. How was I to know? She has a different last name! As far as these drug busts, I walk vacant units every week, and sometimes the keys do not work in the door and I cannot get in. How was I supposed to know that drug dealers were occupying those apartments?" Tony asked. Rick explained that Tony's response was precisely why he was being terminated, because, as a regional manager with over eight years experience in property management, he should have had better control over the property in which he reported to daily.

"I have several deadlines to meet with reports. How am I to control everything that this kid is doing?" Tony asked.

"There are fewer than 250 units here; a child could have better control!" Rick screamed. "This conversation is over. Tony you are terminated effective immediately, collect your personal items, and exit the property, now! You're done."

Chapter 22

Better to sleep with a sober cannibal than a drunken Christian.
—Herman Melville

Several years earlier, city officials passed a law requiring conventional properties to dedicate 10 percent of their total unit count to lower-income tenants. The proposal came at a time when house interest rates were extremely favorable, thus causing record low occupancy in apartment living developments. Avery Heights was a former downtown hotel that soared fifteen stories off the ground. After several years of decay, the building sold and was converted into a 341-unit luxury high-rise community for middle-class residents.

Owners had an idea to segregate the thirty-four units to ensure that Section 8 tenants would not deface the common areas surrounding the higher-paying tenants. However, threats of a class action lawsuit changed the format for such sequestered living quarters. With that being said, owners did hold off on a $3 million renovation project that included a brand-new laundry room with new machines and folding tables in the basement. The renewal project was also due to include resurfaced tennis courts and a swimming pool. The postponed scope even included a full power wash of the building.

Tenants worried and complained that, overtime, the basement had become a haven for criminal elements in the building. Nine months prior, it was necessary for the management company to slightly enhance security services from the whistle-blowing rent-a-cops to licensed and armed guards. The new security guards were supplied with nine-millimeter glocks and staffed each basement and first-floor entrance along with one person driving a patrol vehicle with strobe lights. Two other officers roamed the upper floors and staircases.

As with any other policy or procedure change, there was an unusual incident that prompted such aggressive measures. A local bank was robbed by the children of a building tenant. Three young men—one twenty-six, another twenty-two, and the other seventeen—were tried as adults and charged with armed robbery. Details concluded that the three robbed a franchised bank located less than a mile from the property. The siblings ran while being pursued by police on foot through a propped-open basement door. They hid out in the dark and dreadful laundry room prior to its enhancement. Cops continued in their pursuit, resulting in a shoot out with the suspects. Fortunately, no one was seriously injured. The twenty-two-year-old took a bullet in the shoulder, and one veteran officer took a tethlon-piercing bullet in his ankle.

Soon after, owners decided to heighten security, paint the laundry room, and upgrade the lighting in the basement. "It was a hollow victory," one tenant was quoted saying. A later discovery revealed that the three young men were Section 8 occupants from the tenth floor.

One middle-aged subsidy tenant was responsible for $3 per month in rent, while the government forked over more than a thousand dollars for her two-bedroom apartment. The woman was mentally ill and often paid her rent late—after the 5th of the month—resulting in a $25 late fee. Paying one late fee could have prepaid her rent in advance for eight months! Some months, when she had budgeted properly, she would forget day-to-day that she had paid the rent. She would walk in the manager's office five or six times in one month paying the same rent over and over again. Luckily, the manager was a mature person who had the compassion of Mother Teresa and the patience of Job in the Bible. She would simply accept the checks, write the woman a receipt, and shred the check once the tenant's back was turned. "Bless her heart," Olivia would say.

"Attention, the police are on their way to the rental office after responding to a fight in apartment 313. Do you copy?" Security guard, Tom, announced over the two-way Nextel.

"That's a copy, Tommy," Olivia responded. Two uniformed officers walked into the property manager's office to discuss details of the altercation that took place in 313.

Apparently, the two roommates, Sarah and Casey, had a dispute of some sort. Sarah was in the military reserves working part time at a post office, while Casey was an RN working for a private practice. Casey was a manic depressive who made a recent finding that her boyfriend was sleeping with her half brother. She admitted to cutting up his Suzuki motorcycle with a chainsaw.

Getting back to the fight, Casey's ex-boyfriend, prior to the biker, purchased a Nintendo Wii for the two roommates as a Christmas gift. Both ladies were fitness nuts and commented once that the Wii would be a great exercise tool. He listened and surprised them both with the game system. Since the breakup with the motorcyclist, Casey had been very moody—borderline bipolar—and had been fighting a lot with Sarah.

Sarah, having her own issues, started taking Percocet for mental comfort. Casey expressed her desire to move out of the apartment and find a replacement for Sarah in an effort to save on termination fees. Sarah wanted to screen the potential roommate prior to Casey relinquishing apartment keys to them, especially since she felt she failed terribly at screening Casey. The two bickered for weeks over the alternate roommate, which prompted Casey to vacate the apartment midmonth while still pursuing her replacement.

It appeared that Casey entered the apartment after being absent for several days to remove the last of her belongings. Upon entering the apartment, Sarah was being nonchalant and refused to unlock her bedroom door where the Wii was located. So, in a rage, Casey kicked down the door, and the two tussled with the console. Casey began to cry, screaming that it was her ex who bought the system and that Sarah had no right to it. Sarah, refusing to fight with Casey, dialed 911. Casey begged her to call the police station to retract the call, but she continued to refuse. Casey spotted Sarah's bottle of Percocet and shoved a handful in her mouth. Sarah panicked and picked up the cordless receiver to request an ambulance as an additional emergency vehicle advising, "My roommate is suicidal, and she just swallowed twenty Xanax-type pills!"

Property manager, Olivia Helms, recalled a conversation she had with First Sergeant Bryant regarding the possible split between the two roommates and shared such with the police officers. The first sergeant called to intervene, advising that barrack housing opened up for Private Sarah Blanchard and requested that the military clause be used to emancipate her from the written lease agreement. Olivia went on to say that she had to remind the first sergeant that the military clause only applied to housing that was thirty-five miles or more away from the current location of military personnel. The barracks in question were less than ten miles away.

"You really know your stuff, there," one of the officers commented. He advised Olivia that EMTs took Casey away in an ambulance to pump her stomach and hospitalize her. It would also be necessary to monitor her behavior through the night because of her suicide attempt.

"Thanks officer," Olivia said, as she watched the handsome man in uniform walk out of sight. Manny, the maintenance technician, rushed in and snapped her out of her trance.

"Thanks for letting me take a few hours off today," he said out of breath.

Manny, who lived in Grosse Ile, asked for the half day off to tend to insurance concerns involving his home off the lake. Last Fourth of July holiday, Manny's brother, Thomas, purchased a 1966 thirty-foot wooden Chris Craft Boat with a college buddy of his. Both agreed that due to the boat's age, they would just share maintenance expenses and not carry full-coverage insurance. On the Fourth of July, Thomas' buddy, Francis, wanted to take the boat out to enjoy the fireworks display. Thomas agreed it would be a great family event; however, he had reservations about mixing his children in with a crowd of drinking adults on this boat. As luck would have it, Francis, showing off for boat passengers, sped around the harbor and hit an unknown object, piercing the boat.

Water filled the boat, causing a panic beyond the passengers. According to Manny, instead of calling for emergency assistance, Francis began flooring the boat in an attempt to dock—both engines were blown in such attempt. With help now on the way, the boat was almost under water. Finally, all were rescued from the sinking boat, and the hull was towed to a yard. Instead of scrapping it, Manny asked if the boat could be stored in his backyard to become a thirty-foot playhouse for his children. Unfortunately, it rained and snowed over time and the boat's wood began to deteriorate. "Once the boat became unsafe for my children, I cut the boat up and used the wood in my fireplace," said Manny. However, because the wood was deteriorating and untreated, the unattended fire sparked, caught, and rapidly spread in Manny's family room.

"Luckily my family was on vacation; my wife is in California this week with my eleven-year-old son, who was accepted into Berkley's School of Music. He plays the saxophone," Manny said, as his demeanor changed from panicked father to proud dad.

"Wow!" Olivia expressed in an effort to digest Manny's story. "Well, it's been a day like any other at Avery Heights, and it's budget season; so I'll need your wish list for next year to present to the owners," Olivia concluded, allowing Manny to finally get to work.

Olivia was a good person, a great friend, and an even better boss. She often cooked breakfast or lunch for her staff members and the security personnel. She baked cookies for the sheriffs that would frequent the community to perform evictions. She never bore children, and she had no regrets about not having done so. In her early twenties, she had an extreme case of alcoholism, drinking three pints of vodka or gin per day. She used to wake up to a beer in the morning and fall asleep to a pint with a straw in it at night. Having been clean for close to fifteen years now at age fifty-eight, she would tell countless stories about how she escaped prison so many times by having such an innocent face. "I had been rescued so many times I felt guilty to God. I thought there has got to be someone else who needs saving more than me." That was the day that Olivia took her last drink and enrolled herself into an Alcoholics Anonymous support group.

Once at age twenty-seven, she was let go from a restaurant chain job she'd held for several months, so she thought it best that she sold marijuana for a living. She made tons of money off the pothead friends in her immediate circle and would recoup almost a pound per week from her anonymous drug connection. Once while riding in the backseat of a friend's car, passed out drunk with several ounces of weed under her head, Olivia was awakened by a police officer who had pulled her friend over for driving with expired registration.

Knowing that the charge would result in jail time once Olivia's drugs were discovered, the driver and front passenger pulled over to the side of the road, got out of the vehicle, and ran. The police gave chase and caught up with the two girls who were spotted dumping small packets of marijuana and hash out of their pockets while running. The straggling police officer knocked on the car window with his night stick, waking Olivia and advising her that her friends were going to jail and that she should be more careful of the company she chose to keep. Little did he know, the girls being hauled off to jail had learned to smoke, drink, and deal in drugs all by the hands of the innocent sleeping beauty herself.

On another occasion, while in her twenties, Olivia was arrested for driving while under the influence. She had disappointed her mother so that they were barely on speaking terms. She had burned so many of her siblings and friends that she had no one to turn to for bail. There she sat in the corner of a jail cell crying her eyes out when her name was called, which meant someone had posted bail for her. *But who?* she thought. She hadn't been booked for two hours and definitely did not get an opportunity to make her one phone call for help. It turned out that a bail bondsman was in the lobby assisting a client of his when he'd heard her name being called hours prior. Olivia was so grateful, yet so shocked. She asked the bail bondsman why he chose to help her. He answered like so many had answered before, "You didn't look like you belonged in there," he said. "And when I heard your name called, your Irish name compelled me to help. As you may have guessed it, I'm Irish."

One would never know by talking or working alongside of Olivia about her past. Gospel tunes filled her office, and she always had a kind or spiritual word or advice for anyone she encountered. No one left the rental office without hearing, "Have a blessed day." Olivia believed that God had a special calling on her life, which was why he spared her so many times in the past.

Chapter 23

Success is often the result of taking a misstep in the right direction.
—Al Bernstein

"For many years, this Kansas City block was a symbol of urban decay," the first line in a huge spread read in *The Kansas City Star*. It was a historical moment when a huge investment firm purchased the four-story apartment building, Brandon Park. In addition to forty-five apartments, the revitalized building would include a superintendent's unit, 2,519 square feet of commercial retail space at street level, and a parking garage for ninety-five vehicles.

It wasn't a star-studded event; nonetheless, the mayor of Kansas City invited the retired mayor, Ida Franklin, from the early fifties to late sixties. The former chief of police offered a congratulatory speech for renewing the once crime-stricken neighborhood. He was quoted as saying, "Pulling this eastside community together and making 430 Logan Drive a valuable corner address were no small task."

At the podium, former Mayor Ida recalled the fate of a family she once held close ties to in the four-story structure. With her hair in a back bun filled with ringlets of curls, she told the story of a young Ruth Mills, whose mother and father died in a serious car crash in 1955. Mr. and Mrs. Mills left behind two daughters, Ruth and Claire. In an effort to prevent the two young girls from becoming wards of the state, two compassionate families on the second floor of Brandon Park Apartments, named after the architect's first-born son, stepped up to the plate with strong interests in adopting the orphaned girls. Because of income levels in those days, neighbors agreed to each adopt one. Mrs. Phillips in 2D opted to adopt the younger of the two, Claire, and had dreams of an open relationship, explaining to the juvenile of her adoption status. However, Mrs. Robinson in 2A thought it best that Ruth grow up without knowledge of her paternal parents being anyone except herself and her husband, Mr. Robinson.

Mayor Ida complimented the two women for their acts of kindness and humanitarian efforts. She went on to describe how the minors grew up as neighbors and best friends, but not sisters. Often being enrolled in the same homeroom class as classmates and church programs, the two were inseparable. Ruth soon blossomed into a fine young woman and grew smitten with her college sweetheart, Morris. Her foster mother did not approve of Ruth's selection and was dead set against their engagement. It was said that Mrs. Robinson referred to him as a freckled-face, red hair, and pompous ass. When Morris learned of Mrs. Robinson's face-to-face congeniality and secret disrespect, he decided to take matters into his own hands and push the wedding date up eight months.

Ruth perceived it as Morris' undying love and anxiety to make her Mrs. Morris Carlson, but her foster mother was suspicious of their rush to wed. The wedding was to be held at the local church on a sunny Thursday afternoon. Many family members had drove up to witness the blissful marriage and learn if Ruth was "feeding feet," which meant pregnant in old Caribbean terms. The morning of the wedding, Morris insisted on taking Ruth for a ride. Ruth feared the repercussions of the old superstition against the groom eyeing the bride before the wedding. Morris reminded her of an adage his mother used to say, "White people have money, and black people have superstitions."

Morris whisked her away in his Ford Fairlane to a downtown city county building where records were housed. Ruth was mystified by the sudden trip to the Death and Birth Record Department, but she remained silent. Morris showed Ruth a copy of her mother's birth and death certificate in hopes of breaking the strong bond between her foster mother. The ride back to the church was quiet, yet tearful. "Why? Why?" were the only words muffled by the bride-to-be. Morris did not know if the "why" was for him: as in, "Why did you reveal this to me?" Or "Why did the Robinson family deceive me?"

The wedding went on as scheduled with Ruth growing very distant from her foster parents. She and her new groom did not have money for a honeymoon, so they moved to Jefferson City and started a life together. After three devastating miscarriages, it was soon evident that Ruth would never bare children. Doctors feared her infertility was due to stress.

Approaching their tenth anniversary, Ruth and Morris decided to adopt two children of their own—a boy, they named Morris Jr., and a girl, Jessica. Morris held a stable engineering position with Ford Motor Company, while Ruth was a homemaker studying to be a nurse. Ruth would often carry a forty-five-caliber pistol in her apron as she hung clothes in the backyard of their quaint home due to the close proximity of the Missouri State Penitentiary. Escapees would often run through the yards of homeowners, hoping to hide out in cellars until the coast was clear.

Days before her eighteenth birthday, Jessica confided in her mother that she had been sexually abused by her foster father, Morris, for several years. Ruth cried and held her daughter tight. Her arms were so warm and comforting, but they soon turned to stone when Ruth swatted her daughter across the face in disbelief. Just as Ruth never spoke a word of her discovery with Morris in the downtown office building, she vowed that she would never confront him about the allegation of sexual abuse.

Ruth hung streamers and lace in the living room that day to welcome Jessica home for a famous birthday dinner celebration. Ruth sent Jessica and Junior upstairs to wash up for supper, while she hung a basket of clothes in the yard. The man of the house was preseated at the dinner table enjoying the evening paper and a cup of coffee.

As Ruth reached on top of the fireplace mantel, the unlocked case did not house her forty-five-caliber gun. "Morris, would you have any reason for moving my apron weapon from the mantel here?" she called out. Closing the raised newspaper to turn the page, Morris offered a negative response. "Who could have …" Ruth started to question only to be interrupted by a single gunshot. Everyone bolted to the staircase, where the sound originated. Jessica lay at the top of the staircase where she stood seconds ago before taking her life with one shot to the head.

Mayor Ida went on to describe how the family of three never spoke of the fatal incident and made all attempts to go on with life. As the pages of the calendar turned, Ruth tried to stay busy with church banquets and bake sales. Yet, the two-year anniversary of Jessica's untimely death was soon approaching. Ruth prepared a hearty meal, and the family planned for a quiet, uneventful evening at home on Jessica's birthday. No one vocalized the plans, Ruth just announced, "Dinner's ready," as she wiped her hands on her apron and turned the rear burner off on the stove.

A familiar shot resounded and sent Ruth running once again toward the sullen area of the house. This time, the staircase held the man she vowed to spend eternity with. Morris Carlson Sr. died of a self-inflicted gunshot to the head on the same day of his foster daughter's fatal incident. Ruth had never confronted her husband about the rape; thus, it was suspected that guilt had interrupted everyday life for the adulterer. He had been having trouble sleeping and eating regularly.

There wasn't a dry eye in the courtyard as Mayor Ida recollected the facts of life of Ruth Mills. She closed by congratulating the incumbent mayor and Kansas City housing developers. The former mayor exited the podium to a standing ovation from her political peers and new dwellers of the $11.5 million asset.

There was a brief intermission at the successful re-grand opening of Brandon Park with the grandson of the original architect up next to address the Kansas City residents. Bill Kissinger was a public school educator before he began to model after his grandfather as an architect. Bill's passion for building arose when he noticed the cracked concrete floors, shoddy windows, and unleveled classrooms throughout the building in which he taught. In the beginning, his love for construction proved to be a simple hobby. Soon, he reconstructed areas of the school in which he taught during the off-season and with his own funding. After earning many accolades for his craftsmanship and dedication, Bill decided to do building renovation and architecture full time.

Bill Kissinger, admitting to having a hard act to follow behind Mayor Ida Franklin, took the podium after a fifteen-minute intermission. "Welcome once again to Brandon Park Apartments!" Bill asserted in an effort to warm up the relaxed crowd. "Welcome to amenities that are endless and all yours!" he continued. Bill told the story of when he first fell in love with building architecture. His grandfather, Norman Kissinger, engineered a sixty-story building in downtown Chicago in the early 1930s. The building served as home for an information systems technology mainframe.

It was multifaceted and contained building systems for hospitals, churches, educational institutions, warehouses, and many large corporations. Housing film documents and microfiche of very important data, the building could neither afford to lose power, nor were mistakes possible. Bill recalled that the 40th floor contained model home replicas, much like you would see in an IKEA store. The demonstration homes had roped-off entrances, and all doors to each room were removed. Reporters from major news broadcast stations were present and interviewed different people from all walks of life to get the majority's perspective on the building design.

One reporter approached an Englishman in a derby who described how fascinating and modern the building's design was. "What I can't understand," started the Englishman, "is why aren't there any doors on the bathrooms? Is everyone these days too modern for prĭvacy?" (pronounced with a short "i" versus the long "i")

The crowd laughed in unison, appreciating Bill's rendition of an English accent. Bill described that same sixty-story building that he and his company renovated as a memorial site for his deceased grandfather. As part of the building's upgrade, the security system proved to be the most dramatic upgrade. The security systems consisted of a five fingerprint scan, ID badge scan, photo recognition of associates' faces, and a four-digit pin number. "Though the structure of the building changed, its focus remained the same—to serve as storage for backup data and the mainframe for thousands of corporations, schools, hospitals, and so forth," Bill continued.

"The building services generate $82,000 per minute and contain two thousand backup generators. Unless Jesus himself comes down, there is no natural disaster that will affect the performance of our mainframe. Now that's impressive," Bill arrogated, as the crowd agreed.

"In some ways, I still see myself as that green and naïve kid from Philadelphia, but what can I say … Let's go Royals!" Bill cheered and waved in closing as the audience was delighted and applauded.

Chapter 24

You can go a long way with a smile. You can go a lot farther with a smile and a gun. —Al Capone

County police officers were swarming the apartment complex. "Now what!" Cecily threw up her hands and rolled her brown eyes as an officer approached her office.

"Good afternoon, Cecily. Can we talk?" he asked, motioning with his eyes as he secured and adjusted his service weapon in the rear belt area of his denim pants. Officer Walsh proceeded to explain the incidents of the morning that took place prior to the office opening. "We got a call from a tenant in Tower II, seventeenth floor," he recalled while looking down at notes written on his hand. "A Todd Sheffield claimed that he had just returned home from walking his Yorkie poodle, Chilton, when he noticed that his apartment had been ransacked," Officer Walsh continued.

He went on to reiterate the events as told by Todd Sheffield of 1713 of how his armoire drawers were rummaged through. They took his checkbook, a silver Movado watch, his $400 mobile phone, and, apparently, bottled water out of his refrigerator. "Are you serious?" Cecily asked. The officer assured her that he was giving the story back to her play by play. He went on to describe what happened next, which was while he and two other fellow officers were taking Mr. Sheffield's statement and photographs of his apartment. Todd called his cell phone to see if the thieves would answer, and they did. Another undercover detective instructed Todd to put the caller on speaker phone so that the conversation could be heard by all. The suspect on the other end of the phone instructed Sheffield to go to a nearby ATM machine to retrieve $250 for exchange of his brand-new cellular phone.

"Dude, are you serious? You're holding my cell phone ransom?" Sheffield asked the caller.

Detectives motioned for Sheffield to play along to offer an opportunity to nab the suspects. They arrived at the conclusion that there was more than one after hearing the caller reference the word "we." Sheffield was careful to warn the caller that he would be bringing his cousin along for safety and assurance, but no police. Meanwhile, a plain-clothed officer accompanied Sheffield to a nearby ATM, while the caller remained in close proximity and continued to offer verbal instructions once the funds were retrieved from Todd's account. The caller barked orders, "Cross the street, and pick up the payphone receiver. Now go inside of the McDonald's, and order a sandwich. Walk over to the laundry mat, and wait for more instructions."

During the interval, unmarked police vehicles were traveling the immediate area, and undercover police officers were sitting on a bench at a bus stop pretending to be lovers right outside of the laundry mat. While inside, three scoundrels approached Todd and his "cousin" with the cell phone in hand. "Make it quick, and don't say a word," were the instructions offered from behind. As the two turned to face the criminals, the plain-clothed detective grabbed the suspect holding the mobile phone, while the other two bolted out the door. The remaining officers sitting and fawning on the bench outside noticed the two fleeing suspects and pursued them on foot to no advantage.

"This is like something out of a blockbuster movie," Cecily declared. Seeking an end to the torrid details, Cecily interrupted, "Please tell me that no one was hurt in this sting operation."

The officer assured her that no one was hurt but shared that the suspect they held in custody was a member of a psycho gang that had formed in the area of the apartment complex. "Our gang squad detectives tell us that they have suspicion to believe that gang members are somehow acquainted with occupants in Tower II. This gang has been the target of several investigations involving hate crimes." Cecily felt a huge lump in her throat. "We also believe that gang members are walking the hallways of the buildings looking for unlocked doors," Officer Walsh continued, "I think it would be a good idea to alert your tenants and ask them to keep their eyes peeled for suspicious activity."

Cecily scribbled notes on a legal pad on her desk. "Sure thing," she said.

Cecily walked Officer Walsh to the front door of the leasing office, carrying on a false demeanor as if he were a client. She soon noticed "Bag Lady" pushing her cart along the adjoining sidewalks of the apartment complex. Bag Lady was a long-term resident in Tower I that apparently fell on hard times after her divorce years ago. Rumor had it that she was a licensed real estate agent that was once an attractive and fetching woman. Now, she dressed in dingy and tattered clothing, a wig that was just as forbidding, and ruby red lipstick all over her teeth. She wore long skirts primarily and wouldn't bat an eye before hiking up her skirt to urinate in a nearby bush. Whether she was on the property grounds, had an audience or on the city street, if she felt the urge, she would just hoist her skirt and go. Some feared for her safety roaming the streets from early morning to late night. However, after she was mugged near a 7-Eleven once, she stopped carrying cash with her and could be seen buying her cases of beer and snacks with a Visa card every day.

"We'll let you know when that apartment is ready," Cecily pronounced in a higher pitch, as she winked her eye at the undercover officer who headed back to the station. Cecily returned to her desk to draft the standardized crime memo to circulate to all 500 plus apartments. Instead, she noticed a mystery shopper's report on her desk. Every Monday, shopper reports are faxed to managers from the two weeks prior, outlining the performance of the sales associates at each property. The reports are supposedly based on the unbiased opinions of contracted mystery shoppers. Every industry employs such concept. Grocers contract with mystery shoppers to ensure that tobacco and alcohol products are not sold to underage persons. Retailers have been heavily fined, brought up on charges, and employees have been terminated and personally sued based on the findings from such reports.

The subject of the shop report on Cecily's desk was John Emerson. John was fairly new to the multifamily industry, with only seven months under his belt. John was a former flight attendant for a well-known airline that was bought out by its competition. As negotiations pended and a final decision materialized, John was somehow lost in the shuffle and laid off. The layoff forced him into the café of a Starbucks franchise where he spent a lot of time surfing the online classified ads and updating his resume to post. In the olden days of property management, flight attendants made the perfect candidate due to their hospitality skills and most times bilingual. They were also known for their polished and delightful demeanor, as well as their flexibility as it related to relocating.

John was very charming and charismatic. Some say his homosexuality gave him the edge, because he could help clients decorate their homes or visualize themselves living in an empty apartment based purely on the picture words he'd use to describe them in the empty shell. John lived on-site and maintained an immaculate apartment. He would invite all of his clients to view his fifteenth-floor apartment. His only requirement was that they remove their shoes at the door. Room by room, he would introduce people to the many artifacts and designer sculptures that he acquired from flea markets, boutiques, and even garage sales across the United States. The perks of a flight attendant.

Everything from the bench in the foyer that he found on the side of the road in Cincinnati to the scrapbook materials he purchased at various museums in New York, Texas, Colorado, and D.C. John often told the story of how his mother, who worked part time in a high-end furniture store in Seattle, would use his lifestyle as a way to close the sale on qualified yet skeptical buyers. "You know I can appreciate your reservation on buying this piece," his mother would start, "but I know from personal experience that you will absolutely love this furniture for your home. My son, who's gay, bought this same set from our store in D.C." John chuckled every time he told that story. Everyone knows that gay men have the most style.

The mystery shopping report was personally designed by the CEO of the management company. It was comprised of ten categories for a total of one hundred points, three of which weighed heavily on the subject's overall score, carrying twenty points each. The first question on the report was, "Did the sales agent sell you on the management company?" This meant offering clients positive facts and traits about the company: its ranking in the industry, the number of units managed, mission statement, and so forth. The second question was, "How did the sales agent overcome the discriminatory question you asked?" Mystery shoppers were instructed to ask offensive questions such as inquire about the number of blacks, Latinos, or Asian descent individuals living in the building or make statements expressing their desire to live far away from families with children or from a particular ethnic background.

Sales agents were trained and versed on appropriate responses to such insulting lines of questioning and thinking. The third question was based on the salesperson's performance: "Would you have leased an apartment at the community?" Many sales associates felt that this question was subjective. They felt that they could be scored poorly, based on a particular mood the paid mystery shopper was in at the time. However, owners and executive management felt strongly about the opinion of the "average Joe."

Cecily danced in her chair as she read the report on John Emerson. After all, she also receives a bonus check for favorable reports on her staff. The shopper reported being initially impressed by John's professionalism and genuine greeting. She outlined how he led the tour by asking open questions to encourage engaging conversation. She, of course, described how she loved his apartment and how he promised to help her decorate if she would sign up on the first visit, which created a sense of urgency. The shopper advised John that she did not want to live near any Mexicans. He assured her that the company does not discriminate based on ethnicity or religion. "We lease to qualified individuals based on their credit score, criminal, and check writing history. If you find a place that segregates people based on color or race, my personal advice would be for you to steer clear."

Cecily was planning to approach her regional manager on the subject of recognizing and promoting John when the next opportunity presented itself. Deborah, the regional manager, was also very fond of John. She was quoted as saying to a client who took the time to write a complimentary letter to the corporate office, "John has a genuine and raw talent that he brings to our team and we are most proud of his professionalism and team spirit …"

"Donna, can you announce to the entire team that a staff meeting will be held at 3 p.m.? Please hold all of my calls until after the meeting," Cecily directed.

"Right away," Donna responded. Cecily swiftly prepared the customary crime alert notice to share with staff members. Suddenly, shots were fired and heard in close proximity to the leasing entrance. Cecily instructed everyone to get down on the floor and stay down. She dialed 911 from her desk phone and peeked outside to observe anyone milling around.

A few people were scrambling around to find shelter after hearing the shots ring out, but Cecily could not prepare for what she saw next. She ran out only to notice the words "Faggot Bitch" spray painted on the side of John's Mini Cooper vehicle. John Emerson was laying on the ground with blood streaming down the concrete sidewalk. "John! John!" Cecily screamed, crying profusely.

He opened his eyes with a slight smile on his face, "Well … I guess I can't sue them … for slander … they got it right," he said, as he struggled taking his last breath.

Chapter 25

A mistress should be like a little country retreat near the town, not to dwell in constantly, but only for a night and away.
—William Wycherley

Nervously awaiting the courtroom doors to open, Bridgett reviewed notes provided by landlord–tenant attorney, Richie Budnick. "All cell phones should be in the off position," warned the uniformed court officer. "If Judge Holzman is interrupted by any ring tones or alerts, your cell phone will be confiscated and unavailable for the following ten days," he continued.

There was a slight murmur as individuals lined up to enter the courtroom. Bridgett looked back as she entered, hoping to see Attorney Budnick. *He must be running late*, she thought to herself. There were three trials on the docket this morning for The Madison. One was a fight for possession of an apartment because of nonpayment. Another involved two apartments where eviction was being sought because of a holiday party gone bad, which resulted in five arrests, thirteen police cars on-site, and a total disruption of community enjoyment at 2 am. The third eviction proceeding comprised of a tenant suing the apartment community for a pecuniary award of $100,000—in a wrongful eviction case.

"All rise. The honorable Judge Holzman presiding," instructed the same uniformed officer. Just then, Richie Budnick slipped in the courtroom, closing the door quietly behind him. He spotted Bridgett in the fifth-row bench. She moved her Coach briefcase and amethyst clutch bag from right to left, making room for Mr. Budnick to sit beside her. "Good Morning. You had me worried," she whispered.

"Traffic was a bear on the beltway," he claimed. "Now, they may call Ms. Mings' case first. Do you have the photos of what was removed from her apartment before the locks were changed?" he whispered.

"Here are digital copies and Polaroid copies," Bridgett swiveled to retrieve them from her briefcase. In recent years, courts frowned upon the sole usage of digital photographs because of the ability to make Photoshop alterations to them.

"Greg Perkins, our maintenance manager, is also here today to testify, since he was personally present when the items were removed," Bridgett advised.

"Case Number 08-197559, the state versus Cliff McMillan," a voice resonated from the front of the courtroom. A Caucasian male, in his late thirties, approached the defendant's table with his hands in his pockets.

"Thank you for dressing up for the court today," the judge made an obvious sarcastic observation, as the man stood in denim jeans and a black "members only" jacket.

"Your Honor, Mike Cooley for the state. Mr. McMillan here was cited for drinking a beer at a bus stop on Route 5. Officer Wabash is present in court this morning, your Honor," the attorney assured, as he turned around pointing to a plain clothes officer with a badge hung around his neck.

"Officer Wabash, you are free to go home. I know you work the midnight shift and should not be missing out on any sleep for these clowns;, you are dismissed," the judge demanded.

"Mr. McMillan, were you consuming beer at a bus stop on Route 5?" the judge asked.

"Uh, yes sir," he nervously responded.

"Why?" the judge probed.

"Uh, your Honor, I had just gotten off of work and like to have one or two after a long day," the defendant answered.

"One or two, huh?" the judge asked, shaking his head. "Fifty-dollar fine plus cost," the judge said, as he banged the gavel, and the court officer called the next case.

"Case Number 08-197563, Ms. Sue Moi Mings versus Madison Apartments."

The tenant, Ms. Mings, was sitting on the front row and had already made her way to the plaintiff's podium. She stood alone, which meant she would be unrepresented by counsel. The three for the defendants' podium soon made their way to the front. "Good morning, your Honor; Rich Budnick here for the defendants, The Madison Apartments."

"Morning Mr. Budnick," he responded dryly. "Would the plaintiff state her full name and date of birth for the court?" the judge said, nodding in the direction of Ms. Mings. She responded in pretty good English.

This oughta be good, Bridgett thought to herself.

"Okay, thank you," the judge acknowledged. "Would the defendants state their full name and date of birth for the court?"

"Bridgett Ward, property manager for The Madison, May 7, 1979. Thank you, your Honor."

"Greg Perkins, maintenance supervisor for The Madison, November 4, 1973."

"And once again, your Honor, Attorney Rich Budnick for Madison Apartments."

"Thank you; let's start with you, Ms. Mings. You are suing Madison Apartments for $100K, claiming that you were wrongfully evicted. How were your personal contents removed from your apartment, Ms. Mings?" the judge asked.

"Yes, ya honor; I was living in apartment #357 in the defendants' building, and I had planned to buy a condo, because they raised the rent so high for me to afford." The tenant commenced in pleading her case to Judge Holzman. She went on to explain how her lease was due to expire at the end of March, and she was having trouble getting financed for a mortgage loan. Ms. Mings admitted that she had given a written notice to vacate the apartment on March 31st; however, she did plan on going into the leasing office to speak to "her," as she pointed to the other side of the courtroom, presumably at Bridgett Ward.

"Okay, let me check my understanding of this," the judge interjected. "You said your written lease expired on March 31, and you had given proper notice to the landlord to vacate the premises per your contract. You also mentioned that your next housing plan was to purchase; however, there was an issue with the lender. Had you provided the landlord's office with a retraction notice that indicated you would not vacate your apartment on March 31, but indeed needed more time in the unit?"

She struggled with her words at first, but eventually she communicated that she went into the leasing office on April 1st with her rent check. Ms. Mings said the manager "acted" as if she was too busy to talk to her and demanded that she leave the office. "That is not true!" Bridgett objected.

"You'll have your turn, Mrs. Ward. In the meantime, no further interruptions, *capiche?*" scolded the judge.

He gave Ms. Mings the nod to continue. She went on to say that her rent check was later returned with a note from the property manager, indicating that her lease had expired and was not eligible to renew; thus, she was to be out of the apartment along with her belongings no later than the close of business on April 1st. The tenant explained that on April 2nd she arrived home after business hours to find that her locks had been changed. She went on to explain that the $100,000 she was suing for included an overnight stay at a nearby motel; loss of wages; her expensive furniture pieces, which had been set out on the thoroughfare; and pain and suffering. Ms. Mings claimed that the removal of her personal property in plain view of her neighbors caused her mental anguish, and she could not report to work for at least two weeks thereafter.

"Now, Ms. Ward, in your own words, please describe what took place on April 1st and thereafter," the judge instructed.

"Uh, your Honor, may we present photographs of the expensive, luxurious showroom furniture that the plaintiff described?" Attorney Budnick asked in a condescending tone. The judge motioned for the bailiff to retrieve the items from the attorney. The Polaroid pictures showed a dingy three-cushion sofa with reddish stains all over the smashed pillows. There were two folding chairs near the sofa along with a rubber tree plant turned over on the floor. The bedroom reflected a full-size bed, without bedding on the mattress. There was no headboard, footboard, or any other dresser pieces pictured. The kitchen showed dirty countertops, a disgusting oven range, and hair particles inside of the refrigerator with a box of baking soda, bottled water, and a half loaf of moldy bread. The bathroom showed a cheap shower curtain that could be found at any dollar store and mildew and mold in the tub and shower area. It was obvious when the judge shuffled through to the photograph of the commode, his facial expression indicated a need to regurgitate.

"Bailiff Smyte, would you be so kind as to pass these photographs along to Mrs. Mings," the judge asked, as he handed them over. "Ms. Mings, please verify if the belongings in the photograph belong to you. And have you a list itemizing and proving the total suit of $100K?"

"Yes. Yes this is my stuff, but there was a lot more not shown in these pictures like a forty-two-inch flat screen TV, a mink coat hanging in the closet of my bedroom, a treadmill in the corner of my bedroom, huh ..."

"Ms. Mings, do you have receipts or proof of the additional items that you are naming and claiming?" the judge interrupted. She offered a favorable response as she handed the bailiff two pages of handwritten documents. "Ms. Mings, what is this?" inquired the judge. "I am looking for retail receipts, motel receipts, pay stubs from your employer, and all other documentation that prove loss of wages and so forth. Do you have anything like that, Ms. Mings?"

She trifled through some documents in front of her and began to cry. "They took everything I had ... I have nothing now ... they stole my stuff!" she accused. The judge handed the bailiff a box of tissue to share with the sobbing plaintiff.

The judge in a very empathetic voice explained to Ms. Mings that she did not come to court prepared, nor had she proved her case. He did, however, rule in her favor in the amount of $125 for the items photographed that were trashed prior to her handing in her keys to the apartment. The judge explained to Ms. Mings that because there were no signs of a habitable environment—which is perishable food, clothes, and bedding—once management entered the apartment, they had a right to take back possession of the apartment.

"We will break for a lunch recess; please rise as the honorable Judge Holzman exits the courtroom. We will continue at 12:15 p.m."

Attorney Budnick extended Bridgett his Capital One platinum card, "Buy lunch for yourselves. I need to make some calls from my car." She embraced his offer, took the card, and motioned to Greg to join her at the café adjacent to the courthouse.

Greg was a very observant and knowledgeable person. He received his Bachelor of Architecture at University of Maryland and MBA degree awarded with honors at American University. When hired on with the management company, his resume reflected several years experience as a project manager with a huge development firm out of Illinois. Greg performed asset management analyses and worked on many acquisitions for a one-hundred-year-old firm dealing primarily in high-rise apartment communities, commercial retail, and office buildings.

He had managed projects, including a brand-new 125-unit, high-rise building in Carol Stream, Illinois; renovation and expansion of 3,500 square feet of commercial space in Downers Grove; a sixty-five-unit luxury condominium project in Kewanee; and an expansion plan of a regional shopping center in Naperville, Illinois.

Greg smirked, as he followed Bridgett toward the elevators. Greg and other staff members had suspicion to believe that Bridgett and Rich Budnick had a relationship more intimate than client and attorney. Bridgett had been observed exiting the passenger side of Rich's Mercedes truck during lunchtime.

Once, Bridgett confided in a former leasing agent—who told all— that she and Rich made love in the Jacuzzi tub behind the clubhouse of the apartment community one night after a jazz concert downtown. Also enjoying several bottles of Dom Perignon. It was said that Bridgett spoke candidly about the sexual encounter. She spoke about how she wasn't able to climax through the oral sex he performed, but the actual act of penetration was "everything to write home about."

Greg remembered how Joy, the former employee, mimicked Bridgett's love-struck expressions when she described how she was able to take all eight inches in her mouth. However, the taste of the smegma put an end to her sucking excursion. As most women would, Joy tried to imagine what an encounter would be like with an uncircumcised penis—either the sensation from the extra ripples in the shaft or the softness while in one's mouth. *Yuck!* was the next thought in her head.

"What if a resident had keyed in to use the hot tub that night?" Joy asked Bridgett.

"That was half the excitement, the risk of being caught," Bridgett vaunted.

"Aside from being caught, you could have been fired," Joy scolded.

"If a voyeur wanted to get his or her jollies while watching me get mine, God bless 'em!" Bridgett exulted, obviously not seeing the possibility of an unfavorable outcome to the affair.

Bridgett day dreamed about being scant of breath while frothing on the high-powered attorney's male organ that night.

The two, Greg and Bridgett, finished their sandwiches and returned to the courthouse to win the last two landlord–tenant cases. Mr. and Mrs. Griffith brought suit against The Madison when an acorn on a tree fell and cracked the windshield of their Lincoln Town Car. It was decided that the accident should be deemed an "act of God" and was no fault of the property owner. In fact, Rich Budnick was able to prove that the tree was not on the property's line, but land owned by the city.

The final triumph involved an eviction sought out for nonpayment. Harry Burns of apartment 1411 had a gambling problem and lost several thousand dollars at a casino in another town. Harry confided in a contractor that performed work for The Madison that he had been up as much as $11,000 on the high-rollers' crap table, only to lose it all along with the keys to his brand-new Ford F150. Ironically, the pickup truck was a result of a winning streak he was once on. Harry procured the truck in a sweepstakes at the casino months back.

The case had been heard by another judge two months prior. In that case, the judge sided with Mr. Burns, against the apartment community. Obviously, Rich Budnick appealed, and this case was called in circuit court for a de novo hearing.

When petitioned about his intentions to pay the $5,268.26 in rent arrears, Harry's only defense was that the nonpayment case should be thrown out because of conflict of interest. The judge probed only to discover that Harry was a former client of Attorney Rich Budnick in an inheritance trial ten years ago. The judge failed to find the relevance in the fact and demanded that Harry pay the five-thousand-dollar figure to stay or do the obvious—vacate the premises.

Upon arriving back at the apartment site, Bridgett noticed Heather's

Cadillac Escalade truck parked in a spot zoned for future residents. *I hate when she does that,* she thought to herself. She also thought that it was odd that her supervisor would be on-site unannounced on the first Wednesday of the month, which was always court day.

"Hi. What are you doing here?" Bridgett asked with a fake smile.

"I'm here to see you. Grab two cigarettes, and let's take a ride on the golf cart," the regional manager instructed. Heather wasn't a consistent smoker because of her husband's disapproving attitude toward it; however, she would have a cigarette if she was in the company of a smoker.

Heather started right in, "I'm going to cut to the chase here. The main office has gotten numerous phone calls from your staff members accusing you of stealing, sleeping with the owner's attorney and several of the residents ..."

"Excuse me!" Bridgett yelled on the defensive.

"Hold on; let me finish," Heather warned. "Don't try to bullshit a bullshitter. Obviously, a lot of what they are saying is true. The fact that you and Rich continue to see each other, after his wife took him back, is beyond me. You both continue to use the courtroom and this property as a tryst, and, I must say, it is distasteful," Heather scolded. "There are rumors that you and I made out after the grand opening party held last spring. Rumors that we were wasted, dancing in a provocative manner and making out near the hot tub. It's obvious that you can't hold your liquor or your tongue, because who else would know the truth?" she continued.

"Okay, wait a minute!" Bridgett interrupted again, but Heather cut her off, continuing to describe the details called into HR by anonymous employees of The Madison. Heather narrated how Bridgett had turned in commission claims for the same four clients she moved in months ago. She spoke of how Bridgett brought groceries for her family, was seen unloading her trunk and taking groceries in her apartment, and then turning in a $327 grocer receipt into petty cash, claiming that the property hosted a dinner party for residents. She then described how Bridgett moved in this pedophile who was a pilot for a major airline in exchange for a three-carat diamond ring his ex-fiancé had given back to him when she found out he was cheating with a sixteen-year-old runaway.

"Basically, I have been warned to fire you and make sure you empty your pockets on the way out," Heather said, as she lit up a cancer stick.

By this time, Bridgett was in tears, confessing that her husband left her ten months ago. She related how he stole all of the money out of their joint accounts, canceled all of her credit cards, and had even emptied the freezer before leaving, advising her to "go sell her body" to feed her children—children that were, nonetheless, his biologically too.

"Why didn't you tell me, Bri?" Heather asked in a more affectionate tone. Bridgett answered that she was too ashamed to tell anyone, let alone ask for help. She pleaded for her job and for Heather's friendship in her time of need.

"I know I have a tendency to obscure, distort, and deny the truth. I'm not blaming anyone but myself for my actions. Not that bastard Tom ... not Rich ... not my staff ... and certainly not you. But I am asking for a second chance," she said.

Heather handed Bridgett her lit cigarette, insinuating it was the thing she needed to calm her nerves. Just then, she turned the golf cart around to take the long way back to the property's entrance. "This is what we'll do. I will advise the vice president that I confronted you, and you denied everything and that I believe you. I will tell him that your strong personality may not be compatible with your staff and suggest we transfer you to Tiffany Heights and bring that manager here," Heather articulated, as she hand motioned. Bridgett smiled in relief and hugged her from the passenger seat of the golf cart. "Cut that out before another rumor surfaces!" Heather responded, as she straightened her clothes and partially lost control of the golf cart.

Chapter 26

*We are continually faced with a series of great opportunities
brilliantly disguised as insoluble problems. —John W. Gardner*

"I paid my rent on time, so why am I getting charged these ridiculous
fees?" Carol asked as she entered the rental office without so much as a
greeting or waiting to be greeted.

"We would be more than willing to assist you with your account
questions, Carol; however, there are clients ahead of you. Please have a
seat in the clubhouse and help yourself to the Starbucks coffee station,"
Michelle professionally answered.

Michelle was busy with a potential resident in front of her and
quite annoyed that Carol entered the office with such attitude. With
her cosmetically whitened teeth and close-to-perfect brunette curls,
Michelle immediately converted back to sales mode, attempting
to convince her just-as-beautiful client there was no justification to
her desire to "continue looking around" at other apartments in the
neighborhood. The apartment site consisted of six midrise buildings,
all six stories with three passenger elevators in each, including one
freight. The attractive real estate encompassed 13.3 acres of land, which
offered a total site density of 17.3 units per acre. The buildings were
constructed of wood and concrete frame with lap siding and natural
limestone masonry.

"You loved the island kitchens, the built-in vanity tables in the
master bedroom, and you said yourself your daughter is planning to

enroll in Syracuse in two years. Rent now while the interest rates are less desirable, and buy a town house prior to her freshman year," Michelle encouraged.

"You guys aren't offering any type of incentives? I'd sign up in a heartbeat if the first month was free or at least half off," her client said, leaning in as if to say "it would be our little secret."

"I'd love to Karen. You seem like a nice enough woman, and the stories you shared about your daughter were both sweet and entertaining, but what I offer to you I have to offer to the next six or however many persons that will keep their appointments to view that same apartment this afternoon. We are not oblivious to the fact that our competitors are offering first-month incentives, but guess what? They need to. Because our designer-inspired apartments offer more alluring amenities, and I guarantee that same apartment will be leased by another family the moment you leave my office. Just yesterday, I gave a couple a gift certificate to have lunch at a bistro nearby, and, upon their return, one of the other salespersons had leased their apartment. I felt horrible, and I would hate for that same fate to be yours. Why don't you call your husband, finish your Fiji water, and I will check on my clients out there signing their lease?" Michelle arose from her chair and gave a reassuring smile as she exited the office.

As Michelle entered the clubhouse, she noticed Carol rolling her neck as she spoke to Stuart, the assistant manager. "How are you three coming? Can I get anyone more water, coffee, anything?" Michelle questioned, as she squatted onto the edge of the suede ottoman.

The roommates all smiled and answered in unison, "No thanks." All documents were stacked neatly on the couch table, resting under a paper clip with three pens atop.

"I'm sure it feels as though you have just signed your life away," Michelle said jokingly, "but, in all honestly, this is probably one of the most important decisions you will make in your young adult lives outside of grad school majors. You won't be disappointed."

The roommates all stood as they gathered their empty candy wrappers, napkins, empty coffee mugs, and bottles of water. Michelle grabbed the signed lease and used it to point to the stainless-steel trash can that coordinated with the stainless-steel appliances in the clubhouse. All exchanged handshakes with her and exited the building.

"Is anything wrong, Alexis?" Michelle asked after observing the mysterious expression on her face. Alexis was one of Michelle's clients who had moved in the buildings less than ninety days ago. She moved to Kansas City from Fort Bragg, North Carolina, where she was recently married.

As Alexis toured the community with Michelle just a few months back, she grew very sensitive when Michelle complimented her on her wedding ring. It was a beautiful two-carat bridal set with four princess-cut diamonds coming together in a sparkling center, while several round diamonds framed the center and accentuated the fourteen-carat white gold band. Alexis shared that her parents paid for a lavish $40,000 wedding, while her grandparents' gift to the newlyweds was a fully furnished three-bedroom bungalow just off the military base.

Her wonderful husband failed to disclose to her that while in boot camp a year and a half ago, he had gotten a civilian pregnant and fathered a child—a bouncing baby boy. Two days after the honeymoon, Charles felt the necessity to ask the mother of his child if the baby could stay overnight with him and his new wife.

Alexis returned home from Trader Joe's, excited about preparing the first meal in their new home only to walk in on Charles laying on the carpeted floor playing with the cutest, chubbiest baby she had ever seen.

"Whose kid? He is absolutely adorable," she remembered asking.

"Mine," Charles answered in a low tone.

"Right! No really, are we babysitting for one of your soldier buddies?"

"He's mine okay, and you're gonna have to get used to it!" Charles pounded his fist on the seat of a folding chair nearby causing it to nearly collapse onto little Charlie who happened to be crawling under it at the time.

Crying and calling home to mom didn't make the reality of a baby disappear. Shortly thereafter, Alexis found herself applying for marketing positions with national firms miles away until one in Kansas City, Missouri, called back. In less than four months after her wedding, she was headed to a foreign state, where she didn't know a soul. She thought it would be less stressful if her college girlfriends weren't close enough to drop in on her in her hometown. So she chose an opportunity in a territory where no one would know her story unless she told them.

"Um, I think that guy in the business center is whacking off," Alexis said. Covering her mouth and nose with her right hand and pointing with the left, Alexis was almost embarrassed to speak the words. Michelle placed the lease documents face down on the marble countertop and took off running toward the business center.

"Bob, what do you think you're doing?" Michelle yelled, as she turned the swivel chair that he was sitting in. The seventeen-inch monitor displayed a graphic sex scene involving two busty blondes and what looked to be a very lengthy vibrator. His glasses were fogged and hanging off his face. His trench coat was caught under a wheel of the chair causing him to stumble as he tried to run.

"I'm sorry! Ahh … I was just leaving … I'm so sorry … It won't happen again!" he stammered.

"You filthy disgusting pig! You most certainly are leaving!" Michelle growled while picking Bob up by the shoulder fabric of his trench coat. He pushed his glasses up by the middle bridge while swiftly walking out of the rear glass door of the fitness studio. Stuart discreetly dialed the police after Michelle signaled, extending her thumb and baby finger in the form of an air phone held up to her ear.

"You talked me into it," a familiar voice said from behind. Michelle nearly forgot about her client who was just ending her phone conversation with her husband and was now holding a $500 deposit check between her index and middle finger. The woman had obviously missed what had just taken place.

"You made the right decision, Karen. I'll hold on to this and give you a call tomorrow morning—if that's okay with you," Michelle said, regrouping.

"Wonderful. I'll fax everything else over to the number on your card. Don't work too hard," Karen said, noticing the small beads of sweat upon Michelle's brow. Shortly thereafter, Karen turned and waived good-bye as a call came through her blue tooth headset.

"Officers. Am I glad to see you?" Michelle led them to the lease file cabinet. She retrieved Bob's folder and photocopied the copy of his driver's license. "He's in 44D in building 2630," she said, as she handed one officer the paper with his picture on it.

"He didn't get any on you, did he?" the husky officer asked jokingly.

"No, but I see a little bit of it got on your cheek," Michelle fired back, hardly appreciating the attempt at humor.

Michelle swiftly began the eviction process for Bob in 44D. She completed the seven-day court document and faxed it over to the attorney's office. *Would he dare fight the legality of this eviction?* she thought to herself. Her better judgment persuaded her to continue with the process. Knowing that the embarrassing details would soon become taboo when made a part of court transcripts and possibly evoke fear among a jury of his peers of his pedophile profile, Michelle was convinced that Bob would go away quickly, quietly, and without protest.

While exiting the clubhouse, the officers walked by two college students outside carrying on a conversation about a somewhat mutual friend. "How do you continue to be a friend to a friend who you feel is making a huge mistake?" Shelly asked shortly after closing the passenger door to Rachel's Ford Fusion. In ecru white with champagne leather heated seats, satellite radio, a six-disc CD changer and fold-down rear seats, the Ford Fusion made for a chic accessory on a sunny afternoon. It was all at an affordable price of less than twenty-two hundred dollars, which summed up Rachel's out-of-pocket costs for taxes after she was awarded the vehicle during a holiday give away at the MGM casino.

"Let me guess. Marissa, right?" Rachel asked with the confidence of a psychic hunch. Marissa was Shelly's dorm roommate at Michigan State during their freshman year and Rachel's arch nemesis.

"I know that you do not want to hear another Marissa story, but just because you two don't get along doesn't mean I have to stop being friends with her," Shelly said in defense.

"I have never asked you to. What's the sweet girl up to these days?" Rachel replied with sheer sarcasm.

"She is getting ready to marry a man who is seventeen years her senior!"

"She has slept with all of the men our age; I guess it would be time to settle down with their fathers," Rachel said, as her mind raced.

"She's the same age as we are, so that makes him 42, how sick! My father got my mother pregnant when he was 18 and she was 17, so this guy is old enough to be our father. Gross!" Rachel said, as she added in her head.

"She says he's wealthy, a self-made millionaire," Shelly continued.

"Maybe she wants to be taken care of," Rachel said.

"She makes $70,000 a year; that's not it. He has been married twice before, which means this would make his third marriage, and it's only her first."

"Does he have children close to her age or something? So far, I don't comprehend or sense a problem?" Rachel said, as she began to play the advocate for Marissa.

"Well, he's in the middle of a nasty divorce settlement. From what she tells me, $500,000 to his second wife, several thousand dollars in alimony, and, if she doesn't sell the house in four months, he will need to buy her out at $720,000!" Shelly explained.

"What about child support? Does he have any children?" Rachel asked.

"No, which is why he wants to hurry and marry Marissa. She told me that his own mother told her at the dinner table that she noticed 'things heating up' between them, and she suggested Marissa discontinue dating her son or risk being his third ex-wife," Shelly said.

"Wow! That's pretty mean. Maybe he's really fallen in love this time. Maybe the third time *is* the charm. Maybe his first two wives didn't appreciate him or were unable to bare children or only wanted him for his money. Did you ever think about that?" Rachel asked, continuing to play devil's advocate.

"Oh, did I neglect to mention that Marissa was his mistress during his second marriage, which prompted his wife to file for divorce? She busted them in their house," Shelly said with a smirk.

"Um … Let's just say you failed to mention that," Rachel spoke haltingly as both burst out into laughter.

Chapter 27
(Dedicated to Dr. Jamal-Harrison Bryant)

Every truth has two sides. It is well to look at both before we commit ourselves to either side. —Gandhi

Notices had circulated the day before warning tenants that a new management company would be taking over the apartment complex. It was a troubled asset in downtown Detroit in the midst of a difficult market. Competing communities were converting to condos; there were thousands of layoffs in the pipeline for the automotive industry and cash-strapped owners with skeptical investors. The morning of, property managers and marketing representatives from across the Midwest entered Bristol Plaza to perform final due diligence and interview the current staff.

"Ugh! It smells like ass in this place," the training director commented, as she entered the lobby area pulling a roller bag behind her.

"Let's split into teams," the regional manager said, getting right down to business. "I need two of you to conduct two-minute interviews with all sixteen staff members. Send everyone for criminal background and drug testing immediately. Four of you will split up and walk the units on all twenty-nine floors. In the meantime, I will be ordering supplies, creating a budget template and firing the lead maintenance supervisor. Any questions?"

The groups split into their respective areas, while the existing staff milled around aimlessly unsure of their fate. Stacy and Richard knocked on their first door on the fifteenth floor. Their plan was to work their way down. "Management!" they yelled twice before inserting the master key in the door. No one answered. "Most people will be at work this time of day," Richard said.

Stacy, the hired property manager for the site, entered first with her checklist on a clipboard. She was responsible for noting the serial numbers and model information for all appliances. Richard, a maintenance supervisor at a Pittsburgh site, agreed to notate the overall condition of the apartment: carpet condition, efficiency of the heating and cooling system, any presence of mold or water damage, cabinetry condition, and the life of blinds, appliances, and interior doors.

Just as Stacy looked around the living room observing the burning incense, a stark naked man exited the bathroom in a sort of sleep-walking motion. "Sir! Sir! Please cover yourself!" Stacy asserted, as she covered her face with her clipboard.

Richard stepped in between Stacy and the Mandingo, "Sir, we're with the new management company inspecting units today. We knocked several times before entering. Can you please get some clothes on in the presence of a lady?"

The man just mumbled something, turned, and started toward his bedroom, while Stacy waited in the fifteenth-floor hallway blushing.

Downstairs in the leasing office, security personnel had just escorted Neil Hammond out of the building. "What about that maintenance guy in Chicago, Darnell Higgins? I bet I could persuade him to transfer if more money were on the table," Luanne, the marketing director, suggested.

"How much is he making now?" Jack asked.

"I believe he's making $50,000 plus a 70 percent discount on his apartment," Luanne answered, as she scrolled through the phone book on her cellular phone.

"Offer him $60,000 plus a free unit. Tell him he has an hour to decide and three days to relocate," Jack instructed, as he opened his laptop to work on the asset's current financial budget.

The interviews weren't going particularly well. Most of the staff offered excuses on why they weren't able to take the drug test upon command. Some warned that they were taking antibiotics for cold or flu symptoms. The majority used the fact that they did not own vehicles; thus, they lacked transportation to give a specimen. Attempting to obfuscate the drug test requirement to buy more time to clean their systems. Janet entered the leasing office to warn Jack, the regional manager, of such impeding antics. "I've never seen so many uncooperative people in my life," she complained.

Jack handed her the keys to his rental vehicle. "It's an SUV. Load 'em all up, and transport them to the nearest laboratory—now!" he roared.

The end of the day approached, and Melvin and Janna checked in first after walking floors twenty-nine down to sixteen. "Oh my God! What have we gotten ourselves into?" Janna asked with wide eyes, as she slouched down in an office chair. Jack laughed as he asked for the inspection checklists and a summary of their findings.

"There was an apartment with obvious fire damage that looked as if the tenants skipped out in the middle of the night and never reported the damage to management," Melvin offered the first description.

"Yeah, and they left food out on the stove and counter tops, which left the place crawling with roaches and maggots," Janna said, as she scratched and rubbed her arms as if the insects were crawling on her that very moment.

Melvin chimed in, "Vacant apartments are being used to store supplies and broken-down appliances." He continued, "There is a graveyard of air-conditioning compressors on the tenth floor that just blew my mind."

Jack laughed and confessed, "These are all things that I noticed during my initial visits. Those apartments should be brought back on-line, trashed out, and made ready for clients to move into. It all would realize more revenue for our owners."

The rest of the group began piling in the office. "We've got our work cut out for us. But with a little hard work and a lot of TLC, we can reposition this real estate to compete in the market place once again. Now that we are all here, why don't we call it a night, check into our hotel rooms, and meet back here tomorrow morning at 8:30? Thank you all for coming out and, most importantly, for your hard work and diligence today," Jack praised.

As all had hoped he would, Darnell accepted the lead maintenance position and proved to be just the right skill set for the department and the property. Tall with mocha skin and semi handsome, owners were impressed by Darnell's overall presence, budget skills, and his money-saving techniques. He completed several projects in-house versus contracting them out. Darnell, in his late forties, had eleven children back in Chicago. Needless to say, he traveled home by train every Friday evening to be with his wife and kids. Seven of the eleven were his biologically, while the remaining four were his wife's from a previous relationship that never resulted in marriage. Darnell often joked about his wife's ex being in jail probably plotting to kill him for moving in on his family.

Time went on, and the new management team was making great headway at Bristol Plaza. With very little money available to improve the building aesthetically, much creativity went into marketing and creating demonstration models for potential tenants. On his own time, Darnell took on a project to convert one of the off-line units to a loft apartment. What started off as an appliance graveyard, transitioned into a contemporary loft with exposed metal-beam ceilings, a variety of millwork, cabinetry, and moldings. With rustic walnut flooring in the foyer area, faux painting and dramatic lighting designs, the only thing missing was the rental furniture.

The holiday season approached, and Darnell requested a two-week vacation to be with his family in Chicago for Christmas. Who would object after all of his hard work over the past nine months? In an effort to save money for the holidays, Darnell had not traveled home in the past eight weeks, so he was super excited to go. Jack gave Darnell his holiday bonus early, and he flew home to Chicago. But, after only two days, Darnell was back in Detroit and at work. Everyone questioned his early return, to no avail.

Later that week, Darnell confided in one of his underlings that upon his return home, he was greeted by observing his wife and children decorating the Christmas tree with his wife's jailbird of an ex-boyfriend. Turns out, he was paroled and released early for good behavior. Apparently, all of the money Darnell sent home for gifts was being used to fund a holiday celebration that did not include him. He was devastated—even more so when he was served with divorce papers after the New Year. "You are raising my children around that jailbird!"

Darnell was overheard screaming into his cell phone during a lunch break one afternoon.

It wasn't long thereafter that Darnell's work ethic began to suffer. Jack ignored the obvious for as long as he could, but goals for the New Year and new budget season could not afford to take a backseat while one of his key people struggled with personal issues. Investors had approved several projects, including unit upgrades, lobby renovations, and corridor upgrades. A minority-owned painting company was awarded the $65,000 bid to paint all of the corridors and stairwells with Darnell overseeing the project. Using a minority-owned company offered somewhat of a tax break for owners.

One Thursday afternoon, Jack called Darnell to drive down to his Dearborn office. Darnell never owned a vehicle, so he asked Stacy to drive him. It worked out, because Jack asked her to sit in as a witness. "You know, I have always looked out for you in every situation, because you have worked so hard for me. What are the only two rules I ask in return from my entire team?" he asked. Jack was obviously pissed.

"You asked that no one ever lies or steal from you. Where is this going, Jack?" Darnell inquisitively wondered.

"I have here in my possession a sworn affidavit from Don's Painting Group that you have been squeezing him for money after you guaranteed that he would get the corridor paint contract," Jack said, revealing a notarized statement from the owner of the paint company.

"He's a liar!" Darnell raised his voice and walked toward the door.

"Sit your ass down. There will be plenty of time for you to walk out of that door and never come back. Now …" Jack was interrupted by Darnell's denial and rage. The two exchanged more words as Stacy observed in dismay.

"You are hereby terminated effective immediately. Leave your keys and your cell phone. You have until the end of this month to be out of your apartment and off my site. Do I make myself crystal clear?" Jack asked. Darnell stormed out of the office and to the parking lot to light a cigarette. "Are you okay to drive him back?" Jack asked Stacy, who, in turn, assured him that she has pepper spray "in case he tries anything." The two shared a brief, nervous laugh and parted ways.

The ride back to Bristol Plaza was an awkward one. "I moved away from my family to work my tail off for this man, and this is the thanks I get," Darnell vented.

"In a way, your move was still a blessing, because your ex-wife was only using you," Stacy offered as she yielded for a traffic sign. Darnell just shook his head and rode quietly for the remainder of the trip.

"Come to church with me this Sunday. There you will get all of the answers for your next move. I won't take no for an answer," she said, as she turned the key in the ignition and opened the car door.

Darnell smiled and gave his now former manager a hug, "I'll call you," he said.

Sunday rolled around, and Stacy wondered if Darnell was going to call. She frantically checked her cell phone for missed calls or text alerts, not wanting to initiate a call to him. *I wonder how much money he pocketed. A $65,000 contract—did he demand 10 percent?* she thought to herself. *Why would the contractor lie about anything like this? What would he gain from lying—nothing, right?* Stacy continued with questions that she would never ask aloud. She grabbed her coat and headed to the elevators. She wanted desperately to stop on Darnell's floor. All she could worry about were Darnell's seven to eleven children that depended on his income and medical insurance, because their mother was too despicable to hold down a decent job.

Stacy spoke to the doorman as she exited the building on her way to the 11:30 service. As she entered the parking garage, she disabled her car alarm with the remote. She was pleasantly surprised by who was sitting on the trunk of her car in a grey pin-striped suit, with a pink shirt and grey big block alligator shoes. "Darnell, thank God you're here!" she said. The two shared a friendly embrace and a ride to church.

Darnell looked cumbersome as the usher handed him a tithing envelope. The choir was already singing, and people were standing in rows clapping and singing along in a joyful decorum. "Ain't he all right?" the reverend yelled as he approached the pulpit. He instructed the congregation to turn their Bibles to the Book of Genesis. "I'm going to preach from the topic: God Has a Calling on Your Life," the preacher said, as susurration filled the sanctuary.

The pastor told a story of a fisherman who traveled the ocean biweekly delivering freshwater fish. He traveled from the Florida coast to the Mexican borders on a biweekly basis and had done so for several years. The pastor described how one day the fisherman was approached by two Columbian drug lords who observed his comings and goings. The drug lords inquired how often the fisherman made the trip. "Oh, I come through these parts every fourteen days or so," the fisherman responded.

"And how many times do the coast guards and police stop to search your boat?" one man asked.

"Never. I just waive and go about my business," the fisherman said, as he did just that—went about his business.

During the next trip, the preacher described how the cartel leader approached the fisherman while unloading his seafood. "How would you like to make some real money?" the cartel leader asked him. "I am willing to offer you $50,000 if you can take this bag back with you to Florida," he said. The proposal was made, but the fisherman declined and got back in his boat. Two and a half weeks went by, and the cartel leader approached the fisherman again. "Okay, maybe $50,000 is not enough for the risk, so how would you like to make $100,000 for every successful trip you make for me?" he asked, but the fisherman refused and got back in his boat.

Next time around, the gang approached the fisherman again, "Not enough, huh? How does $150,000 per trip sound to you?"

The fisherman shook his head and assured the drug lords, "I'm sorry sir, but I am afraid you've got the wrong man." Off he sailed in his boat. This went on and on, and the price got more and more attractive—$200,000, $250,000—but the fisherman did not compromise.

Finally, the cartel leader approached the fisherman with a suitcase full of money and said, "You're a smart man. And you drive a hard bargain. How about $500,000—half now and the other half when you return successfully?" The fisherman apologized once again and refused.

The fisherman thought long and hard about the dealer's last offer. He decided it was time to get the police involved. Police interrogated him and made him wear a wire tap. They assured him that he would be in no danger and that DEA agents would be waiting with trigger-happy fingers on the other side of the border. Just as they had previously, drug lords approached the fisherman with duffel bags full of drugs and another full of money. DEA agents swarmed the area surrounding all of the drug lords and handcuffing the fisherman to make it look as though he was also being arrested in the sting. Later, the lead drug enforcement agent thanked the fisherman for his cooperation and said, "I've gotta ask. You have been making this trip for some time now and by your own admission you've been approached by these thugs many times before. Why now? Why are you just now bringing law enforcement into it?"

The fisherman rubbed his wrists in hopes of relieving the pressure from the handcuffs, "I've gotta be honest with you, officer. They were getting closer to my price."

Chapter 28

It is wise for us to forget our troubles; there are always new ones to replace them. —Brigham Young

Welcome to the Greens at the Hamptons, where the color of a good life awaits you! Built in the early 1960s, Greens at the Hamptons was home to many middle- and upper-class suburbanites. Nestled on more than thirty acres of lush greens, with willow trees and man-made ponds, Greens at the Hamptons offered everything from an eighteen-hole tee off to a gala held in the exclusive country club. Located in the heart of Southfield City, the Greens at the Hamptons housed many socialites and celebutantes in its heyday.

Fast forwarding to present day, the Greens at the Hamptons struggled to remain competitive in the housing market. With its wood frame, lap siding and natural limestone, the midrise development had experienced several years of neglect prior to ownership changing hands. Consisting of five midrise buildings with flat roofs, the project was a developer's dream. Upon takeover, the property was reporting 63 percent physical occupancy and 54 percent economic occupancy, an investment nightmare.

The entire staff of thirty was asked to vacate the premise while a temporary team of pros set up to manage the property's day-to-day operations: maintenance, leasing, bookkeeping, and administration. Upon takeover, Rita Sandoval, introduced herself from apartment 2-101. Rita had occupied her apartment home for thirty-six years and was the original and only tenant since 1962. As a matter of fact, Rita rented a brand-new unit shortly after retiring as a music teacher for the Oakland County School District.

She hugged all of the new staff members and owners and invited each of them in intervals to visit her apartment to enjoy a cup of Earl Grey tea. She was the ultra fashion diva, wearing unique crowns and accessories daily. Upon entering her apartment, owners and managers alike were flabbergasted by the original horse-hair-type carpet laid on her floors. Her appliances were outdated but looked like new due to the turtle wax she used to restore their luster over the years. Maintenance personnel tried on many occasions to upgrade Rita's apartment with the brand-new Wolf appliances and wooden blinds they were installing in vacant units upon turnover. However, she cried, grew very defensive and simply refused to let them into her home. After several attempts in coaxing her, all just gave up and left her to her 1963 love shack.

Rita was a widow and lived off of her teacher's pension while investing all of the proceeds from the sale of her husband's business after his death. Rita's CPA, Dmitri, had made her millions over the years and always acted in good faith on her behalf as power of attorney during her battle with senile dementia. One Saturday morning after a great turnout at the pancake breakfast hosted by the concierge team, Rita frantically entered the leasing office screaming that aliens were trying to blow her building up. The property manager, Daniel Honeycutt, pulled her into his office as not to disturb new clients touring the property. After spending several moments trying to calm Rita down and get to the bottom of the "alien attack," Daniel soon discovered that Rita was referring to the burrows dug by gophers near the electrical panel boxes in the ground.

To ease Rita's psyche, Daniel covered the holes with large decorative stones, but that didn't stop the gophers. They dug around the small boulders, and Rita cried and screeched like fingernails on a chalkboard. Daniel contracted with a local cement company to fill the original and new holes made by the gophers near Rita's building. However, that didn't stop them either. They just kept digging. Finally, Daniel contracted with an animal control vendor who set traps for the gophers that were tunneling near Rita's building—she became unglued. "This is animal cruelty!" she yelled. Obviously, there was no pleasing this sweet and nurturing woman.

Seasons changed, and the succession plan put into place for the Greens at the Hamptons was on track. Owners dumped the riffraff and nonpayers in the buildings, increased the rents, and upgraded the aesthetics and amenities while still performing unit renovations. The project was 20 percent complete, and the buzz in the community was becoming more and more lucid. A better demographic of people was attracted to even the unrenovated buildings, because they knew that, eventually, the entire property would be opulent.

At this point, building number five was anything but lavish. Raccoons had built a nest in the ceiling insulation and were often heard scratching and fighting in the rafters. It was suspected that the raccoons had defecated and urinated in the same small area so much so that the drywall ceiling softened and caved in. The collapse happened right before Bobby Knoll's eyes in apartment 5-413. Just arriving home from work, Bobby reacted swiftly by grabbing his puppy and locking himself into his master bedroom suite. Just more than two months prior, Bobby had driven to Intercourse, Pennsylvania, to an Amish puppy mill to purchase a seven-pound Schitzu named Dexter. After securing himself and Dexter behind a locked and closed door, Bobby called the emergency maintenance telephone number to have a couple of guys paged to respond to the crisis.

In the meantime, two extremely large raccoons were totally destroying the apartment on the opposite side of the bedroom wall. The raccoons were running around on the walls at forty miles per hour and breaking every piece of furniture they came in contact with. There were feces and scratch marks in an almost-perfect circular motion on the apartment walls. Every photograph, piece of art, and sculpture were ripped, broken, and ruined. Candles were broken all over the floor, the TV stand was crushed and scratched, the glass dining room table was shattered, and apartment drapes were catastrophic. In the meantime, two seasoned maintenance men showed up with wooden chairs, sticks, and flashlights to coax the raccoons out of the front door of the apartment. "I have never seen a raccoon that large," said one of the supervisors.

"Too bad I didn't bring my hunting gun," the other one joked.

Just before three o'clock in the afternoon, Bobby Knoll was freed from his bedroom only to witness total destruction in the other parts of his apartment. Studying software engineering at Oakland Community College, Bobby was the most distraught over the loss of his sophisticated electronic software and equipment. His couch and love seat cushions, books, and magazines were all ripped to shreds with feces and urine present in every area of the apartment—yuck!

Maintenance personnel expressed their sympathy and reported back to the property manager, Daniel Honeycutt, by taking photographs. The tenant, Bobby, marched over to the management office with Dexter in his arms, "We'll be happy to let you out of your lease agreement," Daniel said almost immediately after spotting Bobby.

"Okay, my place has just been ripped to shreds and shit on by some wild raccoons, and all you can offer is to let me out of my lease?" Bobby asked.

"Conceivably, you're upset, Mr. Knoll; however, I assure you that the raccoons were not placed in the rafters by management, so we bare no responsibility or liability in this," Daniel said, looking Mr. Knoll in the face while attempting to pat Dexter in his arms.

"You go to hell! I am staying in a hotel until my lawyer sorts this out!" Bobby exclaimed while jerking Dexter away from Daniel's hand.

"Please have your attorney fax over a letter of representation … here's my card," Daniel said, as he turned to retrieve a business card from his desk. In the meantime Mr. Knoll was halfway out of the front door.

"You haven't even offered to compensate me for my hotel room. Amazing! When this is over mister, I will sue you, buy you, sell you, and throw away the change!" he cried out prior to exiting. From that point on, everyone referred to that incident as 'Raccoons in the Rafters'.

Just then, three construction men walked in carrying a puffy pillowcase. Evidently, while completing the closet door and bedroom fixture upgrades, members of the construction team found the pillowcase containing $10,000 in cash. "Missa Danyell, we don't touch not'ing. Dis was in the closet, inside," Hector attempted to explain while putting the pillowcase on Daniel's desk. Daniel could not believe the day he was having. He called the non-emergency police to report the large sum of money found hoping to launch an investigation of the occupants and occupations that were occupying the apartment.

The twelve-month employment contract was rounding out, and it was time for Daniel to hire a property manager, his replacement. Daniel was also charged with assisting with interviews for all other property positions: maintenance, leasing, administration, and so forth. He planned a job fair to be held in the clubroom off of the golf course. After his one-year run, Daniel was anxious to take some time off for personal medical reasons.

Daniel's true life calling was as a semi-professional singer. Prior to joining the management team at the Greens at the Hamptons, he was very active in concert performances. Previously, Daniel was being tormented by a sore throat, which prompted him to see a physician. The discovery process indicated that Daniel had a cyst on his vocal cords. Once his property management contract ran out, Daniel had planned to make an appointment to see Dr. Bradshaw—an ear, nose, and throat expert who specialized in the function of vocal cords. Dr. Bradshaw received his medical degree from the George Washington University School of Medicine and completed his residency in internal medicine at Mount Sinai School of Medicine in New York City. There, he also served as an assistant chief resident. Dr. Bradshaw had planned an invasive discovery procedure for Daniel in order to rule out cancer.

Days went by, and the job fair was scheduled to start at 10 a.m. on a Thursday afternoon. The mood was a little bittersweet because of what the day represented. It meant that the time was nearing when all staff members would hand over the baton and keys to a new group of managers, salespeople, and such. Whether the owners had the right idea or not, they brought up an interesting point that all staff members become stale and mundane after a certain period in time. Maybe it was best to bring in and rotate new talent. This sort of temporary contractual method also tremendously minimized turnover. Who wouldn't try something for one year?

The first candidate arrived at quarter after nine. "Good morning. I'm here for the job fair," a gorgeous and polished thirty-something young brunette informed Daniel as he responded to a light knock at the door.

"Absolutely ... right this way," he stammered after being mesmerized by the striking beauty of the very first applicant. Both smiled and lowered their eyes in a bashful manner. Daniel directed the young woman to the conference room where she was to sign in, complete an employment application, attach a resume, and wait to be called for a personal interview.

"Jill Buckley," she said, extending her well-manicured hand toward Daniel.

"Daniel Honeycutt, property manager for the Greens at the Hamptons," he replied.

"Okay, this is a little uneasy—I am here to apply for your position," she said still holding onto his hand.

There was an awkward silence suddenly broken by Daniel, "It's okay. I plan to meet several people who are coming after my seat." Daniel smiled back as he explained the current twelve-month contractual agreement and the owners' reasons for the changing of the guards.

The format of the job fair proved to be a successful one. After many aspiring property management professionals filled the boardroom during intervals of the day, the group would receive an introduction of the property and company—led by the owners and Daniel. After explaining the benefit package and mission statements of the company, candidates were broken into groups to learn more about their desired job descriptions. All would be given a brief tour of the acquisition—amenities, model homes, and grounds. Qualified candidates would be asked to lag behind for a private and more personal interview with the owner representative and Daniel Honeycutt. Others would be offered a trifold brochure and pen with the company's logo and Web site address.

Different groups rotated throughout the day, and many interesting candidates responded to the classified ad. Daniel met a distinguished gentleman from Burkina who managed four-star hotels in West Africa for over eighteen years. It was common knowledge in the property management industry that some of your best people come from the hospitality industry. Landlord–tenant relations or hotel manager–guest relations, the objectives are very similar. The only difference was the length of time between the next guest. The bookkeeper interviewed an account representative from a non-profit organization that funded housing needs for lower-income families.

The job fair wrapped up, and the staff reported to the property the next morning only to be greeted by approximately ten cop cars before breakfast. Police brought a warrant to the management office after busting down the apartment door of Mr. and Mrs. Wesson in 4-112. Many had heard that Mrs. Wesson had taken ill some days ago. She had faxed over a note from an exploratory doctor indicating that she was under his care and possibly in need to vacate her lease agreement by using the early termination clause. Mrs. Wesson worked as an account manager at the city's waste management plant downtown, while Mr. Wesson earned a sizeable living as a mortician.

Less than two weeks prior, Mrs. Wesson had taken ill and passed out at work. She was rushed to the hospital and essentially had not returned to work since. Doctors found a toxic substance in her body that could potentially kill her; thus, she had not been released from their care. Apparently, her uterus and other female organs were suddenly being attacked and proved to be harmful if not fatal. After several x-rays, MRIs and other tests, one exploratory neural surgeon who held special interests in cardiovascular imaging announced the root of Mrs. Wesson's health problem.

The surgeon asked Mrs. Wesson if she worked with or around dead bodies in her line of work. "No, but my husband does. He is a prominent mortician, why?" she asked.

"I'm afraid there may be no easy way to tell you this so I'm just going to come right out and say it," the doctor prefaced. As Mrs. Wesson tilted her head sideways while trying to hold the hospital gown up to her neck, the doctor proceeded to explain that the toxic substance eroding her uterus and other organs had been identified as embalming fluid.

"I don't understand, doctor. Are you saying that my husband is poisoning my food?" Mrs. Wesson asked in total disbelief.

"I know how this must sound, Mrs. Wesson, but I think we need to act fast in bringing your husband in before he is also fatally injured. Your illness is not from an oral intake. It is my professional opinion that your husband is engaging in intercourse with the embalmed corpses and then engaging you at home," the doctor broke the news to Mrs. Wesson as she nearly passed out.

Doctor's assistants and nurses responded quickly in getting law enforcement involved, and a warrant for Mr. Wesson's arrest was drafted immediately. A team of police showed up at the apartment community when Mr. Wesson could not be located at his office. He was mirandized and arrested for attempted murder while handcuffed to a gurney and transported to the same hospital. Mr. Wesson did not seem caught off guard by the arrest. He must have figured some time ago what was eating his wife after she offered him diagnosis from previous doctors. "I gotta tell you, Mr. Wesson. This is some wicked shit. A brilliant scientist like you—what gives?" one arresting officer asked.

With a sort of smirk on his face and blank stare, Mr. Wesson responded, "I could argue your point, but what would be the use?"

Chapter 29

Nothing can be taken for granted any longer. Either you have a basic knowledge about the world, the skills necessary to navigate in the world or you cannot compete. —Phillip Jackson

Everyone dreaded leaving their house on Friday the 13th, especially if you left home only to arrive at 666 Jefferson Court, Presidential Heights. One of the leasing agents, Cole, walked through the door. "Good morning," he said to the concierge, Sandy, who was preparing freshly squeezed lemonade and chocolate chip cookies for refreshments.

"Morning. You sound about as enthused as I am to be here on Satan's day," Sandy retorted.

Cole was the youngest of the team members at the age of nineteen, though he showed resilience and promise beyond his years. His charming nature and smooth demeanor gained him the respect of women of all walks of life—young, old, married, and definitely single. During his interview with the property manager, the two didn't talk much about his skill set and qualifications. The day of the interview, Cole arrived at the apartment community with history books and researched statistics on the current demographic makeup of the building. He was of average height with a dark coffee complexion.

After given the results returned from Cole's behavioral assessment test, Morgan was convinced that he was the perfect candidate for the open sales position. Cole didn't have much sales ability, and he did not possess much experience in important employment roles. His entire employment history consisted of that of a crew member in several fast-food restaurant chains.

The test results revealed that Cole was a helpful, pleasant, tolerant, and precise individual. He worked as a perfectionist in an exact and meticulous manner to avoid making mistakes. Also that he would be analytical, detail oriented, accurate, steady, and conscientious in his work approach. Cole preferred to rely on facts in his work, worked at being objective and rational, was probably very familiar with the difficult areas of his job, and was a loyal individual. He was effective at dealing with detailed information and a very cautious and controlled decision-maker. Cole tended to work better in small groups and work teams. However, the test concluded one flag, which gave Morgan reservations. She overcame such when she identified with herself and her own weaknesses. The flag indicated that Cole would feel stressed by dealing with risky situations, being pushed too hard, and being confronted or argued with.

When Morgan asked, "Why should I hire you?" Cole told a rather bazaar story and series of events in his life that made up his strength, character, and will to succeed. The story explained how his father's absence had a reverse impact on his maturity and focus. Most young men in his shoes would have fallen by the wayside and allowed themselves to become a product of their environment, but he did just the opposite and persevered.

In his father's defense, he wasn't aware that he fathered Cole until his 17th birthday. Cole's mother, Jodie, lacked self-esteem and self-respect for that matter. She would lay down with any man who would give her the slightest attention and believed everything that a man promised her. While in her early twenties, Jodie occupied the lower flat of a Section 8 housing community. Jodie was an unemployed, single mother of a three-year-old baby girl at the time—Cole's older sister. One day while sitting on the porch smoking a cigarette, Jodie was confronted by a technician for the city's gas company. He arrived to disconnect Jodie's gas for nonpayment. She pleaded with the technician, but he assured her that the only way she could reverse his plan was with full payment. "I gotta little girl … and her daddy don't do squat for us … cut me a little slack, huh?" Jodie continued to plead, but the technician did not seem fazed.

"I'll do anything … anything," Jodie continued, while rubbing on the man's back and shoulders. Suddenly, her pixie haircut and fitted shirt showing off her torso caught the stranger's attention. After the two engaged in flirting back and forth, the gas technician finally agreed that he would pay the delinquent balance for a sexual encounter with Jodie. She took him inside and tried her best to show her gratefulness for his kindness. After putting her daughter down for a nap and a forty-five minute frolic, the technician kept his word and left a paid receipt for $172 on the night stand in Jodie's room. Weeks after her sex romp, Jodie began to experience morning sickness and soon discovered that she was expecting a baby boy. Unsure of how the gas technician would react to such news or how to reunite with him—she didn't even get his name—Jodie had to act fast. She reconnected with her ex-boyfriend, seduced him, and laid claim that the baby she was expecting was his.

Jodie's ex, Claude, proved to be very supportive and active in raising Cole as a child. Not having children of his own, Claude was very excited to finally have a son. The two lived together for just over fifteen years, never marrying, when Jodie began to abuse drugs and default on her responsibilities as a mother. Claude soon moved out, leaving Jodie to rehabilitate herself and raise two children on her own. After being coaxed by family members, Jodie decided to take Claude to court for a child support award. Claude begged her not to get the courts involved and tried to explain how his love for her had run its course, and he was no longer in love with her. However, Jodie was soon reminded by her sister that child support was for the child, and she was in no shape to take on full responsibility while Claude was gainfully employed as an electrician.

As permitted in most child support cases, Claude contested the support claim and asked the court for a paternity test. Cole, at age fifteen, had a perfect understanding of how his father was now trying to disown him in an effort to equivocate the financial burden. Cole, his mother, and all of the onlookers in the courtroom that day were shocked and appalled when the judge read the results that Claude had zero percent chance of being Cole's father. "Your honor, I tried to prevent this from coming out, but I was forced to have a vasectomy before I was twenty due to a terrible bike accident," Claude protested. "I knew fifteen years ago when Jodie announced to me that I was going to be a father that there was no way I could have fathered a child. But also for that same reason, I was excited about having a son," Claude continued. Cole ran out of the courtroom prior to his mother's tirade and tantrum when the judge denied her child support claim and scolded her for deceiving Claude, the court, and, most importantly, Cole. Since then—and much like that of President Barack Obama—Cole's values were strengthened more by the absence of a father than the years spent with his "acting father."

The property manager felt such a soft spot for Cole after his story that she hired him—not out of pity—but after looking into his eyes; she believed that he would work hard to succeed, and he did. He continually achieved top sales accolades, and the residents—especially the women—loved him. They would bake desserts for him, buy him things that he would try to refuse, and some would even invite him to their apartment for "a drink."

"What's up?" Paul asked upon entering the management office to retrieve his work orders for the day. Paul Silver was the chief engineer of Presidential Heights, a 390-unit apartment building that soared thirty stories over downtown Columbus. Paul was suspected as being the ring leader behind several thousand dollars in copper that continued to go missing in the community. Life safety equipment that contained copper fittings was inadvertently being replaced with plastic or PVC material. More unauthorized changes included the riser caps in the emergency exit stairwells of the building being replaced, overnight, with plastic caps. Many suspected that he had a drug problem—crystal meth—and he was too slick to ever be caught in the act. He had a smooth gift of gab and backed it up with exceptional engineering skills.

"Paul, it's due to be a quiet day today. I'd like to go over the new budget with you. Can you make time for me this afternoon?" Morgan asked.

"Sure. I had planned to take my guys out to a nice lunch today. Can we connect afterwards?" he asked. Many also suspected that Paul had pulled a few of the other maintenance men in on his theft ring—all except Hernandez. Hernandez was an honest Christian man with five kids, a wife, and a very modest home. Though he had never confided in any authority figure about what he had observed Paul do, his eyes said it all whenever Paul would head a staff meeting or anyone spoke his name. You can tell a lot by a man's eyes.

Once, Morgan ordered a brand-new desktop computer for the assistant manager's desk. Since the assistant manager was responsible for accounts receivables and payables, it was important that she upgrade from the outdated system that constantly froze up while she was in the midst of data entering a batch of rent checks or petty cash receipts. As a national firm, the management company ordered the top-of-the-line desktop systems and loaded all of the necessary software and firewalls for the operator to function at full capacity. Also learning from history, the company never shipped brand-new computer systems without locking the system with a password that could not be hacked. Morgan, being the property manager, was the only site personnel that knew such password to unlock.

The computer arrived via UPS ground on a Friday afternoon, when everyone was too busy to install it; the plan was to install it first thing Monday morning. Upon arrival that Monday, there was no computer. While the assistant manager was furious, Morgan wasn't fazed. She knew that the computer could not be operated unless someone had the password. It would not fully power on; the password had to be entered at the DOS prompt. An incident report was completed, a police report filed, and an all-points bulletin circulated to the entire staff, to no avail. Less than seven days elapsed when the computer miraculously reappeared. *He couldn't get in it*, Jodie thought to herself.

"Happy Friday the thirteenth to you all!" Mrs. Simpson howled as she entered the management office.

"Happy? What's so happy about it?" Sandy asked.

"Don't tell me you all are superstitious?" the resident asked in an unusually perky mood. She'd come in to drop off her rent check for the following month. "I'm going to Honolulu for vacation to visit my sister. She lives on Kunia Island, which is the drier west side of Honolulu." Mrs. Simpson continued as if anyone had asked. "We are planning to go shark diving, whale watching, and fit in some good shopping … I can't wait!"

"Good for you," Morgan congratulated her.

"I am definitely superstitious. Step on a crack, and break your mamma's back," Cole joked.

"Don't forget about this one: never let a black cat cross your path; it is bad luck," Morgan recalled.

"My mother used to always tell me, if a funeral procession rides past your house with the door open, someone in your family would die," Mrs. Simpson volunteered. Morgan hadn't heard of the latter, but she recalled her mother demanding that no one cross the threshold in her house on New Year's Day until a man had done so first. Any diversion was considered bad luck.

While writing a receipt for Mrs. Simpson's check, Cole asked the question, "Speaking of black cats, does anyone know why everything black is considered to be negative or represent something bad?" Cole's question brought to mind all of the dark negative phrases—black cat, black ball, blackmail, black market, and so forth.

Mrs. Simpson smiled as if she was glad he asked. "I'm going to share something with you that a wise person once shared with me, then I will go finish packing," she said.

"Have you ever wondered why they used black velvet backdrops in jewelry stores and diamond showcases?" she asked. The others shrugged as if they had no idea as to the reason. The tenant continued, "The black velvet fabric is used to accentuate, magnify, and illuminate the quality, brilliance, and beauty in the diamonds. So you remember that the next time someone uses the phrase 'black ball' or 'black market' in your presence. Don't marginalize yourself or dummy down to an ignorant person's level," Mrs. Simpson scolded.

Cole began to caress his smoothly shaven face, "That's why I embrace my beautiful dark skin. Black is beautiful, and now I have another form of evidence; thanks for that information," Cole said with a smile.

Mrs. Simpson winked as she retrieved the receipt from his hand, "Bye all!"

Seconds later, the telephone rang, and Morgan was called to line one. It was a vendor representative returning her call regarding a past-due statement amounting to over $35,000. Apparently, the chief engineer, Paul Silver, had been personally picking up copper pipes and fittings from the vendor in his SUV. "I know you guys were renovating over there, so I figured he needed it for a big job. I had no idea he was suspected of stealing. Honest," the vendor recalled.

"I want to be perfectly honest with you; I am going to get my senior vice president involved in this. These invoices may not be paid—they may even be disputed and held up for some time—but effective immediately, I am requesting that you turn this account off. Paul is no longer an authorized person to place orders," Morgan said, making herself clear as steam escaped from her head.

"Not a problem, Morgan. Obviously, I will need to pull my regional sales manager in as well. In the meantime, please make your request to terminate the account in writing," the caller advised.

Morgan placed her head on the desk and screamed. She grabbed her pack of cigarettes and took a walk around the property with her cell phone while bringing the vice president up to speed. "Call his ass in the office right now, and you tell him that we will be scouring every scrap yard within fifty miles of the property. If he is implicated in any way, he will be fired and prosecuted!" the vice president, Jeannie, said; she was taking no prisoners.

"I shudder to think what may happen once this investigation starts," Morgan said with a melancholy temperament. "I wouldn't care if the building fell to the ground afterwards. It would have to fall after Paul was out on his ass. Call me back after your meeting with him," Jeannie insists. Morgan slammed her flip phone shut. She took a few more drags from a cigarette and headed back to her office.

"Paul to my office, please," Morgan said, maintaining a calm tone over the two-way radio. Paul appeared within seconds with a notepad and catalogs in his hand.

"You must be psychic. I was just about to call you," said Mr. Slick as he whistled and walked. Morgan took out the file folder with the past-due copper statements.

"Mr. Silver … come in … close the door … have a seat. Let's talk another form of metal," Morgan said, confronting him about the stolen copper. Instead of denying it, he asked what proof she had. The two went round and round about suspicion versus proof. "Look Paul, as you know you are not a contracted employee, but an at-will employee, which means that I do not have to have a reason to terminate you. Leave your keys, leave your phone, leave any tools that may belong to the company, and security is waiting outside of my office to escort you to your vehicle," she said. Morgan was obviously fed up.

Paul tried to change his tone and asked for one last favor—to retrieve a few contact names and numbers out of his company-paid Nextel. "Make it quick!" Morgan said, as she watched Paul scroll through the menu writing names and numbers on a Post-it note. He extended his hand for a friendly shake and left the keys and phone on her desk.

Days later, Paul called Hernandez on his Nextel to ask how things were going at the building. "You know, it feels strange not to be there at work with you guys," Paul confessed.

Hernandez quickly ended the call and marched into Morgan's office, "How is it that Paul still has his Nextel phone?" he asked.

"What do you mean?" Morgan asked.

"He just called me, and his name came up on my phone as usual. I forgot to delete him out of my phone," Hernandez explained.

"I have his phone right here, so how is that possible?" Morgan queried while retrieving the Nextel phone out of the safe under her desk.

Hernandez turned the phone on and tried to make a call to no avail, so he opened the battery pack in the back. "No wonder ... the bastard stole the SIM card!"

Printed in the USA
CPSIA information can be obtained
at www.ICGtesting.com
CBHW031245160524
8663CB00006B/107

9 781440 140778